CW01500708

For Julie
Enjoy
Mandy x

First published in Great Britain in 2025 by
Hickory Press, Oxfordshire, England

This novel is a work of fiction. All characters and events within this publication, although based at times on historical figures, are entirely the work of the author's imagination.

Copyright © Amanda Roberts 2025
Amanda Roberts asserts the moral right to be identified as the author of this work.

All rights reserved. No part of this publication may be reproduced, stored in a retrieval system or transmitted in any form or by any means, electronic, mechanical, photocopying, recording or otherwise, without the prior written permission of the publisher.

ISBN 978-1-0369-1710-4

Typeset by Hickory Press
Produced in the UK by Biddles Books Ltd

A catalogue record for this book is available from the British Library.

Cover design and illustration: Ali Edwards, Coostie Illustration & Design
Illustrated map: Ali Edwards, Coostie Illustration & Design

www.amandarobertsauthor.co.uk

LADY
OF THE
QUAY

Isabella Gillhespy Series: Book 1

AMANDA ROBERTS

Hickory Press
Oxfordshire, England

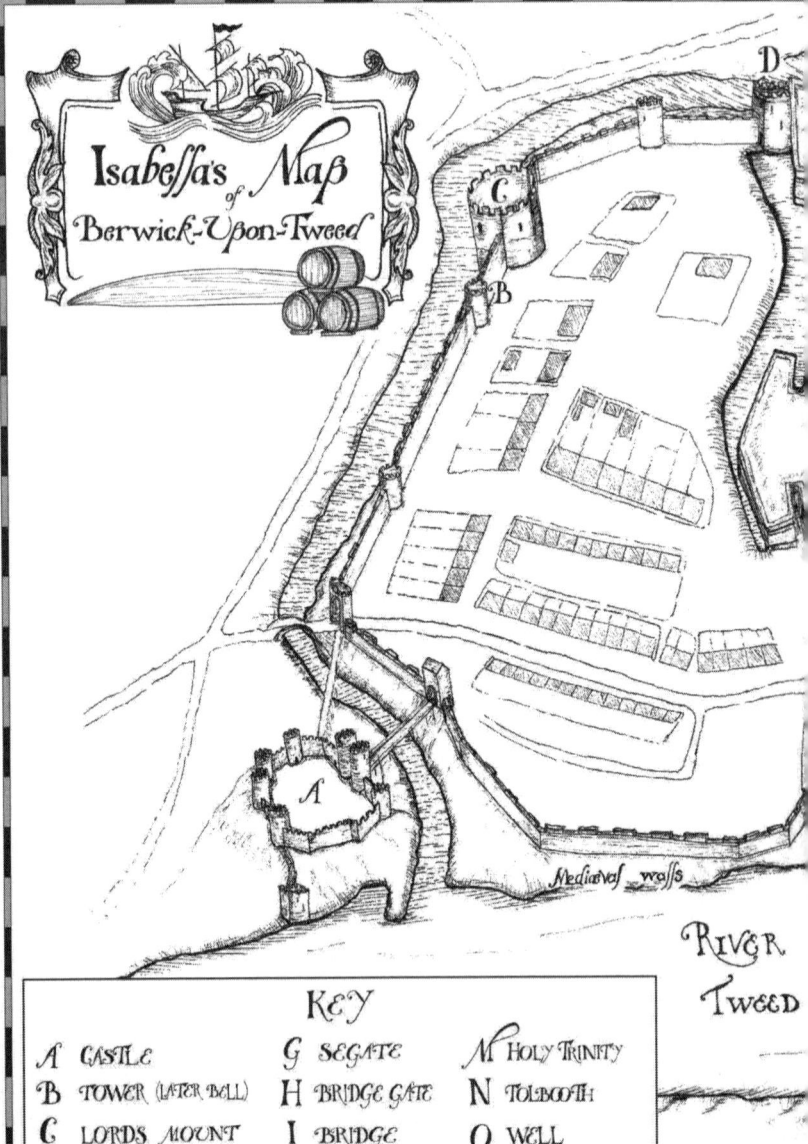

Isabella's Map
of
Berwick-Upon-Tweed

RIVER TWEED

Mediaeval walls

Key

A CASTLE
B TOWER (LATER BELL)
C LORDS MOUNT
D RED TOWER
E BLACKWATCH TOWER
F COW GATE

G SEGATE
H BRIDGE GATE
I BRIDGE
J WHARF
K ISABELLA'S HOUSE
L THE LADY ISABELLA

M HOLY TRINITY
N TOLBOOTH
O WELL
P CUSTOM HOUSE

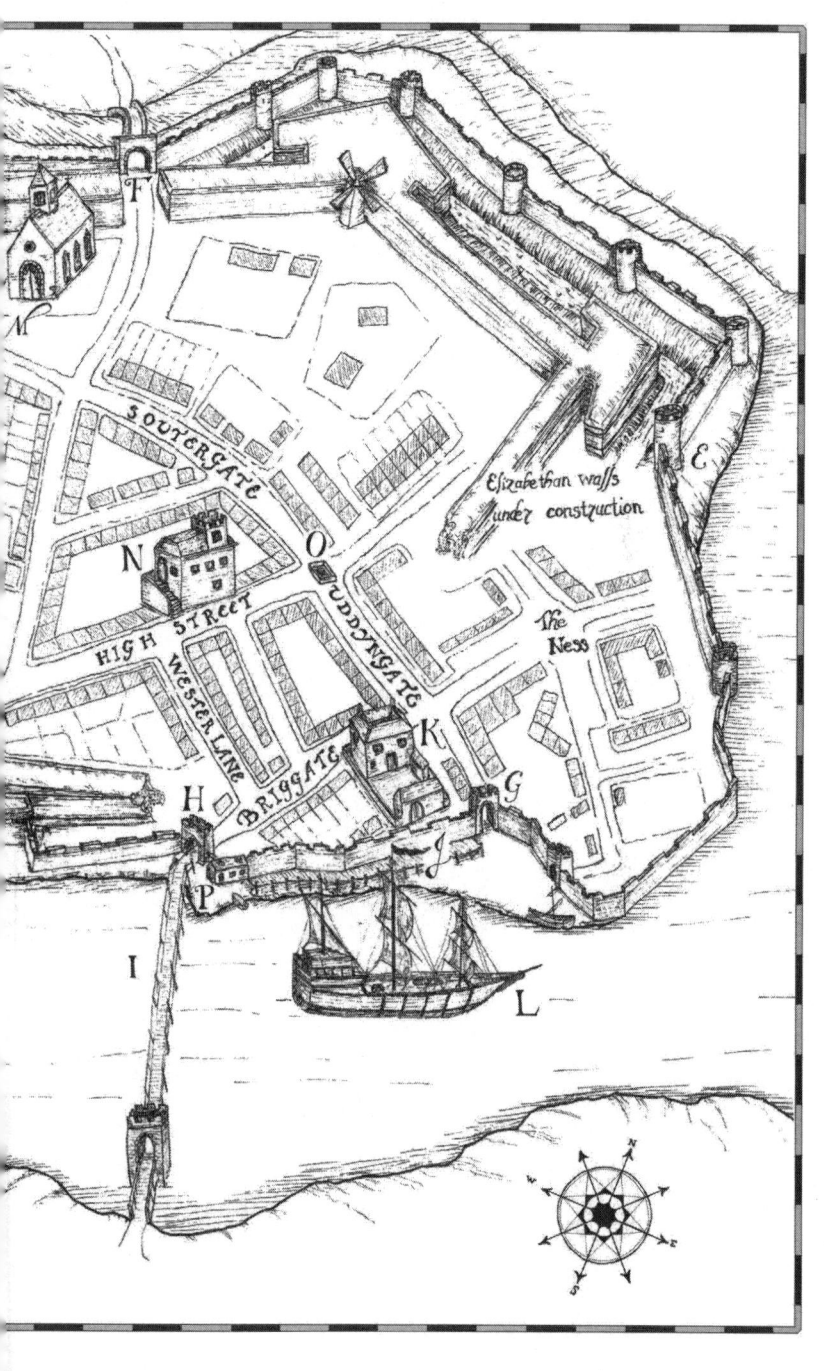

SOUTERGATE

HIGH STREET

WESTER LANE

UDDYNGATE

BRIGGATE

Elizabethan walls
under constuction

The Ness

M

T

N

O

E

K

H

G

P

I

L

Also by Amanda Roberts

The Roots of the Tree
The Woman in the Painting

ONE

1560, Berwick-upon-Tweed, England

I SHIELDED MY EYES WITH my hand, squinting against the wintry sun. It hung low in the sky; a glowing disc squatting by the side of Holy Island like an angelic being descending from heaven. Below me the German Ocean crashed onto the jagged rocks, whipped into an angry white froth by the bitter wind that spattered icy droplets into my face. They stung my exposed skin making me gasp, and the salty tang of the raw air burned my throat. A sharp gust tugged the hood of my thick woollen cloak, pulling it back from my head. In my haste to leave the house this morning I had been clumsy pinning my hair, and it followed my hood in a horizontal stream, billowing behind me like a pennon at a joust.

The Lady Isabella should have been back in harbour two weeks ago. Any delay to her expected arrival was a cause for concern, especially since the fall of Calais to the French had made the route she sailed more perilous. What if … but no, I could not allow my thoughts to travel in that direction.

I turned my back on the ocean, a slow, deliberate movement to refocus my thoughts. Soldiers on the Red Tower watched me with lazy eyes. I was a familiar sight out here on the headland, beyond the shelter offered by the town's ancient defensive walls, hoping for a glimpse of a sail on the horizon, growing taller as it approached land. The outline of a ship emerging from the clutches of the ocean, riding the choppy waters with the grace of a swan gliding across the smooth surface of a mill pond. Arriving in Maison Dieu Quay it would become part of the busyness, the exhilarating hustle and bustle of which I would never tire. I could picture the scene, heaving with activity; dockworkers scurrying around carrying sacks

1

and crates full of who knows what, cargo being lowered on ropes to the crowded jetty or hauled aboard, merchants in and out of the Custom House clutching leather satchels, and above it all, human voices, their shouted commands competing with the cry of gulls.

One last glance at the ocean and I would return home and join my father for breakfast. His mood had been heavy in recent days, his thoughts preoccupied. If I could take him some good news about the Lady Isabella, I was certain it would restore his habitual good spirits. I turned my face back into the wind and scrutinised the churning water, twisting my head from left to right so I could see all approaches to the estuary. A spot to the left of Holy Island caught my eye. I blinked and tried to focus my gaze. There it was again. No more than a darkness on the surface of the water, like a smudge of ink on paper, reaching up for the skies one moment and plummeting out of sight the next.

'Please let it be the Lady Isabella.' I crossed my fingers, not an easy manoeuvre in my thick sheepskin gloves, and watched. The smudge was approaching the coast, and I fancied I could see the glint of sun reflecting on metal or glass. It had to be a ship, but was it mine, the flagship of our fleet, named in honour of my mother, and after whom I was also named? It was not only the cargo she carried that was worth so much to us. She herself was precious.

The smudge was definitely a ship. Its tall sails, puffed out and proud, welcomed the strong wind that was pushing it towards land. As it approached, my eyes searched for our distinctive figurehead, the body of the bear that has been associated with Berwick for longer than anyone can remember, but with the head of a woman. Our bear was rampant and threatening, carved from oak, with a face painted in pale ivory and hair of a dark red falling in tight curls to its shoulders. The lips were parted to reveal over-long, sharp teeth. After a few more minutes of watching I had no doubt. This ship was the Lady Isabella.

I turned, hoisted my skirts above my ankles, and caring not for the opinion of anyone who might see me, ran back towards Cow Gate, the closest of the five entrances to the town. The soldier on duty watched me approach, his eyes exploring the headland behind me.

'The Lady Isabella is on her way,' I gasped.

He smiled and moved aside to allow me to pass. Soon I was in the tangle of narrow lanes and tiny houses that clustered in the shelter of the town walls, where the buildings leaned in towards each other and met overhead. The sun could not penetrate here, so the cobbles were always damp in summer and icy in winter, and the waste that was tipped into the streets gave the surface a permanent sheen of slime and filth. It was a treacherous mix, and I was forced to slow down, even in my sturdy boots that still caused my father to tut with disapproval, although he had long since stopped haranguing me to swap them for footwear more befitting a lady. It was a chance to catch my breath, but the fetid stench turned my stomach and I was relieved when I emerged into the relative brightness of Uddyngate. This was a prosperous street, wider, and lined with warehouses and granaries, as well as larger houses that were home to some of Berwick's wealthiest residents. I had once lived in one of these with my husband, but he had been dead some five years now, may his soul rest in peace, and I had chosen to move back to live with my father.

I hurried down the gentle hill. Our home was on Briggate. It was not as prestigious as those on Uddyngate, but was still one of Berwick's grander buildings, with two storeys built around a courtyard, stables to the rear, and a large warehouse that we used as our stores. As I approached the junction, a boy turned onto the narrow path ahead of me. His head was down, his back bent with the effort of dragging a bulging sack behind him.

'George,' I said before he walked straight into me. His head jerked up and he released his grip on the sack to wipe his nose with a grubby sleeve. 'The Lady Isabella is on her way in. Get down to the quay and tell them to prepare to receive her.'

'Yes Madam,' he replied, a broad grin breaking out across his young features.

'Where's my father?'

3

'Dunno.' He shrugged. 'I 'en't seen 'im today.'

'Never mind. I'll find him. Just get down to the quay.'

George broke into a run, leaving the sack where it was in front of me. Normally I would reprimand him for such carelessness, but today that could wait. I hastened to our house, which was about halfway along the street. Pushing open the front door I was greeted by the familiar smell of beeswax and the gleam of polished wood. Our dining hall was large and empty, both place settings at the table unused. Without pausing to remove my cloak or boots, I crossed to the far corner on my right, passing the hearth but not stopping to warm my hands before the large fire that burned there, and flung open the door that concealed the narrow stairs. I bounded up them, elbows knocking against the walls, feet tangling with my kirtle. It was not like my father to be so late to break his fast.

Our bedchambers were adjacent, at the far end of a galleried walkway. Whilst mine was at the front, with an unexciting view of the houses on the other side of Briggate from the small window, his had a fine view of the town walls and the river beyond. A bowl of clean water stood outside the door.

'Father,' I called, my voice tinged with excitement. 'The Lady Isabella is on her way in.'

I waited for him to throw open the door, relief flooding his face, but I was greeted with silence. I pressed the latch and pushed. The door was not locked and it swung open to reveal an empty chamber. The drapes hanging from the four posts of his bed were open. The covers were turned down and there was not a wrinkle in sight. It was odd that he had not washed if he had already risen, and even more out of character that he had left his bed so neat, but I did not pause to think what that could mean.

There was only one other place he could be. His closet. When shut away in there it was not unusual for him to lose all sense of time, especially when he was working and concentrating hard. He had a private way down to it via spiral steps at the far end of his chamber, but I knew the door to them would be locked. I re-traced my steps across the gallery and slid back down the stairs. The words of a popular folk song drifted towards me from the direction of the kitchen, an indication that Mary was hard at work. I did not stop to greet her. The arched opening to my father's closet at the opposite corner of the hall had been fitted with a solid oak door, of which he was very proud. When I knocked there was no answer. I pushed it open and stepped inside.

The space beyond was dark and cold. I blinked, letting my eyes adjust. It was strange that the shutters were still tightly closed and the fire had been allowed to go out. My father always looked after this room himself. It was his special space; wood-panelled, lined with books and paperwork, large yet still cosy. An imposing fireplace almost filled the length of one wall, across from which stood his much-loved desk and matching captain's chair, set between two windows. I would often tease him that in here he would imagine himself at the wheel of his own ship. But not today. I knew at once that something was wrong. Something did not feel right. As my eyes grew accustomed to the gloom, I saw what that was. My father was slumped in his chair. Head resting on the desk. Mouth slack and open in the parody of a smile. Eyes unblinking and staring, clouded with a suggestion of surprise.

'Father,' I stuttered, icy fingers of fear stroking my veins. 'Nooo.'

I did not recognise the sound that tore from my throat as human; it was more like the cry of an animal in mortal pain. I stumbled down the stone steps and dashed to his side, careless of any obstacles that might be in my way. His hand was cold. Very cold. I backed away, unable to drag my eyes from the vision before me, and collided with something soft, warm and smelling of rosemary.

'Isabella. Whatever be the matter?'

Mary's gentle, lyrical voice could not calm me now. She held out her arms and gripped mine to stop me shaking, taking charge as she always had. I pointed, and then twisted and buried my face in her gown.

'He's dead,' I spluttered.

TWO

MY FATHER COULD NOT HAVE chosen a more unwelcoming corner of the graveyard to lay my mother to rest, and now he was joining her in this cool, dark place, overhung by the dense branches of a row of yew trees. It was a sheltered spot though. I liked to think that the high stone wall protected its inhabitants from the worst of the weather that the German Ocean could throw at them, but there were those who said it was built to such a height to prevent them from escaping and roaming around the town after dark. I shuddered. My father was soon to be one of them.

He would have told me to face my fear, but I was choosing to do anything but that.

I felt the pressure of Will's fingers on my arm, gentle, but reassuring. I was not alone. I turned and tipped my head back so I could look at him. His familiar features were speckled like a miniature checkers board by the fine lace of the black veil that I wore lowered over my face. Will was a handsome man who cared little for his appearance, but today he had made an effort. His thick, black hair and beard were well-groomed and he must have brushed his cloak for there was not a speck of dust on it.

He was watching me, his eyes still and steady, their intense dark blue, almost violet, a near perfect match for the clouds that dominated the sky. Clouds that threatened snow. I tried to return his smile, but it was shaky on my lips. The ground's bitter cold seeped through my boots and I could no longer feel my toes. I stamped my feet, turned away from him and forced myself to look at what was in front of me, at the one thing that I'd been trying to avoid since the Minister, Mr Selby, had led us to the gaping hole that sat like an open wound. A gash in the earth into which the coffin bearers were about to lower my father. His belief had been strong, that by now he would be in a better place and it was merely his discarded earthly husk that would be sealed in this tomb. The thought filled me with dread, and I was certain I would have nightmares about this moment for weeks to come.

I allowed my gaze to travel over the rest of the mourners. The walk from my house to the Holy Trinity church on the other side of town had been slow and busy. My father had been well respected, and it seemed most of Berwick's residents had joined the procession, some in fine black silks brought out for the occasion, others in the only garments they possessed – a well-worn and patched assortment – holding their caps in their hands and bowing their heads. It was a reminder of how my father had transcended the full spectrum of this small town, rich and poor, burgesses, merchants and sailors. *'We are all the same in the eyes of our Lord,'* he had been fond of reminding me. Not for the first time since his death I felt a heavy weight descend on me. How would I live up to his expectations?

Only close friends and business associates had crowded into the old church and now gathered around the grave. Everyone else had remained outside the stone walls, waiting for the procession back to The Sailor's Rest for the wake. I could not see Mary, but I knew she was somewhere behind me. She would not push herself forward into the crowd, but would shed her grief in private. Unlike Widow Swynburn who was making a grand display of sobbing into her handkerchief. She tried to catch my eye, but I refused to oblige her.

The sea of faces surrounding the grave started to waver and melt into one, and my legs trembled. I leaned into Will and his hand moved from my arm to my waist. I would get through this without making a public show of myself, which would do nothing but provide fodder for the gossip merchants in the market tomorrow. I took a deep breath and gasped as the cold, raw air hit the back of my throat.

Mr Selby was looking at me now, his expression expectant, and I realised he had finished and I had not heard a word of his eulogy. I knelt and plucked a handful of half frozen clods of earth from the pile on the graveside. Standing once again, I averted my eyes, threw them into the hole and listened to the ricochet as they bounced across the surface of the coffin. Mr Selby nodded his approval before turning his back and threading a path through the long grass towards the church. The crowd started to drift away too, no doubt eager to get out of the cold and into the warmth of the inn, and the food and drink I had provided. I lingered. As unwilling as I had been to look at my father's grave just a few minutes ago, I was now reluctant to leave him there. The finality of it was overwhelming. I was not ready to let him go. Say goodbye for the last time. He still had so much to show me, and I was finding it difficult to rid myself of the conviction that I had failed him in some way. What if the heavy mood that I had noticed had not been caused by worrying about the Lady Isabella, as I had assumed, but something else? If I had thought to ask him, I might have been able to help. I summoned his face now, but the vision that came into my head was not what I expected. Instead of his familiar easy smile, his features were worn, with deep lines of worry carved around his eyes, and there was a grey pallor to his skin that could not be healthy. I swayed like a man in his cups as a wave of guilt hit me. I had failed to notice there was something very wrong with my father.

'Izzy, we must go.' Will's voice broke into my thoughts and reminded me that I had a duty still to perform. I had to welcome my father's friends and foes – not that there were many of the latter – to his wake. It was expected of me. I gripped Will's arm and allowed him to lead me back towards the path. We were almost the only people left now in the churchyard. Standing at a distance and looking towards my father's grave was a man I did not recognise. His appearance was distinctive for these parts. His red-gold beard and hair were just a few shades lighter than my own, and although his beard was short, his hair was too long. It curled over his stiff white ruff, which was so prominent it would have been more fitting at the Queen's court than in a graveyard in Berwick. I glared in the stranger's direction, wondering what business he could have watching over the private grief of others, and was gratified when he bowed his head and turned away.

Delicate flakes of snow had now started to fall. I found myself thinking that at least the Lady Isabella would not have to cope with blizzards out in the ocean. Then it struck me that my father did not know that. He had died still worried that she – and all on board – might have perished. I stumbled, digging my fingers into Will's arm to stop myself from falling. His muscles tensed to support me and he slowed down.

'I'm all right,' I said, answering the question in his eyes.

Our route to The Sailor's Rest took us along the line of the new town defences. Although incomplete, already the height and thickness of the walls that loomed before us were enough to deter all but the most determined attack from the north. I gazed up at them with awe, remembering as a child how I had been fascinated by the stories my father used to tell me, whilst bouncing me on his knee, of our town being laid siege to and fought over by a succession of kings. In his retelling, the number of times Berwick had changed hands between the Scottish and the English would vary – anything from ten to twenty. I'm sure he did not expect me to remember, and he would look at me in vague surprise every time when I corrected him.

'Papa, it's thirteen times,' I would insist with a giggle and he would frown. I realise now it was a part of a game. He knew all along.

The wake was as dreadful as I had feared it would be. So many people wanted to talk to me, to tell me how much they had loved, respected, even feared my father and how he would be missed in Berwick. Others asked what would happen to his business interests with a gleam in their eye, no doubt speculating whether they could profit from his death. Even if my energy had not been drained by the effort of saying farewell to the person I loved more than any other, I would not have satisfied their curiosity with any response. I had yet to consult with Mr Carr, my father's legal counsel and good friend, but I knew, because he had told me many times, that I would inherit his business and he expected me to use my knowledge of it to ensure his legacy, his lifetime's work and that of my grandfather before him, continued to thrive. I would do my best to honour his wishes, but there was now nothing to stop me from making the investment in a new ship that I knew was well overdue.

Mr Carr would be here somewhere. I drew myself up onto the tips of my toes in an effort to see over the top of the crowd and scanned the room. There he was. In a corner near the table where the food was set out, clutching a platter piled high with pies that would contribute more substance to his already portly girth. I crossed the room, avoiding being drawn into conversation with anyone, accepting condolences with a simple nod.

'Madam Gillhespy,' Mr Carr greeted me. He patted me gently on the back, as if I were his favourite dog and I stepped away. He'd known me since I was a baby, and sometimes I thought when he looked at me he still saw me as a child, not as a mature woman, and widow. 'How are you my dear?'

I shrugged. How did he expect me to be?

The heat in the room was unbearable, and the smell of food, ale and too many human bodies crammed into a small space was quite nauseating. The peace and comfort of my home was what I needed now.

'I must leave. Will you come by the house in the morning and we can discuss what happens now?'

'Of course, my dear. Do not worry about anything.'

I nodded and repeated my tip-toeing exercise, this time searching for Will. I spotted him with his good friend Arthur. The two of them had pulled apart from the main crowd and were occupying a window recess. Will had a way of throwing his whole body into a conversation, and he was doing that now, gesticulating with his right arm and tapping his foot, whilst Arthur wore an expression of faint amusement, or maybe frustration. As I approached his countenance changed, and he welcomed me with a sympathetic smile before taking my hand and pressing it to his lips.

'Please let me add my condolences to those of the rest of this room,' he said. 'Your father was a fine man. This town will miss his wisdom and kindness.'

It was such a simple exchange, but it lifted my spirits. His warm brown eyes crinkled at me in a way that left no doubt that his words were spoken in earnest. Little wonder that his company was so sought after at dances and other social occasions in the town. If I did not have Will I could almost see myself joining the queue of ladies waiting to have their hearts broken by such a charming rogue.

'Thank you,' I murmured, withdrawing my hand and turning to address Will. 'I'm exhausted. Would you escort me home please.'

I hated having to ask, but in spite of our new Governor's efforts to curb the more unruly elements of the town, it was no place for a lady to be alone after dark. Besides, I had promised Mary.

We walked back through streets now carpeted in a covering of soft snow, which was still falling, the flakes bigger and denser than earlier, its whirling whiteness muting the dark night under the starless sky. Will offered me his arm and I took it, not because I needed it, but because doubts were besieging my mind and I craved the reassurance of physical contact with another human being.

'I cannot help thinking that I could have done something to prevent this,' I said. Will dipped his head towards me and I looked up at his puzzled expression.

'What do you mean Izzy? Mr Hedley said his heart failed. What could you have done?'

'If he was ill, why didn't I notice?' I demanded. 'Why didn't I press him when I sensed there was something wrong? If he was ill, the doctor may have been able to treat him. Do something.'

My voice had been rising in pitch throughout this outburst. Will stopped walking. He pulled me towards him and enfolded me in his arms, holding me so close that I could feel the beating of his heart reverberate through my body. My breathing slowed to keep time with its rhythm.

'Don't torture yourself so,' Will said. 'I'm sure there's nothing

11

you could have done. Only God can decide when a man's time on this earth is at an end.'

Will's grip on me relaxed and with one of his hands he cupped my chin, tilting it up and bending his neck so our faces were almost touching. My back arched in response, thrusting me towards him as a seedling to the sun. The brush of our lips sent a surge of desire through me, reminding me of how long it had been since I had enjoyed the embrace of a man. For Will and I there should not be much longer to wait, except that now I must observe a decent period of mourning. We would have to instruct Mr Selby to postpone the reading of our banns and set a later date for our marriage. Will's arm started to curve around my waist, but I pulled away and we resumed our steady pace towards home.

Once back in the house I shook the snowflakes from my cloak and hung it on a hook, removed my veil, and pushed open the door into the small parlour that adjoined the dining hall. The fire had been lit and a candle flickered on a table in the corner, illuminating the intricate gears on the clock that my father had loved to watch as they clicked and whirred, charting the movement of the planets as well as telling him the time of day. The welcoming familiarity was just what I needed, and I vowed not to torture myself with thoughts of what I could have done to keep my father by my side, nor think of the churchyard for what was left of the evening. I sank onto the settle in front of the fire, arranging the cushions behind my back so the hard frame would not dig into my spine, and tried not to look at the empty chair facing me on the other side of the fireplace. Will poured two tumblers of whisky and handed one to me. I sipped at it and he swallowed his in one gulp, turned back to the drinks cabinet and poured another. He ignored my father's chair, for which I was grateful, and instead joined me on the settle.

'Izzy,' he said, 'we need to talk.'

I had been gazing into the fire, but the seriousness of his voice drew my attention. What could be so important that he needed to raise it now, after the emotional exertion and exhaustion of the day?

He put his tumbler down and reached for my hands.

'I understand you want to delay our wedding day, but I think we should keep to our original plans.'

His eyes were boring into mine with an intensity that made my insides melt. Even so, what he was suggesting was impossible. I had thought we were in agreement on this point. Watching his face, those features that I could read so well, I realised we were not. With a sigh, I shook my head.

'No. Much as I want us to be married, I will not disrespect my father by doing so whilst I am in mourning.'

'I know it feels wrong, but your father would have understood. There's going to be so much that needs your attention and I want to be with you, to help. Besides, I think we have waited long enough. We could have a quiet, private ceremony out of respect for him, and celebrate in a year's time.'

I pulled my hands out of his and leaned towards the fire. A log cackled and spat a puff of sparks into the air.

'What are you saying? I'm already familiar with my father's business. I know what needs my attention, Mr Carr is there to advise me, and I am capable of making decisions.'

Although I tried, I was unable to keep a sharp edge from creeping into my voice. Today had been draining, and I did not need or desire an argument, especially with Will.

He reached for my hands again, which I had clasped together in my lap, and encircled them in his.

'I know you are,' he said. 'I'm saying that you are going to be vulnerable and there are plenty who would seek to take advantage of that. Not all of your father's business associates are of the kind you would invite to dinner.'

It was difficult to argue with Will's calm analysis, because even though it pained me to admit it, there was some truth in his words. The comments and looks I had noted during the wake had shown me that much, and of course Will worked at the Custom House. He saw the rougher side of the merchant's trade in Berwick. The side that I knew my father, and my husband, had kept from me. But I was not going to hide behind a man. I was on my own now. The business needed me. I was not expecting everything to be easy, and I would have much to learn, but I was equal to it, whatever anyone else might think.

'I'm trying to do what is in your best interests.' Will's hands relaxed and I wriggled my fingers, releasing them from his grip. He pulled away from me, his eyes narrowed and his lips set in a hard line. 'Don't you want me by your side? If you've changed your mind you only need to say so. I won't hold you to a betrothal and a future that you no longer desire.'

'Of course I want you by my side.' I sighed, raising my eyes to the ceiling. Saint Oswald give me patience. It was unfair of Will to push this conversation on me now, when he knew the guilt I was battling with. It could be that I was over-reacting, but I did not have the energy to soothe a wounded ego.

I took a deep breath to smooth the tension from my voice. 'You know that is what I want, more than anything. And you will be, but please do me the courtesy of allowing me to mourn my father first, even if that means we have to wait a little longer. We have the rest of our lives together. There is no need to rush.'

Will stood up and returned to the drinks cabinet. He kept his back turned towards me and poured himself another measure of whisky. That's three, I found myself counting. My father would never have more than two of an evening, but Will was not my father, and this had been an exceptional day. I waited for him to speak again, but it was the loud rattle of metal on metal that interrupted our silence. I was not expecting anyone to call this evening. Most of the town would still be enjoying my hospitality, and who would be so insensitive to call at the house after I've just buried my father?

'Did you …?' I started to ask but he stopped me with a shake of his head.

I imagined Mary grumbling under her breath as she roused herself from the warmth of the kitchen fire. Then footsteps on flagstones and the swish of skirts told me she was crossing the hall, before the murmur of voices and a gentle knock at the parlour door.

'Come in Mary,' I called. A blast of cold air accompanied her into the room, fanning the flames on the fire and making the shadows dance on the walls.

'Sorry Isabella, but there's a gentleman to see you. He wouldn'y give me his name.'

I frowned. 'Tell him to come back tomorrow would you please. This is not a good time.'

'I did, but he insisted. Says it's urgent.'

I sighed and stood, folding my arms in front of me in a stance that I hoped would be unwelcoming, if not intimidating, and convey to this visitor that his timing was deplorable.

'All right. Show him in,' I said. Will put his tumbler down and we both watched the door.

The man who appeared silhouetted in its frame seconds later was tall and slim. His cloak and hat were covered with snow, and flakes clung to his red-gold beard. He pushed the door closed behind him, removed his hat and bowed. A gold ring bounced from his left ear, and I stared at it, having never seen a man wearing such an item before. It glowed in the candlelight as he took a few steps towards us.

'Madam Gillhespy?' he asked. "Isabella Gillhespy, née Lilburne?'

His accent was quite strange, with an odd inflection on the vowels.

Will cleared his throat, a hint that an answer was expected. For a moment I could not articulate a single thought that was inside my head, because I recognised him as the stranger from the churchyard earlier, the one who had been looking over towards my father's grave. It was an uncomfortable feeling, that he knew my name and where I lived, yet I had no idea who he was.

'And you are?' I asked, trying to sound composed.

'Richard Elliott.' He bowed again. When he raised his head his eyes met mine, and there was something in them that made me think he was waiting for a reaction. That his name should mean something to me. It did not. I waited for him to say more, to explain, but he remained silent. Will crossed the room and leaned against the hearth behind me. He placed one hand on my shoulder and I raised one of mine and let it rest, lightly, on his. Funny how a few minutes ago we had been arguing. Now we were united against this stranger.

'Well, Mr Elliott, nice as it is to meet you, today has not been a good day. Whatever business you have with me can wait until tomorrow. Why don't you call on me in my stores, say 3pm?'

I did not bother to tell him where the stores were. He'd found my house, he could work it out for himself.

'No.' His hand strayed to his ear and he twisted the gold ring between his thumb and forefinger. 'I'm sorry, this is not how I'd planned this at all and I'm making a bit of a mess of it.'

'Sir, we have just buried my father, and I'm really not in the mood for guessing games.'

'I know, and that's why I'm here.'

'Did you know my father?' Now my curiosity was piqued.

'We met on only one occasion, just over a week ago,' he said, dropping his hat on a chair and taking a few steps towards us. He was a man who was sure of his reception. His stance was confident, his smile engaging, but I was not in the mood to be charmed. 'I came to Berwick to find him, because my mother's name, before she married, was Elizabeth Lilburne. She is your father's sister.'

I stared at the stranger, opened my mouth to speak and closed it again to stop myself repeating his words back to him. I had never met my aunt. She had left Berwick before I was born, broken all ties with the family when she had married against my grandfather's wishes. I had never thought that she might have had children, or that I would one day meet them.

If this man was indeed her son, it would make him my cousin. Had he been lingering in the churchyard earlier hoping to speak with me? It made no sense. If he had arrived in town a week ago, why had my father not mentioned him to me? Introduced us even?

Will's hand tensed and his fingers dug into my shoulder. It was a reminder that he was there, but my entire being was focused on this stranger, who was watching me with equal intensity, gauging my reaction and the impact of his words. He was rewarded for his patience as my confusion raced across my face. My lack of knowledge made me weak, and I sensed the situation slipping out of my control.

'I wrote to your father when I arrived in town,' he explained. 'He invited me to meet with him, at the office of his legal counsel, a Mr Carr. He was eager to hear news of his sister after all these years. Mr Carr was more concerned about confirming my identity. I presented him with my documents and references for him to check, which is what he has been doing this past week. I was saddened to hear of your father's death, and wanted to pay my respects earlier, but Mr Carr requested that I wait until he had completed his investigation. I did attend the funeral service. I believe you noticed me in the churchyard.'

'I'm sorry if you were expecting a warm welcome, Mr Elliott, but this is all a bit of a shock and also quite a large coincidence. If you are indeed who you say are ...'

'I understand that you may doubt me,' he said, his voice edged with indignation that told a different tale. 'I spoke with Mr Carr this afternoon and he's satisfied that I am who I say. He wanted me to wait, to allow him to speak to you first before I introduced myself, but that feels somewhat impersonal.'

'Please don't interrupt me.' I drew my shoulders back in an attempt to assert my authority on the situation. 'I was going to say that I need some time to get used to the idea that I have a cousin.'

He stretched his mouth into an even wider smile, but it no longer reached his eyes and the effect was unsettling.

'Don't worry about that. We've got all the time in the world.'

He strolled over to the hearth, paused in front of me and then settled himself into my father's chair. My fingernails dug into Will's hand and I sensed him tense. This stranger seemed oblivious to the fact that he was not welcome, and if his behaviour was intended to provoke, he was succeeding. He crossed his legs and brushed a speck of dust from the cuff of his shirt with fingers that could have belonged to a lady they were so smooth and white. I watched him, too astonished to speak. He did not once acknowledge Will's presence, but focused his attention on me, and time seemed to slow down until his next words, spoken in a soft tone, shattered the illusion. 'You see, the reason I left London and travelled here to find my uncle was something I discovered, quite by chance. Madam, you and I are now partners.'

THREE

AFTER THE EMOTIONAL ENERGY OF the day I longed for the oblivion of deep sleep, but it eluded me. My head was too full of Richard Elliott's ridiculous assertion that he and I were partners in my business, and the disagreement between Will and I about what I saw as the need to postpone our wedding day. I rose early, tired and irritable, and took out my bad temper on Mary. She had helped me to prepare my father's closet for the meeting with Mr Carr, and I snapped at her for spilling ink on the leather inlay of his desk. I apologised immediately of course, but she gave me one of her looks that made me feel as though I were a child again, and as soon as we finished she returned to the kitchen, leaving me alone with my thoughts to wait for Mr Carr and Will to arrive.

Before he had left last night, Will had asked me if I wanted him to be there for this meeting. It had not occurred to me that he would not. Just because I wanted to be able to mourn my father, did not mean I no longer wanted to marry Will, and it puzzled me that he could not understand that.

Will was in a position of some authority at the Custom House, which was how I came to know him. He often had business with my father and was a frequent visitor to our house. However, he was married, so I did not think of him in that way. I accepted my father's choice of husband for me, a linen merchant associate of his, and had been happy during the four years of our marriage. Then my husband was killed in a riding accident, and a few years later, Will's wife died from consumption. He was lonely and would often join us for supper, sometimes sitting with me in the parlour after we had dined if my father wished to return to work. On those occasions we would talk about everything, from religion to poetry, and the minstrels who would pass through the town with their songs and masquerades. It was surprising how often we were of the same mind.

I had accepted his proposal of marriage four months ago, and since then I had been counting the days to our wedding in May. Mary and I had spent many an hour planning what I would wear, and the Lady Isabella had brought back a bale of silk in an exquisite shade of red ochre to complement my hair. I had a fitting booked with the seamstress who was to make my gown, and my excitement had grown to a level that far exceeded the experience of my first wedding, but my father's death had not so much dampened my pleasure in anticipation of the day as drowned it, because he would not be there. No-one was more disappointed than I that we would have to postpone, but it was clear to me that there was no alternative. I hoped I would be able to make Will understand that, because I needed to focus all my energy on the very real problems that I knew I was going to have to face, first and foremost being the matter of Richard Elliott.

Whilst my thoughts had been roaming free, I had been wandering around the room, plucking books and folders of paperwork from the shelves lining every inch of wall that was not occupied by windows or the fireplace, then returning them without bothering to open them. I paused now behind my father's desk, the surface of which had been untidy when I'd found him, with papers strewn all over it. That was an indication that he had been hard at work when his heart had stopped beating, because he never left his desk in a mess at night. I did not have the stomach for going through these yet and had already stacked them in a neat pile.

My hand brushed against the back of the chair positioned behind the desk. My father's captain's chair had been removed, at my instigation. I'm not sure where George took it – probably to the small office in our warehouse. It did not concern me, because I would never sit in it. I'd already replaced it with one that had been in my old nursery. It was solid and heavy, with a high, carved back and chunky arms that made it too big to push under the desk. Countless nannies, and then governesses, had sat in this chair, attempting to instruct me in everything from reading, writing and arithmetic, to flower arranging and the correct way to address a Lord or Lady, should I ever meet one. Eventually I'd defeated every one of them, and my father had conceded that he was wasting his money. This chair, though, remained a symbol of authority to me.

I had never thought that might be important, but after last night, I was not so sure. First, Will's warning that people would seek to cheat me, that because I wear skirts instead of hosen I will be easy to deceive and take advantage of. Then Richard Elliott turning up, purporting to be my cousin, and making his ludicrous claim to my business. A business that he knew nothing about, whereas it had always been a part of my life. After the last of the governesses left, my father had instructed me in the running of it, and before long I was helping with the paperwork, as my mother would have done had she lived. Even during the years of my marriage, I had still helped my father as much as I could. He had made no secret that after he died I would inherit, but neither of us had expected that day to arrive so soon.

I turned my back on the chair and the desk, sat down in one of the room's four window seats and gazed out at the courtyard. The snow was no longer falling, although it must have done so for most of the night. Where it lay undisturbed it was deep, reaching almost to the seat of the low bench in the courtyard that Will and I had often sat upon, in the late days of summer before the weather became too cold to make such a pastime enjoyable. An area had been cleared in front of the door set into the middle of the far wall of the courtyard. Even so, the chickens that would normally be strutting around, pecking at the ground, remained in their coop, built on to the kitchen wall. Thunder would be in his stable beyond the courtyard. My father's old horse would be wondering where his master was. If I had time, I would go to him now, wrap my arms around his solid neck and draw comfort from his soothing presence. A lump rose in my throat. I gulped and swallowed. It would not be appropriate to allow my grief to surface now. That would have to wait.

Muffled by the snow and my emotions, I almost did not hear Will's knock at the door – always three, evenly spaced, short raps. I left Mary to answer it and settled myself into what I would think of as my captain's chair. On an impulse, I grabbed a quill and pulled some papers from the top of the pile so they sat in front of me. If I wanted to show Will that I could cope, it was best to appear calm and confident, and let him think that I had been busy. Lest my eyes were shiny with unshed tears, I did not raise my head until he was striding across the room towards me. I put the quill down and folded my hands together on the desk to stop them shaking.

'Izzy, you look exhausted. Are you sure you're ready to do this?'

I almost laughed. At least there was to be no great distance between us after yesterday's argument, although I wished he would be a little less forthright. A compliment on my appearance would have been welcome, even if not warranted. He hovered by the side of the desk.

'We can ask Carr to come back tomorrow.' His voice was gentle, and I'm sure he meant well, but I needed answers, and another sleepless night, or a day of wondering if Richard Elliott's claims held any element of truth, would not provide them.

'No. It's best I face this now. Sit down won't you?'

I had placed two chairs across from me on the other side of the desk. Will's eyes travelled around the room and I thought he would prefer to join me on my side, but eventually he sat down, facing me and to my right. He removed his gloves and placed them on the corner by my father's stack of papers.

'What do you know of your aunt?' he asked.

'Not much,' I admitted. 'My father had mentioned her, but we never discussed her, or what had happened in any detail. It did not seem important to me, and I'm certain he didn't say anything about her having a child.'

'And he didn't mention anything to you about this Richard Elliott having arrived in town?'

'No.' I shook my head.

We did not have to wait long for Mr Carr to arrive. He took the vacant chair, placed a leather folder padded with paperwork on the desk in front of him, withdrew a sheaf of papers and cleared his throat.

'Ord,' he greeted Will with a nod and turned to face me.

'Mr Carr. Something happened last night that you need to know about, but first, please tell me, my father made me his heir, didn't he?'

'My dear, I have all the paperwork here, if you'll just bear with me for a moment.'

He started shuffling through the papers. A few fell to the floor and drifted beneath the desk. He dropped to his hands and knees to gather them. Standing up Mr Carr was a stout figure, but crouching down he was even rounder, and it was a tight squeeze for him between the chair and the desk. It was quite comical. Will caught my eye and I noticed his mouth was twitching as he too tried not to laugh.

I waited until Mr Carr had reinstated himself on his chair before addressing him again.

'A young man turned up here last night – a stranger, saying he's my cousin, and claiming part ownership of my father's business. Please tell me that isn't true.'

As I spoke, my eyes did not leave his face, which was a moving picture of surprise, dismay and agitation, in that order. I could no longer hold onto the shred of hope that I had been clinging to. Richard Elliott had not made all of this up. If he were indeed my aunt's son … I found I could not articulate the thoughts that followed, even inside my head.

'He did not heed my advice then,' Mr Carr spluttered.

I spread my hands on the surface of the desk and waited for him to continue. A lump of something hard and icy descended into my stomach. I both wanted, and dreaded, to hear more.

Will got up and moved to stand behind the desk, by my side. 'Carr. It's clear that you know something of this individual. Perhaps you could explain?'

It is not often that a man of the law loses his gift for words, but Mr Carr opened and closed his mouth several times without uttering a sound. Eventually he cleared his throat and the words that had been stuck there came spewing out. 'Madam Gillhespy. First of all, I deeply regret that the young man showed such insensitivity and did not do as I requested and allow me to speak with you first. With the exception of a specific bequest for Mary, your father did leave you all of his possessions and assets. But perhaps, if you will allow me, I should start at the beginning.'

The lump in my stomach shrank to a more manageable size. My father had indeed left me everything, but Mr Carr's words made it clear that this situation was not going to be as simple as that. I was in thrall to my rising curiosity, and I cursed myself that I had not been more inquisitive when my father had spoken of his sister. If I had known how important it would become to know what had happened to her, I am certain I would have pressed him for more information. Now I had to rely on Mr Carr's account. I drummed my fingers on the arm of my chair, waiting for him to speak.

He shuffled his papers again, without dropping them this time, and then replaced them all on the desk. He steepled his hands and rested them over his ample stomach, rubbing the thumbs together.

'Your aunt's name was Elizabeth, and she was younger than your father by about twenty minutes.'

He paused. This was not the beginning I had expected. My brain stumbled, trying to catch up with the meaning of his words.

'I didn't know they were twins,' I gasped.

Mr Carr inclined his head, but his eyes were watching me. I twisted my neck so I could see Will's reaction. I detected my surprise reflected in his face before his brows twitched and his expression closed down. I turned away.

'Go on, please.'

'They were very close – as close as you would expect twins to be, even though they were boy and girl. There were no more siblings. There had been an older brother but he died of a small pox when he was about eight years old, and after the twins your grandmother had been unable to carry another child successfully to birth.'

'Elizabeth was a wild child though, and spoilt. Your grandfather thought it would be best for her to marry, and he lined up a match with a wealthy merchant, a business associate of his, who had recently lost his wife. Of course, Elizabeth was not happy with his choice. Your grandmother tried to keep the peace, tried to persuade her of the advantages of the match, and the life she could expect to lead as the wife of one of Berwick's most prominent citizens at the time, but all she could see was that he was old; his youngest daughter was several years older than Elizabeth herself, and he had a number of grandchildren in various nurseries already. Your grandfather was enraged and humiliated by his daughter's refusal to obey his wishes, and your grandmother was unwilling to force her. The result was a disaster.'

Although my memories of my grandparents were hazy, I do remember being terrified by my grandfather when he was in a temper. I would run to the kitchen and hide beneath the table, comforted by the warmth and the appetising aromas. Mary would slip me pieces of cake or a scone whilst pretending not to know I was there. Elizabeth's situation had been similar to my own, yet I had been willing to marry the man who was many years my senior and had a son only a few years my junior. Elizabeth had not, and she had my admiration for daring to defy my grandfather. I wondered how my father would have reacted if I had refused to marry Mr Gillhespy.

'I already know she left Berwick, having married against my grandfather's wishes,' I said, prompting him to move his narrative on to what happened next.

'Let me tell you the whole story,' he insisted.

Will's fingers tapped my shoulder. A sign of his own impatience perhaps, or a caution to me to contain mine?

'She ran away, and when she returned a few weeks later she was with a sailor, whom she introduced as her husband.' Mr Carr's shoulders quivered. 'A very unsuitable chap he was too. His name was James Elliott and he was known to your grandfather. He was fond of the drink, and a gambler, but he was a handsome fellow and he could talk well. Elizabeth was enchanted by him and he seized his chance, expecting, I imagine, that she would be provided for by her family and not cut off without a penny.'

'And is that what they did? Cut her off without a penny?' I was leaning forward in my chair now. My aunt had spirit for sure. I think I would like her.

'Not quite.' Mr Carr closed his eyes for a moment. 'Elizabeth had hoped her father would capitulate in time and invite her sailor husband into the business, but she miscalculated. Your grandfather made it quite clear that he would never, ever, accept his new son-in-law.'

'So what did they do?'

'They left Berwick, went south and never returned. Elizabeth only got in touch once more. She wrote to her parents to tell them they had a grandson, but promised that if they were not prepared to accept James they would never meet his child.'

'She was stubborn,' I muttered.

'Indeed she was, and so was he. It's a family trait, I believe.'

I looked up and saw the flicker of a twinkle in Mr Carr's eyes. Recognising that as a joke at my expense, I glared at him and the gravitas of the situation cloaked his expression once again.

'And my father tried to find her?'

'After your grandfather died, he never stopped trying to find her, and he tasked me with helping him. We were given addresses, and we wrote letter after letter but received not a single reply. We had no idea whether the letters were reaching her or not.'

All of my life, my father and I had formed our own, small family unit and I had never known the extent of his emotional connection to another person, and what's more, a person I did not know. It brought an uncomfortable realisation that our relationship may not have been as close as I had always thought.

'Why did he keep this from me?'

Mr Carr thought for a moment before replying. 'Only your father would be able to answer that in full. I do know that he found it very painful to discuss, and he knew it would be difficult for you, or anyone, to understand how he could feel so close to a sister who had walked out of the family, who had left him, her twin brother, behind, because of the strength of her love for another man. A sister who had made no effort to contact him for nearly thirty years.'

There was something about the way Mr Carr was addressing a spot beyond my shoulder rather than meeting my eyes that worried me. It was a sad story, but nothing he had said so far told me what I needed to know.

'There's still more though, isn't there?' I demanded.

Mr Carr leaned back and his chair groaned in protest beneath him.

'What does all of this have to do with Richard Elliott claiming to be a partner in my business?' The lump in my stomach swelled again, and I pressed my hand against it to ease the sharp pain whilst I grappled with a horrifying thought that had just popped into my head. 'No, he wouldn't have left his nephew, whom he had only just met, a share of his business. I don't believe it. Can we challenge it?'

I cast a desperate glance at Will but he did not respond. His eyes glittered with an intense scrutiny that was focused on Mr Carr. Through my skirts I could feel the jerky motion of his leg as his foot tapped at the floor.

'No, my dear, it's not that at all. As I said, your father left you all of his assets.'

'So tell me then.'

'Your father did not own all of the business. When your grandfather died he split it in equal measure between your father and Elizabeth's son, Richard. His share was to be held in trust until he should choose to claim it, and the condition of his inheritance was that he return to Berwick and work in the business.'

His words fell like a sledgehammer on my past and my future, shattering both into tiny fragments that I was desperate to catch but they slipped through my fingers.

The betrayal was one thing. My father had allowed me to believe in a reality that did not exist. What was even worse though, was that he had failed to prepare me for this moment. Will squeezed my shoulder but I brushed his hand away, pushed my chair back and leapt to my feet. I needed to get out of this room, away from Mr Carr and his 'my dears'. Even away from Will, who had not said a word but I could feel the tension oozing from him, as thick and viscose as honey. I swept out of the room, not sure where I was heading. To the comfort of the kitchen and Mary's kind face and words? No. Solitude was what I craved. I crossed the hall, my feet finding their own way as my vision was a blur. Once in the parlour I leaned against the window frame, pressing my nose to the glass and trying to blink back the welling tears.

Betrayed. I had been betrayed.

I missed my father so much, but he had kept such secrets from me. And now, what was I supposed to do about Richard Elliott? The thought of handing over half of what was supposed to be mine to a complete stranger was one I could not bear to contemplate, and the prospect of working with that stranger, being expected to defer to his decisions, was beyond my comprehension. But it seemed I must do both. I clenched my fists and raised them to the window. The front door slammed and I looked up. Mr Carr waddled away from the house clutching his folder of documents.

'He's gone to find Elliott.' Will's voice was soft. I had not heard him enter the room, but I was pleased that he had followed me.

'Why?' My breath misted the glass. I unballed my fists. My nails had left crescent-shaped marks in the soft flesh at the base of my thumb. I rubbed at them, erasing them with my fingers, and turned to face Will.

'Because you two need to talk.'

He was right, of course, but what was I going to say?

'Izzy. Are you all right?'

'I'm fine.'

I resumed my study of the street, so he could not see in my eyes how distraught Mr Carr's revelations had left me. If he had reached out to touch me, even just the lightest brush across my arm, I believe I would have been unable to hold back the tears any longer, and they would have burst from me like waves on a strong tide, sweeping away everything that lay in their path. I did not need to see him to know he was watching me, and the slight shaking of my shoulders would tell him I was not speaking the truth.

'Do you want me to talk to him for you?'

'No,' I said. Part of me wished I could accept his offer, but if I was going to have to fight for what was mine by right, it would do me no good to back away at the first sign of battle. Besides which, it would convince Will that he was right about not postponing our marriage. The snow was falling again, tiny flakes swirling in a vague pattern, as if they were dancing to a tune I could not hear. I lifted a finger to the glass and tried to trace their movement, aimless and elegant, the complete opposite to the turmoil in my mind.

'Why didn't he tell me?' My voice was little more than a whisper. 'Secrets. If ever I have children of my own, I swear I will not keep such secrets from them.'

Will moved so he was standing by my side. He leaned with his shoulder against the window, watching me. His tall frame blocked much of the dim light and drew my attention away from the snow. My mind started to clear, and I raised my eyes to his face, inviting him to answer. His shoulders flexed and he appeared ill at ease. Another thought occurred to me.

'Did you know?' I demanded.

'No.'

The speed of his denial made me suspicious. He held my gaze and I believed him, but I was also certain he was hiding something from me.

'Fathers don't always tell their daughters everything, especially when it involves events that occurred long before they were born.'

'My father shared everything concerning the business with me,' I countered.

It was habit. That is what I had always believed. I had yet to come to terms with the reality, which was that he had not shared everything with me. What other secrets had he guarded? I shook that question away. Will was watching me, waiting for me to say more, and I was grateful that he did not point out how wrong I was.

I swallowed and smiled. 'Let's welcome Mr Elliott and see what he has to say.'

An hour later I was reinstated on my chair behind my father's desk – my desk – when Mary ushered my cousin into the room. I had half expected Mr Carr to be with him, but he had come alone. My legal counsel did not have a stomach for confrontation, or perhaps he was being discreet, allowing us to have this difficult first conversation in private. Will sat in the same chair he had occupied earlier. The advantage was now mine. Whatever Richard Elliott had to say, the situation could not be any worse than it already was. In a strange way the thought was comforting, and it emboldened me. I waved my hand at the empty chair. He sat down and flashed me a smile, which I did not return.

'So, Mr Elliott. Why now? It's obvious that the letters my father sent reached your mother or you would not have known to come here. So why now? Why have you waited all of these years to return to Berwick?'

My father had always told me when facing a difficult business negotiation to seize the initiative. *'Strike the first blow,'* he used to say. I could hear his voice now. What would he have done if Elizabeth had responded to him? Would he have welcomed his nephew into the business? That was not a difficult question to answer. He would have honoured the conditions of my grandfather's will. Given what Mr Carr had said about the depth of the bond between them, he would have been excited about the prospect of working with his sister's son.

'Because I didn't know,' Richard Elliott was saying as I dragged my mind back from the past and reminded myself of my father's other often repeated piece of advice. *Don't forget to listen.'*

'My mother kept it all from me – a little like your father appears to have forgotten to share with you. She's a bitter woman with a long memory. She had no desire to return to the family who had spurned her, and no intention of allowing me to do so. Indeed, she told me she was certain it was a hoax – the business, the inheritance – an elaborate fabrication on the part of her brother to persuade her to leave my father. You see, she never forgave her brother for not taking her side, and she loved her husband in spite of his faults. I found out quite by accident when I was looking for something among her papers. She was adamant that I should not come, and I was equally adamant that I should. I'm afraid we did not part on good terms.'

He leaned back and crossed one leg over the other. His hosen were a fine wool in a deep shade of blue, and his black doublet was embroidered with thread of a matching shade, fastened with a row of shiny buttons. He wore the same ruff as yesterday. He was a man who took care with his appearance, unlike Will, who had perfected a certain crumpled look, and who I had never seen in a ruff. I glanced at him now, but his expression was inscrutable and fixed on the man to his side.

'What is it that you want?'

'I would have thought that was rather obvious. I want my inheritance.' He picked at a loose thread on his sleeve, a slight frown creasing the skin between his eyebrows.

'What do you know of my father's business?' My words were chosen to provoke, but he showed no sign of being ruffled by them.

'Our business.' He corrected me. 'I'm a fast learner.'

I swallowed hard and forced myself to continue. 'And what have you learned so far?'

'I'm not a complete novice. My own father worked for a merchant in London.'

'He was a sailor, I believe. It's hardly the same.'

'He was, at first, but then as he grew older, proved he was trustworthy and demonstrated a shrewd business sense, he ran the wharf operation for his employer who was trading in fine silks, spices and gold beyond your imagination, and from much further afield than the Low Countries. You need to think on a much bigger scale Madam Gillhespy.'

He grinned, a wide, jubilant smile. If I could have erased it from his face and ground it to dust beneath my feet I would have. Of course I could not, and as I was too much a lady to put into words the thoughts that were running through my head, I had to content myself with loading all my anger into my expression. Even so, it took more than a few seconds before his smile faded and he cast me a puzzled glance, rose to his feet and bid Will and I good day.

FOUR

'HOW DARE HE TELL ME how I should run my business,' I raged, when Will and I were alone again. I had abandoned my chair and was pacing up and down the length of my father's closet. Will remained seated.

'Izzy. Slow down. I'm exhausted just watching you.' As I approached the desk again for the fifth or sixth time, he seized my arm and forced me to stop. He stood up and pulled me towards him. I resisted at first; I wasn't ready to be placated, but he was firm and I deflated into his arms, resting my head on his shoulders. He held me, and gradually my breathing slowed and my thoughts started to resume order from the jumble the confrontation with Richard Elliott had left behind.

'You have to admit that he has some grand ideas,' Will said.

I lifted my head from its cradle on his shoulder and pushed him away. Taken by surprise, he dropped his arms and I stepped back.

'Grand ideas! Is that all you can say? I know what this business needs more than anyone, and I certainly don't need a stranger to advise me.' I turned my back on him and bit my lip in frustration.

In truth, Richard Elliott was saying nothing more than I had already resolved upon, but it was his smug complacency and self-assurance that had fired my temper; the way he had started to tell me what we needed to do, without even bothering to ask me what I thought. People would listen, because he was a man, and he had just swept in from London. Though for all of his big ideas, his true knowledge of this business would fit with ease into Mr Hedley's smallest medicine phial.

Once again I was reminded of Will's caution about the difficulties that lay ahead. Difficulties that had taken on another layer of complexity since the arrival of my cousin. Already I could feel my influence being diluted. Richard Elliott would become the authority, and receive the credit and respect for having the knowledge and vision to refresh this business. It would rankle with me like a sore, if I allowed it to.

My fingers stroked the bunch of keys hanging from my waist. The cool metal soothed my skin and strengthened my resolve. This was my business and I would fight for it. In public I might have to defer to my cousin, but in private I would not. I would make him listen to me when I gave him some of the hard facts about the condition of our most important ship. The Lady Isabella was ageing. Like a battle-scarred soldier, every time she returned she bore new wounds inflicted by the waters on which she sailed. I had tried to persuade my father that it was time to retire her to local trips and invest in a new ship to make the arduous, but more profitable voyages to the Low Countries and back. Ever cautious about spending money, he had not agreed, but now he was no longer here to object.

I thrust my head high and turned back to Will. He was leaning against my desk, hands resting on its surface, one leg crossed over the other, watching me with appraising eyes.

'We have to invest in a new ship,' I said, deciding to forgive him for his insensitivity and save my energy for the real battle ahead. 'I've spoken with Captain Thirlwell. After that last trip the Lady Isabella is barely seaworthy. She must be moored for a period of time so the work can be carried out properly. I cannot send her out and risk the lives of all the crew, not to mention the value of the cargo. None of my other ships are big enough to make the long journey viable, and besides, they're needed for our local trade.'

Will raised his eyebrows. 'You often have to make tough decisions in business,' he said.

'But not irresponsible ones,' I replied, meeting his eyes.

We remained like that, locked in silence for a long moment. Will's work gave him a good understanding of the shipping trade, and I know he and my father had often discussed business. Indeed, my father had valued his opinion. For the first time it occurred to me that he might have sided with my father's more cautious approach rather than my vision for expansion. Of course we had talked of my plans, or at least I had talked and he had listened. I cannot remember him ever disagreeing with me, but then I cannot remember him agreeing with me either. His eyes slid away from mine. The uneasy feeling that there was something he was not sharing with me returned.

'What are you thinking?' I asked him.

'Just that ships not at sea are not earning money.'

It was a trite response that annoyed me. Did he think I did not realise that? I watched his face for any sign that he was joking but there was none. The expression in what I could see of his eyes was unfathomable. I bit back the cutting reply that I felt his comment deserved and moved away from him towards one of the window seats. Leaning against the wall, my gaze travelled out to the courtyard. A robin perched on the naked branch of the apple tree, its red breast a dramatic contrast to the crisp white coat worn by the rest of the courtyard. It cocked its head towards the window, and for a moment I fancied that it was watching me, encouraging me.

'Izzy.'

Whilst I had been looking at the robin, I had not noticed Will move towards me until he was so close that his breath tickled my neck and my insides squirmed. He rested his hands on my shoulders and turned me around to face him.

'Have you thought any more about what I said, about not postponing our wedding?' he asked, stroking a loose strand of hair with his long fingers and tucking it behind my ear. 'As your husband, I can deal with Elliott, and I promise I will make sure your voice is heard.'

'You're asking me to be disrespectful to my father's memory. It goes against everything I believe.'

I pulled away from him, unwilling to allow him to sense my hesitancy. Without the presence of Richard Elliott I would not have faltered, but his arrival had changed everything. Will and I working together, side-by-side, was what I wanted, but it should not be like this. I should not be forced into a corner, choosing between submitting to the authority of one man or another, when all I wanted to do was grieve for the one I'd just lost.

I decided to change the subject.

'Mr Young has asked me to meet with him this afternoon,' I said. 'And I intend to see what we can do about making the investment in this business that my father had put off for far too long. If that means that we have no ships at sea for a time, well, so be it.'

Will was slow to respond and when he did, his voice was soft, his tone measured.

'What does he want?'

I shrugged. 'He didn't say, but I will find out soon enough.'

'I can get away for an hour this afternoon. I'll come with you.'

His presumption staggered me, but I chose to ignore it. 'That won't be necessary. Mr Young has invited me to meet, and I do not recall him advising I would need a chaperone or a man to speak for me.'

'Izzy, please, I'm begging you. Let me help you. The likes of Elliott, Young and even Captain Thirlwell. It's a rough world ...'

'Are you sure you don't mean it's no place for a woman?' I snapped.

'There are many who would hold that view,' he retaliated, thrusting his hands towards me and then withdrawing them. He raked his fingers through his hair until it resembled a bird's nest of intertwining twigs with random bits sticking out. It would have made me smile, but I was too cross with him. 'But that isn't what I was trying to say. I meant that even though you think you understand your father's business, and he did share much with you, there is also plenty that you don't know. The quay and the men who work there don't belong in polite society. You have no experience of dealing with them, and they may not wish to deal with you. I worry that you will put yourself, and the business, at risk.'

His words made no sense to me. I was as familiar and comfortable with the quay as I was with this room. It had been my playground when others of my age were tossing knucklebones or spinning tops. I had been around it all of my life, often against my father's wishes. Will was not saying what he meant, I was sure of it, but what did he mean? I wanted to challenge him – I was more than capable of dealing with the men at the quay if I needed to, although it seemed I would not be allowed to demonstrate that, but I had not been talking of them.

'Doesn't Mr Young belong in polite society?' I asked, directing the conversation back. It was a disingenuous comment. Mr Young was by far the most successful and wealthiest merchant in the town with the biggest ships and an office next to the Tolbooth. It was also a well-known secret that he was prepared to lend his wealth to others, for a small premium on repayment.

'Young is a man of business. He will pursue whatever is in his interests, not yours.'

I chose not to answer. He pulled me closer again and murmured into my hair.

'You have just lost your father, and then the shock of Elliott turning up. It's a lot to cope with.'

I think it was the sympathy in his voice and his proximity that was my undoing and I could no longer hold back.

'I miss him so much.' I swallowed hard, trying to choke down the sob that was rising in my throat, but it was too powerful. Giving in to a moment of weakness that I hated myself for, I buried my head on Will's shoulder and let the grief flow out of me as if it were the Tweed emptying itself into the German Ocean.

After Will had gone I still had plenty of time to fill before my meeting with Mr Young, and I intended to go to my warehouse. With Will's help I had already supervised the offloading of the Lady Isabella's cargo – mostly woven linens and tapestries, glazed pottery from Antwerp and wine. Dockworkers had barrowed everything to our stores, using one of the narrow stone passages through the walls that were so useful for merchants like myself with premises on Briggate. I must ensure everything she had brought back with her had been stored according to my instructions, and do a proper inventory. Something else my father had instilled in me, *'Always know what you've got, and check it often.'* He did not trust anyone. I had been so busy with the arrangements for his burial that I had not yet had the opportunity to address this.

First, though, I had a craving for the quay. I wanted to taste the salt and feel it stinging my skin as it hustled across the estuary, carried on the breeze from the ocean. I wanted to hear the shouts of the men busy loading and unloading boats, and inhale the unmistakeable smell of the fish which Berwick traded with our neighbours down the coast. The quay was in my blood, and without it I was not fully alive. In spite of Will's words, I belonged there.

Wrapped in my thickest cloak and warmest gloves, I set out, intending to approach through Segate, which afforded my favourite view, with the industry of the wharfside framed by the low wooden bridge that spanned the Tweed and led to the south. Beyond the bridge, the castle dominated the landscape, protecting the town from attackers who might try to approach along the river. The snow had stopped falling, and already the hooves of horses and wheels of carts trundling along Briggate towards the bridge had churned and mixed it with the mud that lay beneath, whilst to the sides the surface had been compacted by many pairs of human feet. It was not at all like the pristine, white surface that, as a child, I had loved to be the first to spoil, hopping through it like a rabbit and looking back over my shoulder at the tiny footprints I'd left behind.

I skidded along the icy surface, grateful once more for my sturdy boots that kept me from slipping to the ground more than once. I could almost hear my father tutting. How he would reprimand me for going to a meeting with Mr Young in the footwear of a labourer, but part of me thought it appropriate that I was wearing men's boots. Perhaps I should buy a pair of hose and a doublet too! At the thought, a low chuckle escaped my throat, and with it some of the tension that had built up through the stress of the past week evaporated.

The guards nodded to me as I passed through the gate and emerged onto Maison Dieu Quay, which was busy. When was it ever not? I gulped in the air, relishing its wildness, and the sharp tang of the ocean as it hit the back of my throat. Several of the dockworkers called out to me or acknowledged me as they bustled past, loaded down with crates and sacks. This was my world. How could Will even suggest that I did not understand it, or its people?

He would be at work now, at the Custom House, which was ahead of me, close to the bridge. I picked my way along the quay, trying to avoid the iciest patches of compressed snow and dodging boys wheeling barrows loaded high with fish, eggs and grains. The Lady Isabella was anchored midstream, fighting to hold her position in the ebbing tide. When I reached the small wooden jetty, I paused to look across at her, wishing she was closer so I could go on board. I would need to have a conversation with Captain Thirlwell soon, to assess the work that needed to be done, but that would have to wait for another day. Her sails had been taken down, and from this distance she did not look too tired, but appearances can be deceptive.

I preferred to remember the Lady Isabella as she had been when my father had taken me on board for the first time, when I could have been no more than four years old. It was one of my earliest memories. My father had gripped my hand as we crossed the gangplank from the jetty, and the captain had been waiting on deck to greet us. I fell in love that day, with my namesake, but I was also in awe of her power and beauty. After he'd finished talking business with the captain, my father had hoisted me onto his shoulders and taken me around the deck, pointing out the rigging for the sails, the masthead and the castle, which I had found disappointing since it seemed to be just another part of the deck and did not resemble any structure that to my mind was worthy of the name. His pride in our ship was infectious and remains with me to this day, even though he has not.

I was unwilling to tear myself away from this scene, allowing its energy to revitalise my spirits, but I could tarry no longer and I turned towards the walls and one of the passageways back onto Briggate. My mind moved on to the meeting with Mr Young. Immersed in my thoughts, I did not hear someone approaching me from behind.

'Madam Gillhespy.' Richard Elliott's voice was a most unwelcome interruption. I thought about ignoring him, pretending I had not heard, but that would be very impolite, and much as I disliked him, I would not be rude. Instead, I stopped and turned back to face the river. As I did, the wind whipped my cloak and dragged me sideways in an unruly stagger that would have deposited me on the ground had I not collided with him first. His arms reached out to steady me, but I recovered my balance and pushed them away.

'Mr Elliott, forgive me.'

I stepped around him, the ice and snow forcing me into a slow pace, and was both surprised and a little annoyed when he fell into step beside me.

'I'm pleased to see you. I went to take a look in our warehouse, but when I got there it was all locked up and appeared to be deserted.'

I suppose I should have expected this. Of course, he would want to see what riches this business possessed. A few weeks ago, by his own admission, he did not know it even existed. Now, half of what I had was his, and he had not so much as lifted one of those soft white fingers for a half penny of any of it. I stopped and regarded him closely. I could imagine him rubbing his hands together with anticipation, greed in his eyes, and I wondered how much money he needed to make before he would leave us in peace and return to London. A dandy like him must have a sweetheart waiting to marry him, especially if his pockets were filled with my money from my inheritance.

'You must think I'm a dreadful opportunist, but I can assure you I'm not. I'm willing to work as hard as anyone so our business flourishes. Please allow me the time to prove that to you.'

'I believe I have little choice,' I replied, resuming my slow progression. 'It so happens that I'm on my way there now. Perhaps you would care to join me?'

I was proud of my store. It had heavy double doors, painted black, with a solid iron ring latch above the lock of the left side. They were imposing, and to my mind quite impressive. I reached for my father's keyring that I now wore hanging from a length of cord I had fashioned around my waist, selected the biggest key, which was longer than my hand, and unlocked the door.

The air was as cold inside as out. I flung the doors open to allow us a little light – there were no windows and I did not intend to be there for long enough to go to the trouble of lighting candles.

'Well, here we are. I like to think of it as our emporium.'

As I spoke, I swivelled around on the spot, letting my eyes adjust to the gloom before moving further in so I could peer into the deeper recesses of the building. The space was neat and tidy. Everything appeared to have been stored as I had instructed. Bolts of cloth wrapped in paper filled the highest of the shelves that lined the walls. Beneath them were crates of pottery and tapestries, and barrels of wine were lined up in rows on the baked-earth floor. I nodded with approval.

'I need to do a full inventory of what the Lady Isabella brought back on her latest trip,' I said, watching Richard Elliott stroll up and down the rows, disappearing into the shadows and then re-emerging into the light as he approached me, his eyes travelling from floor to ceiling. The store was not completely full, but I thought it looked impressive.

I prised open one of the crates closest to me and pulled out the large water jug that nestled in a bed of wood shavings to protect it from damage.

'Is all of this stock sold?' he asked as he drew closer to me.

He could have commented on how well the space was organised, the quality of the cloth, the richness and variety of the wines, or the beauty of the Dutch pottery that I held in my hands with its delicate yet vibrant shades of blues painted on the creamy white surface, but of course he didn't, and I chided myself for expecting anything other from this man. All he could see in front of him was money, pure and simple.

'Some of it will be, but until I've done the inventory and checked my father's paperwork I cannot be sure,' I replied, reluctant to admit that at the moment I did not know the answer.

'I can help with the inventory,' he offered, his disembodied voice bouncing towards me from the dark of a far corner.

I did not want his help. I wanted him to leave. Could I even trust him to do an inventory? His tour of the warehouse came to a halt by my side.

'I told you, I'm here to work.'

I inclined my head in acknowledgement. What else could I do? His expression was serious and he sounded genuine, but I still had my doubts whether he knew what it meant to do a day's work.

'How long will it take to get the Lady Isabella fully loaded and ready to sail again?'

I shook my head. 'We're in no rush. Our seas at this time of year are treacherous and she needs work. Have you seen her yet?'

'Only from a distance. I've a mind to go there now.'

'Perhaps you should. Then you may understand that we cannot just load her up and send her back out again.'

'Why ever not, Madam Gillhespy? Surely that's what this business is all about?'

'This business needs a new ship, Mr Elliott.'

'Forgive me, but doesn't it take months – years even – to build a boat the size of the Lady Isabella? What are we supposed to do whilst we wait for that to happen? Sit here and watch the mist rolling in and out with the tide?'

'There's no need to mock,' I retorted.

'But there is a need for some realism.'

We were glaring at each other now. He was the first to look away, and as he did, his eyes fell on a small pile of cards stacked in a silver tray on the table just inside the entrance. I had drawn these for my father in my very best handwriting.

Joseph Lilburne, Briggate, Berwick

He plucked one from the top of the pile.

'Nice,' he said. 'Your work?'

I nodded and picked up the rest of the cards.

'I guess we won't be needing them any more. When you can find the time, perhaps you should do some new ones. Richard Elliott esquire and Madam Isabella Gillhespy. Has a certain ring to it don't you think?'

He smiled at me and I scowled back.

'If you'll excuse me, I have an appointment,' I said.

I stepped outside. He lingered for a moment, his eyes sweeping over the stores as if committing the contents to memory, before following me. He stood by my side, watching me lock the door, his fingers twisting the ring in his ear and a thoughtful expression on his face.

'Is that the only one?' He nodded towards the key.

'I assume you mean the key, and yes, it's the only one.'

'Better see about getting another one cut then.' He smirked. 'Oh, and I think we ought to call each other by our first names? All of this formality between partners and cousins is somewhat irksome, don't you think? Good day to you Isabella.'

I watched him saunter away, willing him to slip on the icy ground in his fashionable boots, but he was careful, or maybe lucky, and his feet remained in contact with the rough path. I could think of no polite response to his parting jibe. Instead, I bent down and scooped up a handful of snow, which I rolled into a hard ball in my gloved hands and threw, aiming at his retreating back. It landed a little short and shattered into compacted fragments that skittered and bounced after him, as if they were in pursuit. I thought I heard him laugh as he vanished from my sight, swallowed up into the gloom of the town walls on his way back to the quay.

What had I done to deserve Richard Elliott in my life? What crime had I committed? I had been composed, my thoughts focused in preparation for my meeting with Mr Young, infused with energy and optimism by my visit to the quay. Now I was unsettled, my mind unfocused and flitting away at tangents, and my skin itched with the unpleasant sensation that an army of ants, or a battalion of spiders, were crawling beneath it. I squeezed my eyes closed, counted to ten, and when I opened them again I started walking, across the common ground in the direction of Segate, then turning left, up Uddyngate towards the town centre. Richard Elliott might think this was all a big game, but the last laugh would be mine. I wondered what he would say if he knew I was going to meet someone to talk about raising the money for a new ship.

'My dear Madam Gillhespy,' Mr Young greeted me at the door to his office and lifted one of my hands to his lips. A wave of heat hit me from the roaring fire and I leaned towards it, welcoming its warming embrace. I removed my cloak. He took it from me and hung it on one of an elaborate series of hooks on the wall behind the door. He was one of those men who suited his name. He was not young – far from it – but as his hair gave up its own battle for survival and became thinner, paler and downier, sitting in soft, tight curls close to his head, it gave him the appearance of a chubby-faced cherub, which his faded blue eyes with their milky whites did nothing to deter. I knew I should heed Will's caution that he was a man of business though, and not let his appearance, or his long association with my father, dull my wits when talking to him of my plans.

I had not been here before and I looked around me now, startled by the opulence of my surroundings and curious about the type of man who would create it. Designated an office, I had expected a sparse, functional room, but this space was anything but. It was more richly furnished than my father's closet. I supposed it was designed to make an impression on his many clients. It oozed success and wealth, from the gilt cornicing that surrounded the fireplace and window frames, to the deeply-piled and vibrantly-coloured rugs scattered around the polished wooden floor, the gleaming silver and brass plate on display and the floor-to-ceiling tapestry that covered one entire wall.

At Mr Young's invitation I settled into a capacious chair set to one side of the fireplace. My fingers traced the outline of the leaves and flowers carved into the arms whilst I waited for my host to occupy its matching pair facing me.

'The loss of your father was such an untimely tragedy,' he said, stretching his stubby legs out in front of him and smiling.

I inclined my head to acknowledge he had paid his respects.

'Thank you for inviting me to call on you, but I imagine this is not a social occasion,' I replied. I could not allow my thoughts to dwell on my father, accompanied as they would be by emotion and grief, neither of which had a place in this meeting.

He raised one eyebrow and a flicker of something crossed his face, but before I could identify it, he'd replaced it with an encouraging smile.

'Indeed. These must be difficult times for you, but you are showing great tenacity in confronting your problems like this. Your father would have been proud.'

His choice of words took me by surprise and I puzzled over them for a moment, staring at him. It seemed strange to describe my father's death as a problem. But if that is not what he meant, then to what was he referring? To hesitate, or show my confusion, would be construed as a sign of weakness, and instinct warned me that would be foolish in front of this man. I crossed my legs at the ankle and bent my knees, which pushed me into a more relaxed sitting position, and addressed him in a casual tone.

'Actually, I was pleased to receive your invitation, because it pre-empted my own intentions to request a meeting,' I paused to recall the words I had prepared with care and rehearsed in my chamber. 'I want to talk to you about investing in a new ship. The Lady Isabella is ageing and none of our other boats are suitable for expanding our trade routes into new areas. It's something that my father should have already set in motion, but he was ever cautious and he disliked change.'

Mr Young's smile faded and his lips parted as if he were the one now taken by surprise. I waited for him to respond. He swallowed several times before a loud rasp emitted from his throat. When he did speak, his voice was tight and clipped, all pretence of friendliness banished. 'I see. And how do you plan to make such an investment?'

I kept my eyes fixed on his face. Its hue had changed from the healthy, pink cherubic glow of a few minutes ago and his cheeks were now splattered with heightened red spots. Perhaps that was the effect of the heat, which had intensified from a pleasant, welcoming warmth into an overbearing presence, pressing down on me as a wind in the ocean would beat down on the Lady Isabella. I did not think so, though. He had shifted his position so his body was angled away from me, as if he found me – or something I had said – distasteful. Will had warned me that Mr Young would do whatever was in his best interests, but if he profited by loaning some of his wealth to others, why was he so slow to take my hint? If this was some kind of a strange game, it was clear that I did not understand the rules. No matter. I was on my own, and I would have to do this my way, so I decided to abandon the subtle approach I had thought appropriate, since usury was prohibited, and be more direct.

'I rather thought I would look to secure a loan, and it is my understanding that you are the person to talk to. Or am I mistaken?' I asked with the hint of a smile.

Mr Young emitted a strange noise resembling a grunt, which he tried to disguise by pulling out a handkerchief and very loudly blowing his nose. I watched and waited in silence. His behaviour was quite perplexing.

'When I requested that you meet with me, it was not to discuss lending you more money, and nor indeed is that the conversation we need to have.'

'I'm afraid I don't know what you mean,' I responded, sensing this exchange of words was slipping out of my control.

He stood and crossed the room to his desk, on top of which sat a thick document folder which he picked up. 'Madam Gillhespy, Isabella,' he said, as he walked back towards me. 'There is really no easy way to say this, so forgive me. I had thought you would be better acquainted with the state of your father's business – your business – but it's clear that you are not. You see, I have already lent your father as much money as is prudent. Indeed, more so. And, in view of the, er, unfortunate change in circumstances surrounding those loans, with your father no longer able to take responsibility, I must insist on their prompt repayment in full. So you see, I'm not in a position to extend more credit to you.'

What Mr Young was saying was incomprehensible to me. My father had never mentioned any loans, and nor had he ever given me so much as the slightest indication that our finances were anything other than healthy. If not a new ship, what had he needed to borrow money for? I wanted to challenge Mr Young. Insist that there must be some mistake. He was standing in front of me now and I opened my mouth to speak, but he shook his head and I closed it again. I watched with a horrible fascination akin to dread as he opened the document folder, extracted two thick sheets of creamy parchment and handed them to me. A voice inside my head urged me to refuse to take them. That way it might not be true, but I could not. The thick parchment was luxurious to my touch, the sort a man of influence and vast wealth would commission. I lowered my eyes and read one sheet and then the other. Stunned, I read them again.

'I see,' I said, although I did not.

Mr Young cleared his throat with fresh gusto, and turned back to face me. The red spots on his cheeks had gone, and his pale eyes were no longer soft and welcoming, but hard and flint-like. 'There are two loans, totalling three hundred ducats,' he confirmed, just to leave me in no doubt.

I looked again at the two pieces of paper in my hands and my father's neat signature, and for the second time in as many days my world changed. First my cousin, and now this. What else had he kept from me? And what had he needed to borrow three hundred ducats for? Our business had accumulated healthy profits over many years, so there could be no need, and I had noticed no recent extravagant expenditure. All of the confidence with which I had walked into this office not ten minutes ago drained from me, seeping into the floorboards at my feet and disappearing, like a mug of spilled ale. I wanted to ask what the money had been for, but anything I said now would only make me appear more foolish than I already did.

'I appreciate this has come as something of a shock to you, and I'm not so unreasonable that I won't give you a little time to pay, especially with respect to the memory of your dear father and our long-standing friendship. Shall we say four weeks? Repayment in full, plus my consideration of course, or property to the value of.'

His smooth tone implied he was granting me a great favour, but the way his eyes bored into me left me in no doubt that this supposed friendship would count for nothing if I failed to meet his terms. I had to get out of that room, away from its suffocating heat and his odious presence before the flashes of white inside my head exploded and I could no longer see. I gripped the chair arms and pushed myself to my feet.

'Thank you for your time,' I managed to say in a level voice, holding my head high. I would leave this interview with my hopes for the future in tatters, but my pride intact. 'I'm sure you realise this has come as a bit of a shock. I trust that this conversation will go no further, until I have had the opportunity to look further into my father's affairs.'

'Of course. When you're ready to discuss the matter, please make an appointment and I will be happy to help in any way I can.'

I gathered my cloak and left, not trusting myself to utter another word. The young clerk seated at a desk in the outer office smiled and said good day in a cheery tone. I pushed past him and out onto the street where I welcomed the numbing coldness of the raw air on my cheeks as Mr Young's words tumbled around inside my head, his expression imprinted behind my eyes. *'Repayment in full … or property to the value of.'* Did he mean my business or me? I would die before I allowed him to lay a finger on either.

FIVE

'NEVER, NEVER, NEVER,' I RAGED under my breath as I hurried down Uddyngate, cold already gnawing at my bones. Widow Swynburn approached me as I passed the town's public well, but I was in no mood to make polite conversation and pretended not to notice her. I longed for the refreshing vitality of the quay, but even that would not soothe my present mood, and when I reached the turning for Briggate, I forced myself to go straight home. My head was a spinning top of thoughts, all whirling around, bumping into each other and jostling for space. My father's death had brought me personal grief and many other problems – my disagreements with Will over our marriage plans, the appearance of Richard Elliott in my life, what to do about the Lady Isabella – but never once had I thought about my financial circumstances. I did not know I had to. We were wealthy. We are wealthy. I would know. I'd been running the household for years. Never once had my father so much as hinted that I needed to be cautious with expenditure in any way.

'There is also plenty that you do not know.' That's what Will had said. It would appear that he was right, and it struck me that he might have known about this. That feeling I had experienced more than once, that there was something he was not telling me. What if he had known my father was in debt, and why?

I stumbled through my front door, bolted along the hall and into the closet. My cloak fell from my shoulders as I hurried to my father's desk, reaching for the bunch of keys at my waist as I moved. The desk had one long drawer that ran along its full length, and below it two smaller, deeper drawers on either side of the footwell, the lower of them finishing almost at floor level. I tugged open the middle drawer on the left, pulled out the small metal box that fit snugly inside it and fumbled with the small key. The box held about

10 shillings and the same again in smaller coins. It was no more than I'd expected. This was where we kept our float for daily expenses, and so we always had change to give to customers purchasing from the store. My father kept his real money in two hiding places in his bed chamber.

I locked the box and shoved it back into the drawer. My steps slowed as I crossed the closet, ignoring my cloak which lay like a puddle on the floor. In the hall, I crept past the screen to the kitchen as if I were a house thief, lest Mary come out to greet me. On the gallery, my fingertips brushed the smooth oak of the bannister, my steps slowing as a feeling of dread gathered in my stomach, stretching its tentacles around my limbs until my movements became sluggish and ground to a complete halt outside the door to my father's bedchamber.

Surprises. I hated them. Always had. But I had to know. My hand hovered above the latch and I tried not to think about the last time I had stood in this exact spot, waiting for my father to throw open the door, his dear face lighting up when he heard my good news. I shook those thoughts away, pressed the latch, pushed the door and stepped into the cool darkness of the room. It was of generous proportions, comfortable but not lavish in its furnishings. I had not set foot in here since his death, and I expected to be greeted with that distinctive staleness to the air of a room that has been neglected, but I was wrong. It smelled of wax polish. Mary had not been as squeamish as I about entering.

I flung open the shutters, which had been left closed in a mark of respect. The fading afternoon light that drifted into the room was dim, but sufficient for my purposes. The window recess was deep, and topped with an embroidered cushion. I knelt in front of it. There was a pressure spot in the wood panel facing the room. It was not visible and you had to know exactly where it was. I pressed my fingers to it and the panel swung open to reveal another behind, made of plain wood and fitted with a lock, which was stiff and the key did not want to turn. I persevered, cursing under my breath, and after several attempts it clicked open to reveal a space built into the walls of the house itself, occupied by a stout wooden chest. I gripped the chest with one hand on either side and dragged it from its hiding place, but before I even inserted the key I knew what I was going to find. The box was too light. I flipped the lid open. It contained a handful of sovereigns whereas it should have held one hundred or more.

I crossed the room to the fireplace and dragged the settle to one side. Beneath where it had stood, a loose floorboard hid another secret cavity. I prised it up to reveal a shallow space in which a cloth bag snuggled. I removed it but did not bother to look inside. It contained trinkets, which I knew were worthless. They were meant to fool anyone who should not have been looking into thinking they had found the hidden treasure. They had not. I crouched down so I was almost laying on the floor, inserted my arm and stretched it out under the floorboards. My fingers pressed around in the dust until they found a thick leather cord. I grabbed it and pulled. The cord was attached to another, smaller chest, more of a casket in truth. Easing myself into a kneeling position I extracted the casket and shook it. There was a pleasing rattle from inside, but I was not deceived. Like the larger chest, it was not heavy enough. My fingers were shaking so much they struggled to hold the key. When at last I managed to release the lock and tip the contents out into my lap, a few crowns and maybe a dozen shillings was all it contained.

'No.' I shook my head. A dark despair infused my thoughts. The sum total of these two chests should have amounted to several hundred sovereigns. It was all of our savings, and the money to fund the next trip for the Lady Isabella – wages for the crew, food and ale for the journey. What had he done with it?

'Noooooo,' I shouted, elongating the vowel until my breath expired and I had to gulp in air. I threw my hands up, sending the coins rolling and spinning around the room, and then brought them down onto the boards with a crack of bone against wood.

I probably would have stayed there all evening, cradling a sore wrist, if Mary hadn't interrupted me, her heavy tread across the gallery warning me of her approach.

'Isabella, are ye hurt?' Her voice was muted by the closed door that separated us, but even so there was no mistaking the solicitude it was loaded with. She had heard my outburst and would not be fobbed off with ease, but I could not tell her the truth.

'I'm all right Mary, just give me a moment please.'

I listened to her footsteps retreating until the stairs swallowed them up, then I crawled around the room, hampered by my skirts, collecting up the coins and replacing them in the casket, before returning it to its hiding place under the floorboards and pushing it as far in as I could. I replaced the larger chest too and the panels that concealed it. The room looked as it had before. Finally, I closed the shutters. In the darkness, I fumbled my way back to the door and let myself out.

The clatter of spoons on dishes told me that Mary was preparing the table in the dining hall below to serve me supper. A lonely supper, for one person with no appetite, but I did not have the heart, or the energy to stop her. She turned towards me as I reached the bottom of the stairs. Candlelight softened the grey in her once flaxen hair and smoothed the laughter lines at the side of her kind eyes, so she could have passed for a woman ten years younger than her true years. The light did not disguise the sympathy and concern that were stamped on her face. It was that of a mother for her child, that endures no matter how old the child becomes. With one glance my composure dissolved, swept away by the revelations of the day. I stumbled to her side and placed my head on her shoulder. She stroked my hair, her fingers gentle and soothing.

'My poor bairn,' she murmured. 'Ye must miss him so much, but it will get better, I promise.'

What could I say? I had to let her believe that the cause of my anguish was grief over my father's death, because I could not share

my recent discoveries with her. If Mary left me I did not know what
I would do.

Eating alone at the vast table, which could seat a dozen people
with ease, did nothing to improve my attitude, or my mood, and I
vowed that unless I was entertaining I would take my meals in my
closet from now on. Yes, I had to try to think of it as my closet now.
I retired there after I had eaten, and although I relished the silence,
I was not yet comfortable with the void that my father's absence left
in the space. With the shutters closed to deny the outside world, I
settled by the fire and tried to cocoon myself in memories of him,
but I could no longer trust my own mind. To keep secrets had not
been in his nature, and yet that is what he had done. And these
were not just any old secrets; they were big, black, ugly ones. How
was I supposed to reconcile the man I thought I had known so well
with the person I was now discovering? He had been the pivot of
my existence for most of my life, my moral and spiritual guide and
a person respected by all who knew him, but who was he really?
The shock of Richard Elliott's sudden appearance was as nothing
compared to the news that my father had borrowed money with a
recklessness that was not in his nature. And what had he done with
it? Even worse, how was I going to repay three hundred ducats to
Mr Young in just four weeks? I had some savings of my own, but
not enough. My husband had bequeathed me an amount on his
death, to be paid every year, but that was not all available to me
now. If I tried to sell some of our silverware Mary would be sure to
notice, and then I would have to tell her the truth.

I was surprised to find I had drifted over to the shelves containing
books and manuscripts along the far wall, although I could not
recollect having risen from my chair. The candles had burned low,
so the hour must be late. My fingers trailed along the leather-bound
volumes. I should retire to bed, with a book. That might divert my

thoughts from the problems that were crowding in on me. In the morning, with a clear head, I would be able to come up with a plan. Thomas Malory's Le Morte d'Arthur should provide a good enough diversion – I had always loved tales of the legendary court of King Arthur and his knights – but the well-worn copy that I know we had somewhere eluded me. Aching with fatigue, I settled instead for Geoffrey Chaucer's Troilus and Criseyde.

When I awoke several hours later I discovered the book laying by my side, open and face down on top of my bed covers, and the candle had burned to its wick. My father would admonish me for damaging the book's spine, so I picked it up and closed it before I remembered that my father would not admonish me for anything ever again.

The hour was early still but I was wide awake. Floorboards creaked at the other end of the gallery where Mary had her chamber and then relaxed into silence. She must have gone down to the kitchen using the steps that led there from her room. While I dressed, thankful that my wardrobe, befitting a woman in mourning, comprised only simple garments that were easy to lace up myself, I outlined a plan in my mind to discover, if possible, what my father had done with the money, and to work out how I would repay Mr Young. It was a plan with many gaps, because in truth I did not know what I could do, but I would challenge Will later to find out what, if anything, he knew. I would keep searching amongst my father's belongings for something that might give me a clue, and tackle the inventory of stock so I could start selling it – I would let it be known that even though I was in mourning, my stores would re-open for business, so I would need to employ someone because I could not be there all of the time. First though, there was something else I needed to do. It would not provide any answers but it would make me feel that I was not so impotent.

Mary was already busy in the kitchen, measuring flour into a bowl with a large wooden spoon. She was alone. Anne, the young girl who came in to help her had not yet arrived. 'Isabella.' She looked up as I entered the kitchen. 'Ye gave me a start there. I wasn'y expecting ye to be up at such an early hour.'

She put the bowl and spoon down on the table, and studied my face. 'Ye've a bit more colour to yeself today.' She nodded with approval. 'There isn'y a meal ready yet.'

'I'm not hungry. Would you help me with something first? Find George as well please and join me in the closet.'

I turned and left the kitchen before she could question me, or object that the bread would not bake itself. Standing on the top step of the closet, just inside the door, I cast a critical eye over the room, but I already knew what I wanted to do. Just replacing my father's captain's chair with my own was not enough. By the time I had removed everything that was loose from the surface of the desk Mary had arrived with George, entering through the low door at the rear that was almost hidden between shelves. It led out beyond the courtyard, past the buttery to the stable and then the stores. As well as Thunder, the stable was home to a cow and a goat. George slept in the loft above. The pungent smell of animals and dung followed him into the room and it was comforting in a strange way. He had straw clinging to his hair.

I told them what I wanted to do, and very soon all three of us were breathing hard with the exertion of moving the heavy desk so it was angled across the far corner. From this vantage point I could look out across the entire room, with the fireplace to my right and all the windows stretching in front of me, revealing tantalising glimpses of the courtyard; broken paintings viewed through a series of small panes. We moved one of the chairs that had been either side of the fireplace into the corner of the room diagonally opposite my desk next to the steps down from the hall, and left the other by the side of the fire with a low table next to it. I draped a shawl across its back. Crocheted in all shades of the sun – from the buttery cream of a winter's morning to the bright yellow of midday in summer and the deep red of a glorious sunset – it was a colour palette that I loved and which lifted my spirits at a glance. The final touch was a rug in a gorgeous shade of russet that I had spotted in the warehouse yesterday when I had visited with Richard Elliott. I'd already sent George to bring it to the house. It was almost the length of the room, but not very wide, so it ran just along the centre, like a path designed to take a person from one place to another. I left the portraits of my parents where they had always been; one hanging either side of the fireplace, my father handsome with kind brown eyes and hair that was already thinning on top, and my mother young and beautiful, wearing a low-cut gown and matching ruby earrings, tiara and necklace that I had inherited but would not dare to wear. When we had finished I stood with my hands on my hips, looked around and nodded in satisfaction. The room was no longer borrowed from my father, it was mine.

'George, will you go and find Captain Thirlwell when you've finished your chores for Mary and ask him to come and see me this afternoon – tell him he can find me in the warehouse from two o'clock.'

'Yes Madam.' George ducked under the door at the back of the room, and the aroma of stables followed him.

I turned to Mary. 'No need to prepare the table for me to eat,' I said. 'I'll break my fast in here this morning when it is ready. I have to start going through my father's paperwork.' Not only had I put it off for too long, but if I was going to work out where all my money had gone I needed to scrutinise every receipt, every order, every letter, everything I could lay my hands on. My father must have bought something with it that I could perhaps sell to recover the money. It could not just have vanished, like the mist over the ocean under the heat of the sun.

Mary lingered. 'Are ye going to tell me what's wrong? Is it something to do with that young man? Is he really Mistress Elizabeth's boy?'

'He is,' I admitted, smiling at how she referred to the aunt I had never known as if she were still a child.

'He's got the look of her about him for sure.' Mary nodded as if she had just made a profound discovery, and waited for me to say more.

I rearranged the ink pot and quills on the desk, giving myself a moment to think. Much as I might wish to confide in her, I knew I could not, but she might be able to help me. After all, she had served my father for many years, and not counting myself, she was the person who knew him better than any other. She might know something.

'Mary, before my father died, had you noticed anything to indicate he had not been well, or that his mind was preoccupied?'

I watched her expression change. She had not been expecting me to switch the conversation from my cousin to my father, and she hesitated, her brow puckering into pleats. I fancied she was choosing her words with care, weighing up what she should say.

'Please, whatever it is, don't keep it to yourself,' I prompted.

She nodded. 'I thought he hadn'y been himself these past few weeks, but when I tried to ask him he looked at me in that way of his and said there was nought wrong.'

I reached behind me to feel for my chair and lowered myself into it. Mary had been more observant than I, which did nothing to assuage my guilt. Her keen eyes were on me now.

'I know he was worried about the late return of the Lady Isabella, and I cannot stop thinking that I allowed that to blind me to anything else,' I said. 'A man's heart doesn't just stop beating without warning. I should have noticed that something was not well and made him call Mr Hedley, or tried to talk to him about what he had on his mind. Things might have been different.'

'Don't Isabella,' Mary spoke firmly but with compassion. 'That way lies madness. His time was up. God has called him. There's nought ye could have done.'

I bowed my head in submission, willing to concede to Mary's religious beliefs which were unshakeable, and relieved that she believed my melancholy was due only to my torment that I had failed to notice that something was ailing my father. Our exchange had convinced me though, that I ought to have another conversation with the physician, Mr Hedley. My father could have confided something of his worries in him.

'I'm going to the Scotch Market later this morning,' Mary said, changing the subject. 'I may be a little late back.'

'Hmm,' I grunted. I knew that meant she was going to spend some time with Douglas Lumsden, her sweetheart I suppose you would call him, although the idea that someone of Mary's age could have a sweetheart made me want to laugh. I couldn't though, not in front of her, because that would have implied that I approved of their friendship, which I did not. How could I, when marriage between the Scots and the English was unlawful in Berwick and it was forbidden for any Scots person to reside within the town walls? They were laws that were applied with a lack of fervour, but nevertheless they were laws.

'Are you sure that's wise?' I asked her. I had hoped that since the Queen had ordered the Scotch market be moved outside the town walls it would dampen Mary's enthusiasm for visiting, and for Douglas, but it appeared not.

'Tush,' she scolded. 'Why can't people leave us be? Folks in this town don't care. Most of us have got mixed blood if ye care to look.'

She stared at me, defying me to argue with her further. I could forbid her to go, but what would I do if she chose Douglas over me? Nevertheless, there was something about him that unnerved me. It wasn't just that he was Scottish, or that I did not like him, so much as I was not sure I trusted him.

After Mary had brought me some food and ale I settled down and braced myself to start work, beginning with the papers that had been on top of the desk. These needed my attention anyway, and I might find what I was looking for among them and have to search no further. Although I had no idea what I was looking for. With a heavy sigh, I pulled the pile towards me.

The task was as arduous as I had feared it would be. Nor did I find anything very interesting, and my father kept pushing his nose in when I did not need him. There were a number of bills, but only household-related, as well as lists of goods sold and new orders to be fulfilled. *'Make sure he pays before he collects.'* My father had drummed into me about one customer whose order for a set of small tapestries woven in Brussels should have been among the Lady Isabella's latest load. *'Yes father, but where has all the money gone?'* I silently asked him back, and he vanished. There were forthcoming schedules for the smaller ships, which I filed, and a notice about a meeting of the burgesses. I had hoped to take my father's place as a burgess. Indeed, he had often voiced that as his wish, for there had been no-one else to protect our interests as one of the town's most significant merchants, but I had heard nothing from the other burgesses. I suspected they would not welcome a woman into their midst, and that honour would probably be bestowed on my cousin instead. Nevertheless, I recorded the date and time of the meeting.

After two hours the desk was almost clear, except for the big ledger detailing the goods that had come in with the Lady Isabella. Captain Thirlwell had delivered it to the house a few days ago. I would check this against the stock in the warehouse after I had done the inventory later. Everything else I had filed away, using my father's system for now, although I intended to make some changes. Nothing I had found so far shed any light on the big questions I needed to answer. There was nothing unexpected, and no correspondence with Mr Young – although that did not surprise me, as these transactions were by necessity clandestine in nature.

I drummed my fingers on the desk, thinking, whilst my eyes swept the room, making sure I had missed nothing, but the closet was now neater than I could remember it being for a long time, with everything in the place I had allocated to it. Why had I never thought to discuss our financial position with my father when he was alive? I had taken our wealth for granted, but if I had not, he might have confided in me. I would not make that mistake again.

I pushed my chair back as far as it would go and tugged the

brass handles on the top drawer of the desk. It opened with the smoothness of a length of silk slipping through my fingers, and I cast my eye over a neat arrangement of new quills, ink, blotters, paper, candles, wax and my father's seal. Nothing of interest. I opened the other drawers in turn. As well as the money box they contained writing paper, details of customers and notes written in my father's hand. There was nothing out of the ordinary or of particular interest. The bottom drawer on the right, though, would not open.

Locked drawers hold secrets, and these particular drawers were never locked – not even the one with the cash box in it. I knelt down on the floor, removed the keyring from the cord around my waist and tried every key of a suitable size in the lock. There was one to fit every other drawer of the desk, but not this one. I thumped it with the flat of my hand. At the very least, that drawer must hold a clue to what my father had spent so much money on, and if there was any left, where it might be. I was certain of it, but where was the key?

I was still pondering that question when the click of the door to the closet opening was followed by a low whistle.

'My, my. Someone's been busy.' It was Will. I stuck my head up over the desk. 'I like it.'

He was standing on the top step, just inside the door, dressed for the cold weather. The high collar of his thick cloak was pulled up to his ears, hiding the lower part of his face, and his hat was low on his head, so I could only see his eyes, which twinkled with amusement. He removed his cloak, hat and thick gloves and threw them over the chair. I frowned, thinking I would need to get some hooks for George to fix to the back of the door.

'What are you doing on the floor?'

'I dropped something,' I said, pushing myself to my feet and smoothing my skirts, hoping the lie would not show in my face. He did not seem to notice. I could not match his good humour though, troubled as I was by my suspicion that he knew something he was not telling me, my certainty that the argument about our marriage plans was not yet over, and the new burden of my father's debt.

'I wasn't expecting you this morning.'

'I've got the customs statement for you from the Lady Isabella's last shipment,' he explained.

I took it from him, dropped it on the desk and moved to the window closest to me, where I sat down and pressed my nose to the glass. It was cold, and through its mottled lens the courtyard glittered under the rays of a weak sun, dreamlike and not quite real. Will joined me on the narrow seat, raised my hand to his lips and I longed to rest my head on his shoulder, letting him take the weight of my worries. I could not do that though. Not now, perhaps not ever. I pulled my hand away.

'You knew my father well. What did you know of his dealings with Mr Young?' I twisted my head from the glass so I could watch Will's reaction. He looked at me with a quizzical expression.

'They were associates, rivals even. Both burgesses. Common interests. What's this about? You know this as well as I do. Beyond that though, your father did not confide in me. Why would he?'

Will leaned towards me. In the confined space of the window seat we were almost touching. His proximity was intoxicating; his musky smell mingling with the crisp freshness of the outdoor air that clung to his hair and his skin. I stood up and moved towards the warmth of the fire. At once, the freshness was replaced with the bitter tang of smoke. When I turned to face him he was still sitting in the window seat, watching me. He appeared thoughtful, and his shoulders were hunched.

'What is it Izzy? Let me help you.'

'You can help me by telling me what you know.'

He pursed his lips, held his hands out and then dropped them again to his side.

'I don't know what you want me to say. What do you think I know?'

'Did you notice anything unusual about his behaviour recently, or did he seem as though he had something on his mind?'

'No. He may have been a little more distracted than usual, but like you, I would have said that he was worrying over the Lady Isabella's late return. Please tell me what's wrong. What did Young say? This is something concerning him isn't it? What did he tell you?'

If Will did know about the debt, he was doing a very good job of pretending otherwise, and in all the time I had known him I had never thought he had a particular talent as a player. I still could not shake off my conviction that he was keeping something from me, but if not this, then what?

'My meeting with Mr Young was not what I had hoped,' I admitted. My tongue felt too thick for my mouth and I found it difficult to form the words. I swallowed and tried again, aware of Will's attention, focused on me with a new intensity. 'He said my father left an outstanding debt that would have to be settled before he is able to consider further loans.'

I wished I had not moved away so I could see his face more clearly, but the way his shoulders jerked back and his mouth fell open was enough to remove my last shred of doubt. He knew nothing of this. He was as shocked as I had been, and I shuddered as I recalled the moment – was it really only yesterday afternoon – when I had read my father's signature on those pieces of paper. So innocuous, just a squiggle of ink, but what a blow it had dealt.

Will was on his feet now, and in two brisk strides was by my side. He put his hands on my shoulders and pulled me towards him. I had always liked the way my head fitted into the hollow beneath his chin when he put his arms around me. Nuzzled there, like a foal with its mother, taking comfort from his solidity, I could almost believe that we would find a simple solution to this. And then he spoiled the illusion.

'Why didn't you send for me yesterday evening?' There was an edge to his voice that I did not like.

'Because it's not your problem and I needed to think,' I said, pulling away from him. His eyes were bright and dark at the same time.

'I'm trying to help you, if you would only let me. Damn it! I knew I should have gone with you. I warned you, but you wouldn't listen.'

'What difference would it have made? Do you think if you'd been by my side he would have delivered a different message?' I brushed away the hand he stretched out towards me. 'That would not have changed the situation.'

I spoke the truth. It would not have taken away the debt, but I had little doubt that on one level Will was right. The tone of the interview would have been quite different. Unfair though it was, Mr Young would not have spoken to me the way he had if Will had been by my side.

'Tell me what Young said,' he demanded.

The exact words were fixed in my memory as firmly as if branded there by the blacksmith himself. *'Repayment in full, plus my consideration of course, or property to the value of.'* They had been ringing in my head ever since he had spoken them, but I hesitated, looking at Will, his features twisted with anger, and I made a decision. I would not tell him everything.

'I've told you.'

'But what was he borrowing money for?'

'I don't know. He told me nothing about any loans.'

'How much?' Will persisted.

'It's not important.'

'How much?' he repeated. His tone was softer now, more cajoling.

'One hundred ducats,' I snapped, crossing my fingers behind my back to ask forgiveness for my lie. 'I'll pay him back and raise the money for a new ship some other way.'

A heavy silence hung between us, and then Will turned and pummelled the mantel above the fireplace with his fists and kicked the basket of coals that stood inside the hearth. I had never seen him so angry, and I did not stop to think, but moved behind the chair, putting more space between us.

My reaction seemed to diffuse his anger. He spread his palms against the mantel and rested his head on them.

'Forgive me Izzy. That was inexcusable. I didn't mean to alarm you. It isn't you I'm angry with.'

He turned around. His expression had softened and his eyes pleaded with me to believe him. I relaxed a little.

'But what did he spend the money on?' Will repeated.

I watched him for a moment, wary that his temper might flare up again, but there was no sign that he was anything but his usual, calm self.

'I don't know – I've spent all morning going through paperwork but I've found nothing. There is something odd though.' I stepped around him, moved behind my desk, and pointed at the drawer that would not open.

'This drawer is locked and I don't have a key that fits.'

I leaned over and rattled the handle. Will squeezed behind the desk by my side. He leaned over my shoulder and his hair brushed my cheek, as soft as a child's. My fingers longed to stroke it, but instead I ducked away to the end of the desk, out of his reach. His attention was focused on the drawer. He knelt down and examined it.

'The lock's been changed,' he announced. I edged back towards him and peered over his shoulder. He pointed to the escutcheon. 'Can you see around the edges where the wood is scratched and not quite the same shade?'

He was right, and I knew with even more certainty that whatever I needed to find would be in that drawer, but I did not know where to look for the key.

'And you're sure there isn't a key for it on that ring?' He nodded at the bunch that I had left on top of the desk.

'I'm sure, but you're welcome to try.'

He did, then he opened each of the other drawers, peered inside them and probed with his fingers. When he stood up, running his hands through his hair, he shook his head.

'Nothing,' he muttered. The frustration in his voice matched my own. 'We could force it.'

'No. Let me look for the key first. If I cannot find it, then we'll force it.'

'As you wish,' he said.

He withdrew to the other side of the desk and I thought he was going to gather his belongings and leave, but he stopped and turned back to me. 'Izzy, do you think his death might not have been natural?'

'What … what do you mean? You think he might have been …' I could not finish, could not bring myself to say the word. Who would have wanted to murder my father? I sank into my chair.

'No, no, of course not.' Will fidgeted as if he was finding something uncomfortable. 'I meant, could he have taken his own life?'

Will and I stared at each other, our eyes locked together, I do not know how long for. It was probably only a matter of seconds, but if anyone had asked me I would have said it was much longer. The idea was just too horrible and I was shocked that he had even suggested it. He must have read that in my expression and he backed away from the desk.

'I'm sorry. It's just that if he had debts, what other problems might he have had? Then Richard Elliott arrives, expecting to claim his share of a healthy business, and your father cannot bear the shame of admitting the truth. Perhaps he could not see a way out, and well, he wouldn't have been the first man to believe that was the only option left to him.'

'He wouldn't. He would not do that to me.' Even as I said the words I realised that I no longer knew my father, so how could I assert, with any degree of conviction, what he would or would not do? A fragile silence now hung between us, suspended like the fine gossamer spun by a spider. Will broke it.

'I have to get back to work. I'm meeting Arthur at The Sailor's Rest later, but I could cancel if you need me to help try to make some sense of this?'

'There's no need to change your plans on my account. Besides, I have to go to the stores and do the inventory and I don't know when I'm going to be able to look for the key. It would be foolish for you to waste your evening.' What I really meant was that I was glad to have the opportunity to find the key and inspect the contents of that drawer alone. Although I was not being completely dishonest, because I had told Captain Thirlwell I would be at the stores and I could no longer put off doing the inventory, especially now that I had to find 300 ducats to repay Mr Young.

I stood up and led the way across my new rug to the door.

'So be it.' Will nodded. 'You know what this means though don't you?'

I paused and turned back towards him.

'You're going to have to send the Lady Isabella back out as soon as possible.'

He was right, but I did not like it one bit, and there was another problem. One that since I had opted not to tell Will the full truth of my situation rested on my shoulders alone. How was I going to pay for it?

SIX

'WHAT WERE YOU INVOLVED WITH father?' I tipped my head back and studied the sky, as if I might find the answer there. Thick, dark clouds obliterated the sun, which boded ill for more snow. It was only just past midday, but already it had the feeling of night.

I had let myself out of the back of the house through the low door at the rear of the closet. Thunder whickered in response to my question from the shelter of his warm stable. George had cleared a path through the snow and I kept to it, looking out for icy patches and frozen-over puddles that would pull at my feet and have me sliding down the gentle slope unable to stop, in spite of my sturdy boots.

Thunder's large chestnut head was hanging over the top of the stable door. He snorted as I approached, his breath misting in ghostly fronds, and nudged me none too gently with his nose.

'Careful boy. You'll have me on the floor like that.' I stroked his nose with one hand. The other I held out to him, palm flat. On it sat a carrot I had fetched from the kitchen. His breath tickled my wrist, and the wet warmth of his mouth enclosed my hand for a moment as he took the carrot and tossed his head to chew it with gusto, before turning back and nudging me again.

'No more,' I said, and pressed my cheek against his velvety neck, breathing in his horsey smell.

'If only you could talk to me, Thunder. What secrets might you hold?'

It was true. Thunder might hold the answer to whatever my father had been involved with, just by knowing where he had been and with whom he had met. But of course, he could never share that knowledge. Who might my father have confided in? I could think of no-one, and it hurt that he had not felt able to share his troubles with me, his only child.

The conversation I had just had with Will had not improved my state of mind. Tormented as I was that I had failed to notice my father was ill, I could not stop thinking that he might have taken his own life, which intensified my sense of guilt threefold. Captain Thirlwell would not be arriving at the stores for at least another hour yet. I could make a start on the inventory, or I could attempt to ease my troubled mind by going to see Mr Hedley. Patting Thunder's neck and promising to take him out soon, I continued down George's icy path to the warehouse, but when I got there, instead of reaching for the heavy key to unlock the doors I turned away, towards the bridge. A little more than five minutes later I stood before a tall, narrow house on Wester Lane. I knocked on the door, which was set between two blackened posts of timber and slanted with the incline of the street, giving the whole a crooked appearance.

The assistant who let me in answered my query as to whether the physician was at home with a curt nod. The room I entered was cramped and cluttered, the space almost entirely filled by a long table that creaked beneath the weight of the books and papers that were piled upon it. Behind it, potions in jars jostled for space on shelves and strips of cloth sat in layers waiting to be used as bandages. The assistant passed through another door, partially hidden behind a screen, bidding me to wait, and moments later Mr Hedley appeared.

'Madam Gillhespy! To what do I owe this honour? Please come through. Will you take some wine, or ale?'

I declined any refreshment and followed him into a room that was even smaller, but appeared so much larger because it was almost empty. It contained only a desk, the surface of which was tidy, and two chairs, one behind the desk and one in front of it. A merry fire burned in a small hearth. A tiny window provided almost no natural light.

'Please sit.' He positioned himself behind the desk and indicated the other chair.

Mr Hedley was a man of medium height, a few years younger than my father, with greying hair that was still thick and kind eyes framed with fine lines etched into the skin that stretched across his cheek bones.

He smiled and the lines deepened. 'How are you faring?'

'I ... well, you know, I'm as well as can be expected in the circumstances,' I mumbled.

I had rushed here on an impulse and now I realised I had no idea how I would broach the worries that were pressing on me. Mr Hedley sat in silence, demonstrating the patience of a man with the wisdom of many years who understands how to listen.

'Actually, perhaps I will take some wine after all,' I said.

He did not ring for his assistant but left the room himself, returning after a few minutes with a tray containing two goblets. It was enough time for me to gather my thoughts. I sipped the wine and then placed the goblet on the desk.

'Physically, I'm quite well, but I have something on my mind that I just can't resolve. The more I think about it the more I believe I have failed.'

'Go on,' he prompted when my voice faltered. 'If I can help in any way at all you know I will.'

'I think you can help me to set my mind at rest. You see, I'm convinced that I could have done something to save my father. To stop him from dying.'

Mr Hedley's eyebrows arched and then relaxed.

'But whatever makes you think that?' he asked. 'Your father had been dead for several hours before you found him.'

'No, I mean, was he ill? Had he consulted you about anything at all in the weeks, or months, before his death?'

The physician steepled his fingers and thought for a moment.

'The last time I saw him was socially. I don't think I've seen him in a professional capacity since he had that fall last year and twisted his ankle.'

I remembered that occasion well. He'd been ordered to rest

with his leg elevated on a chair, but my father had been a most uncooperative patient, and had insisted on hobbling to the stores and the quay daily using a hefty stick for support. I had tried to persuade him to do as he had been instructed, but he would not listen.

'Why do you ask?' Mr Hedley peered at me. His eyes, fixed on my face, assumed a shrewdness that had not been there before. I sensed him probing, trying to identify the true meaning behind my words. He must be accustomed to people speaking to him in couched language, full of hint and innuendo rather than saying what was on their mind. But how could I admit that if there had been nothing wrong with my father, there was reason to suspect that he may have committed the sin of taking his own life?

'It's just … I can't help thinking … I mean, why did his heart just stop beating if there was nothing wrong with him? And if there was something, I should have noticed. Done something about it. Or persuaded him to.'

'Oh my child.'

If anyone else had called me a child I probably would have snapped that I was a grown woman and a widow, but coming from his lips it sounded perfectly natural. He rested his arms on the desk, leaned towards me, and spoke in a soft voice that was little more than a whisper.

'There's so much that we do not yet know about the human anatomy. Why does one man's heart thrive until old age whereas another's falters and fails when he still has so much to give? Your father was not a young man. He'd had to bear the pressures of business and the worries that come with it. He would not have been alive if he didn't have his own problems. But I cannot tell you that he had an illness that made him more susceptible to a failed heart, because if he did I knew nothing of it. I think you must stop tormenting yourself. There's nothing for you to blame yourself for, and I'm certain there is nothing you could have done to prevent it.'

This was a long speech for Mr Hedley, possibly the longest I had ever heard him make. He was trying to soothe my conscience, but I thought he was also telling me what he believed to be the truth, rather than what he thought I needed to hear. It did help to be reassured that I had not failed to notice my father had been ill, although it did not make his death easier to accept, and it still left the other question hanging over me. The question I could not voice.

'Thank you,' I said, rising from my chair. 'You've helped to put my mind at rest. I'll leave you to your work.'

He stood too and eased by me to the door where he paused, his hand on the latch. 'Any time you need to talk, please, you know where to find me,' he said.

I hurried back to my stores, aware that I had lost track of time and in all likelihood would be late for my meeting with Captain Thirlwell. No sooner had I dismissed one problem from my mind than others crowded in to take its place. My father had been preoccupied with something, and if it wasn't his health it must have been concerning the business and the debt. I had to discover what he had done with the money and find a way to repay Mr Young, which would mean selling as much stock as I could, so the inventory was more urgent than ever. And then there was the question of the Lady Isabella. I had to face the fact that my financial position meant I must send her back out to sea as soon as possible, but how could I do that, knowing what I did about her condition? And how would I fund the voyage? I hoped my credit was still good in the town because I would be living on it before long if I could not find any answers.

Captain Thirlwell was waiting at the entrance to the stores. When he saw me he removed his hat and inclined his head. He was a large man – not tall but muscled from a life at sea – with a face that I had never seen, because it was almost entirely covered by his thick beard, bushy eyebrows and mop of wild hair. When he first joined us I was still a little girl, and I had asked him why he had so much hair on his face. My father had scolded me for being impertinent, but the captain had knelt down so his head was on a level with mine and answered me as though my question deserved some serious attention. It was to give him protection against the rough weather he experienced at sea, he had said. In those days his beard and hair had been a rich brown, the shade of Thunder's coat, giving him a resemblance to the Berwick bear on which our masthead was modelled, but the chestnut was now flecked with grey. There was nothing faded about his eyes though. They were as vibrant as the slimy green weed that cushioned the rocks at low tide, with a twinkle that belied his reputation as a hard and ruthless taskmaster.

'Captain. Apologies. I've kept you waiting,' I greeted him and he grunted in reply.

I unlocked the door and paused inside, blinking whilst reaching for the tinderbox that we kept on a shelf above the table. I swapped my gloves for a special pair that had the fingers cut from them. It was a clever adaptation I had made, enabling me to handle a quill and other items, whilst still affording me some warmth. The captain strode past, leaving me to light a candle, which I placed within a glass lantern so I could carry it around with ease. He stood with his hands on his hips, facing into the large space, and I joined him.

'I feel your loss,' he said. 'Your father was a good man.'

Was he? I no longer knew.

'We've a good, full stores,' I replied. My fingers reached out to caress the bolt of cloth, a fine linen weave, that was on the shelf closest to me.

'What are you going to do now?'

'I'm going to run this business.' I turned to face him and paused, wondering if he would be my ally or refuse to accept my authority. He remained silent so I continued. 'How long do you need to fix her up, get her back out to sea?'

He shrugged. 'How long have I got?'

Not long enough was the only honest answer, but instead I offered, 'Two weeks, maybe three.'

He threw his head back and laughed.

'I know that isn't sufficient, and I had hoped to be able to delay for longer, or even retire her to local trips only, but it appears that isn't an option at the moment.'

His laughter faded and his eyes blazed into mine. 'I'll do it for you, and the memory of your father, but not for that pasty-faced foreigner.'

'I assume you mean Richard Elliott.' A voice inside my head rejoiced that the captain was my ally. 'You and I would appear to be in agreement about my cousin, but I'm afraid we're stuck with him, for now at least.'

'The rumours are true then? That he inherits through his mother?'

'Yes,' I confirmed. Although it occurred to me that my father's debts might be the means of ridding myself of the nuisance that was Richard Elliott, and I allowed the idea to take shape.

Captain Thirlwell bowed. 'We have an agreement,' he said.

I watched the captain leave, closed the door and set my mind to the task that I could no longer avoid – completing the inventory. The sheets I had designed for this purpose were in a desk in the small office just inside the entrance. My father's system had been so haphazard that the finished result always had the appearance of ants swarming over the surface of the paper and I could make no sense of it.

I extracted a few sheets, a quill and ink pot and set to work, starting at the end of a row furthest from the entrance. The darkness here was dense. Even in the height of summer the light did not penetrate this far into the stores, and with the shelves piled high with goods, the very walls seemed to close in, swallowing a person up into their blackness. I kept the lantern by my side, knowing that I would have itchy, sore eyes long before I had finished my task, as a result of working in the dim light it cast.

Sure enough, after less than an hour of climbing up and down the steps, counting and recording the details, my back was aching and I had rubbed at my eyes with dusty fingers, making them more irritable. A noise from the front of the stores, very much like the door opening and closing, reminded me that I had left it unlocked.

It was our habit, so customers could call in if they were passing, but since my father's death we had been closed to business and I was not expecting anyone this afternoon.

'Who's there?' I called into the gloom, wishing I had thought to light another candle and leave it on the entrance table. Unease stirred the hairs on the back of my neck. Being alone here had never made me nervous before, but then nothing at the moment appeared as straightforward as it once did.

A light flared and my tension lifted, to be replaced with annoyance. I could only see the back of his head, but the red-gold hair was unmistakable.

'Mr Elliott, you startled me,' I reprimanded him. 'What are you doing here?'

The light flickered as he approached me and his features became clearer. He was frowning.

'I've a perfect right to be here, as you well know.'

His reply was a rebuke, but I could not think of him as my business partner, even if he was. He strolled towards me with the air of a man who has not a care in the world. If only he knew the truth. I wondered if I should tell him, there and then, and whether that would send him scuttling back to London where he belonged. But what would I tell him? How could I admit that my father had kept me so much in the dark, had trusted me so little with his business dealings, that not only had I been unaware that he had borrowed such a lot of money, but I also had no idea what he had done with it? No, it was best that I wait until I was better informed.

'I didn't mean to alarm you Isabella, please accept my apology. I've been strolling around the quay, talking to people, getting to know the trade here.'

'You've been to see Captain Thirlwell?'

'Amongst others.'

Of course I knew he had, and I wanted to laugh, remembering the captain's contemptuous dismissal of him. I waited for him to elaborate but he remained silent, his eyes roving over the stacked shelves of the stores. His attire was more casual today, although still meticulous. The ruff had gone and his hosen and doublet were a plain dark brown. It occurred to me that he was a man who knew how to dress for the occasion, and had the means.

'What are you doing?' He peered at the paper in my hand.

'The inventory,' I replied, not bothering to keep an edge of sarcasm from my voice. What did he think I was doing? For a man who professed to have learned so much of the business of a merchant from his father it seemed a remarkably dumb question.

The sarcasm washed over him like waves on the rocks.

'Let me help you.'

I shrugged. If he was going to persist in hanging around here, he might as well make himself useful. 'There are more of these sheets, quills and ink in the office.' He turned and started to walk away from me.

'Wait,' I said. My tone was sharp and he stopped. 'I haven't told you what to do.'

'I can do an inventory,' he snapped. He swivelled around to face me.

'But can you do it the way I want it doing?' I asked, placing the emphasis on 'I'.

'As you wish. I am your pupil.' He mocked me with a bow and I thought about telling him to leave, there and then, but I doubt he would have listened to me.

'I have a system,' I explained, keeping the rising anger out of my voice. 'It makes it easier for me to collate afterwards. If you want to help, you need to use the same system.'

I explained how I wanted him to list items and their precise description in the left hand column, and then, where there were multiple identical items, use tally marks to record them. He nodded, as an attentive student would, but I suspected he was not taking me seriously. We worked in silence for a little over an hour, by which time we had finished what had been an onerous task and I was grateful for his help.

'What happens now?' He handed over a wad of sheets.

'I'll cross-reference against the last inventory and sales since then, double-check Captain Thirlwell's ledger and the customs bill, work out what the stock is worth and how much profit we can expect, and start selling.' I started to tidy up the office, replacing quills, ink and unused stock sheets in the small desk, and sliding the completed sheets into a leather satchel that was hanging from a hook behind the door. I would take them with me to study later.

'Where are all those records kept, because they clearly aren't here?' He gesticulated with his arm towards the empty surface of the desk and the walls, which were bare, devoid of shelves or anywhere for storing ledgers or paperwork of any kind.

'At the house,' I replied. 'It's more comfortable there and my father often worked late into the evening.'

'That's all very well, but it may not be very convenient now,' he mused.

I did not rise to his barb. If he thought I was going to come down here to work when I could be in the comfort and warmth of my own closet, with Mary to bring me food and drink, he was very much mistaken.

I extinguished my candle, replaced the lantern on the entrance table, swapped my gloves and moved towards the door where I waited, with one hand on the latch, for him to follow. He was in no hurry.

'I must say Isabella, the people in these parts certainly like their wine. We appear to have a huge stock.'

'It will go quickly.'

'The tunnage on wine isn't affecting sales?'

It was true that this had gone up dramatically. King Henry's debasement policies had reduced the value of our coins to such an extent that the revenue collected via import and export duties had plummeted. In response, Queen Mary had increased levies, so we had to charge our customers more, but it had not dampened demand. We had yet to discover what Queen Elizabeth's policy would be.

'It would appear not. Perhaps the people of Berwick are made of hardier stuff than your London clients.' I flicked the latch and pushed the door open.

'Hmmm,' he replied, not rising to my taunt, but taking the hint that it was time to leave.

Whilst we had been cocooned in the warehouse, night had set in. Delicate flakes of snow fluttered from a sky that was impenetrable in its blackness. The air was so raw that it hurt to breathe.

I slung the satchel over my shoulder and locked the door behind us.

'We have some very fine cloth as well. I've a mind to have a new doublet made.'

He was right. My husband had advised my father well, and we were renowned for the quality of our cloth. Indeed, I would contest that I have not seen better offered for sale in these parts, but he could have chosen a better time to raise the subject than outside, after a tiring day, whilst the snow fell on my shoulders and clung to my hair, and the cold was already seeping through my boots and holding my feet in its icy grip.

'I will gladly sell you some cloth, Mr Elliott,' I replied, trying to keep the impatience from my voice.

'At a discount, I hope.'

I could not decide if he was teasing me or not, and in the darkness, with his hat pulled down over his forehead, I could not read his face.

'I must bid you good night,' I said, turning away from him, already picking my way with care back along the path George had cleared towards the house, my boots squeaking as they sank into the carpet of fresh snow.

'Now would be a good time for you to show me the records you keep at the house,' he said.

I did not need to turn around to see he was following me, his voice bouncing in my ear told me as much. Although I was grateful for his help, I'd had my fill of Richard Elliott this afternoon.

'Mr Elliott, I've had a very long day. All I want to do is have some supper and retire for the evening, alone.' After searching for a missing key, I added inside my head.

'You can keep putting it off, but I'm going nowhere and I have every right to look at the records. Why can't you realise that and stop fighting me?'

Everything about the man was insufferable. I tried to bite back my anger and hoped he would slip and fall on the snow, but of course he didn't. I kicked open the back door and stood aside. 'After you,' I said, with a smile that I hoped did not reach my eyes.

A candle burned fiercely inside a glass lantern lighting up the boot room, which was little more than a cramped passageway that led to the kitchen on the left and the low door to my closet on the right. Footsteps echoed in the kitchen.

'Mary,' I called, shaking the snow from my cloak. Moments later she stepped out from the shadows. She appeared flushed and there was an air of contentment about her. Was that as a result of the afternoon she had spent with Douglas Lumsden I wondered, and then pushed the thought aside. I did not and could not approve of that relationship, and I hoped it would not end by causing her heartbreak, or worse.

'Mary, Mr Elliott and I will take some supper in my closet. Please send George to make up the fire and hang our cloaks to dry.'

She held out her arms to take our cloaks and retreated to the kitchen.

My cousin did not comment on my new arrangement of the closet, although he did pause to look around before settling into one of the chairs in front of my desk. If I did not know that he had been in this very room just a few days before, I would have thought he was seeing it for the first time and taking stock of his surroundings.

A few hours later I had shared most of the details of the business with him. I still had not told him about the financial situation, but I explained the ledgers, the filing system, customer correspondence and my father's arbitrary pricing system. He was very attentive and listened with few interjections. In fact, I would go so far as to say that his powers of concentration were impressive. Nevertheless, I was impatient for him to leave. I tried to stop my eyes from straying to the locked drawer. If he had not insisted on returning to the house with me, I could be searching for the key now and might even have found it.

Mary had served us with a casual supper of smoked and dried fish, pickles, cheese, bread and wine.

'We could build this into something truly special, Isabella,' he enthused, piling food onto his plate.

'I certainly intend to, Richard,' I replied, deciding to join him in dispensing with the formality of address.

He raised an eyebrow and his lips moved into a half smile before he took a large bite of fish. I watched, amused, as he grimaced and chewed slowly. His throat bobbed and he swallowed with a gulp.

'You may not like me, but I didn't think you would try to poison me,' he exclaimed, draining his mug of wine.

'It's a local speciality, and it may be an acquired taste,' I admitted, taking a small bite myself. 'Try it with the pickles. They either improve it, or they take away the taste. I'm never sure which.'

He shook his head. 'Forgive me, but I'd rather starve.'

As the hostess, I should have been offended, but I found his petulance amusing. I bit my lip and turned my head to one side, so he would not notice I was trying not to laugh. It would not do to let him think I was enjoying myself in his company.

'I've had some ideas about how we could expand by increasing the goods we trade,' he said after eating some bread and cheese.

I watched his enthusiastic chewing and waited for him to say more.

'Spices,' he announced, pronouncing the single word with pride, as if it were some profound revelation.

'Spices,' I repeated. 'You mean like pepper and garlic? I regret to inform you that we are not so behind the times here. We do have spices.'

'No, I mean exotic spices, from faraway places that you and I can only imagine, like cinnamon, cloves, saffron and nutmeg.'

'What are you suggesting? That the Lady Isabella should sail to the other side of the world? Because if so I fear you are gravely over-estimating her capabilities.'

'No, no, no. You don't understand. The Portuguese ships dominate this trade and they have a strong influence in Antwerp. I believe we could buy a good quantity there to bring back here.'

There was a hint of impatience in his voice. His fingers strayed to the ring in his ear and he twisted it.

'In London these spices sell in small quantities for vast sums. I've asked around since I've been here in Berwick and no-one is importing anything of the like. We could be the first, and we would have every wealthy household from here south, as far as Newcastle, maybe even beyond, queuing at our door to buy from us. We could set up a trade with shopkeepers in Newcastle, Durham, Whitby even, to stock our spices. Everyone gains because if we are bringing them in directly from Antwerp we would be able to offer a better price than the London merchants are able to, when their goods have to be distributed by land or transferred to a different ship to sell in the north.'

He was on his feet now, the impatience replaced with excitement, eyes shining as he enthused about his idea. And it was, on the surface, a good one. King Henry's love of such spices had generated a great demand for them among those who could afford to pay the high price they commanded. However, I feared his enthusiasm was blinding him to the possible obstacles of such a trade.

'Your idea is interesting,' I conceded. 'But what do you know of the practicalities of such a trade? I mean, how do these spices need to be stored, for instance, so that they don't spoil?'

He dismissed my objection with a flick of his wrist. 'Remember, they are already travelling by land and sea from Asia. We're not pioneering anything new. We will simply replicate how the other ships store them for transport.'

He made it sound so easy, but I had an inherent dislike of anything I did not understand. My father's voice popped into my head. *'Caution, Isabella. He who makes a rash move in business may live to regret it.'* The laugh that I could not prevent escaping my lips was bitter. How many times had I rejected that approach, and he was in no position to preach to me about caution, even from beyond the grave. In that moment I made up my mind. I would go along with Richard's idea, but his enthusiasm, which was bordering on recklessness, would be tempered by proper consideration of the practicalities.

'No fortunes will be made by our smaller vessels shipping eggs and grains to our neighbours up and down the coast, although if we trade more goods it will help. We can use them to distribute our spices as well.'

'Richard, slow down. I'm not opposed to your idea, but there is much planning to do first.'

'We must get the Lady Isabella out again, without delay,' he countered.

I stared at the candles, which were burning low.

'You mentioned that you had met with Captain Thirlwell. If you had listened to him you would know that the Lady Isabella is barely seaworthy at the moment. Before I will risk her – and her crew – on the German Ocean at this time of year, she needs repairs.'

'I listened to him, but I do not see any activity. Why aren't the repairs being organised?' The lightness that had been in the air just a short time ago had vanished, hidden behind eyes that were hard and unblinking. This might have been the time to tell him about the huge debt that had to be repaid, somehow, to Mr Young – it would give him something else to think about – but I could not bring myself to do so. Nor could I bring myself to tell him that Captain Thirlwell and I had already spoken about this and agreed a target that neither of us were happy with. That admission, I was sure, he would interpret as defeat, and I could not explain it without alluding to the reasons behind it.

'This is not London,' I said, refusing to meet his eye. 'We don't have skilled labourers for the picking. I want only the best to work on the Lady Isabella and we must wait for them.'

A strange noise erupted from the back of his throat. 'That's a lot of blather, if you don't mind me saying, dear cousin. Her crew is the only skilled labour she needs.'

I did mind, and of course he was right. A wave of fatigue swept over me and I knew I could not take much more today. 'Perhaps we should continue this conversation another time,' I suggested. 'It's late, and I have much to do tomorrow.'

He rose to his feet and nodded. 'I fear I have outstayed my welcome,' he said.

It was very tempting to agree that had he even been welcome in the first place he would indeed have outstayed it, but I was better bred than that. I satisfied myself with inclining my head.

'But I would like to continue this conversation at the earliest opportunity. Tomorrow?' he said, reaching for my hand. For a moment I thought he was going to take it and raise it to his lips. I snatched it away and he bowed instead.

After he had gone, I leaned my head against the door. It was late and I was bone-tired. George was hovering in the shadows at the back of the hallway.

'Shall I bank the fire?'

'Yes please. Where's Mary?'

'She's to bed already,' George said scuttling into the closet.

There was no longer any question of me searching for the missing key tonight. Much as I wanted to, I did not have the energy. I would resume my efforts in the morning, which arrived earlier than I had expected. It was still dark when I emerged from a deep sleep, woken by a loud hammering at my front door. I rubbed my eyes, and pushed myself up onto my elbows.

'Open up,' commanded a voice I did not recognise.

I slid out of bed, pulled a thick shawl over my shift, unlatched the window and leaned out. It was not ladylike, I know, but if I did not put a stop to this everyone from Briggate to the quay itself would be roused and amusing themselves at my expense. It was no longer snowing, and a thick fog hovered in the cold, damp air.

My window overhung the street. I looked down on a man cocooned in a dark gown with a hat pulled down over his ears. He was holding a lantern in one hand, and in the other, a long staff which he was using to beat on my front door.

'What is the meaning of this?' I demanded, trying to inject an imperious tone into my voice.

The man raised his head and removed his hat, revealing a large, round bald patch surrounded by wispy grey hair, which merged with the swirling fog. It gave him the appearance of a disembodied, featureless head floating on the surface of a river, hair spread out around it. He tipped his head back so his face was angled up towards me. I did not recognise him.

Mary's heavy tread clipped along the hall downstairs from the kitchen to the front door, and the bolts grated in their brackets as she drew them back.

'Madam Gillhespy? I have orders to take you to the Tolbooth immediately. You need to come with us.'

The fog seeped in through my open window and its clammy fingers stroked my skin making me shiver. The Tolbooth was where law-breakers and trouble-makers were taken. I was neither, so why was I being summoned there?

'On whose authority?' I challenged, with more confidence than I felt. He did not scare me, but a shift in the foggy darkness behind him revealed that he was not alone. Several men stood in the shadows. I could not tell whether they were wearing the uniform of soldiers, or the town guards, but the sight of them sent a chill down my spine.

'Lord Grey de Wilton,' he said. His words turned the chill into ice. Our new town Governor reported to the Queen's principal Secretary, Sir William Cecil, and was the highest authority in Berwick. What could he want with me?

'What is this about?' I asked.

'I could not say. You need to come with us,' he repeated. 'My orders are to escort you by whatever means I deem necessary.'

Was it my imagination or had the figures in the shadows inched closer? The man beneath my window spoke softly, but there was an undertone of authority that convinced me he would not hesitate to carry out his orders.

'There's no need to threaten me,' I countered. 'I will come with you, but perhaps you will do me the courtesy of allowing me to dress first?'

He grunted and mumbled something. I did not care to know what. 'If you allow Mary to come back upstairs to help me it won't take long.'

I did not wait for his further reply, but closed the window and selected a gown woven from a heavy woollen cloth with a high neck to keep out the worst of the cold. Mary's face was pale and her fingers fumbled with the stays as she helped me to dress. I did not need her help, but I wanted to talk to her in private.

'Don't worry Mary. I've done nothing wrong,' I whispered.

'What do they want?' she whispered back.

'I don't know, but I'm sure I will find out soon enough. Send George with a message to Will. Tell him what's happened.'

The hammering began again. 'Madam. My patience is wearing thin.'

I nodded to Mary and followed her down the stairs, the candle that she held lighting our way. In the hall, I paused to pull my cloak around my shoulders and raise the hood before opening the door, my head held high, my hands in their thick gloves clasped together so no-one could see how they were shaking. Then I stepped out of my house and the thick, swirling fog wrapped itself around me and swallowed me into its darkness.

SEVEN

THE ROOM IN WHICH I was left to wait was small and bare – the only furniture two chairs facing each other across a table, the surface of which was scuffed and pitted with divots. Although the ceiling was low, the single window set into the wall above my head was too high for me to see through. It was tiny, and fitted with heavy metal bars, which cannot have been to deter escape since even a small child would struggle to squeeze through it. A single, tallow candle shed a pool of dull, yellow light and filled the space with its rancid smell. My escort had locked the door behind him, leaving me in no doubt but that I was a prisoner.

There was a hearth, but no fire. Left here, alone, my apprehension intensified the chill in the room and I shivered. My hands in their gloves were warm, so I wrapped my arms around myself and huddled inside my heavy cloak. That kept some heat in my body, but did nothing to raise my spirits. It would not do to give way to fear, so instead I fuelled my indignation about the treatment I had been subjected to.

I had not appreciated being marched through the streets like some common thief. There were few people about, but those who were had stared at me in a most unpleasant way, bordering on insolence. Judging me for some imagined crime. Me, Isabella Gillhespy. One of the most respected merchants in town! I did not recognise any of them, although it was quite possible that I paid their wages. I had tried asking my escort what this was all about, but he'd ignored me. The guards had pressed close to my back, making me feel claustrophobic, but not nearly as claustrophobic as I was now, trapped in this airless room, below the Tollbooth in the very heart of the town. It was a building I knew well, as this was where the burgesses met and conducted the business of the guild, but I had never seen this side of it before.

The minutes ticked by, and although I tried not to dwell on why I was here, I could not help myself. In this building all manner of petty thieves, whores and drunks were held awaiting trial or for punishment to be meted out, and it was humiliating to be counted amongst their number. More serious villains – those accused of murder or treason – were also detained here these days, deep in its bowels, rather than in the dungeons at the castle, which was sinking further into disrepair. Some of those, once incarcerated, never saw the light of day again, except on their final walk to the gallows.

With only my thoughts for company, I fancied I could smell the fear and the dread that would have consumed many when entering these walls before me. I had to draw some comfort from the knowledge that, grim though this room was, it would be as a palace compared to the accommodation being suffered in the true cells below. That had to be an indication that my supposed crime was not so great, or maybe it was a mark of my status. Whichever it was, I had to hold onto the belief that this was a positive sign.

After a while of standing I resigned myself to a possibly extended wait, and sat down on one of the chairs. It was as uncomfortable as it looked – the seat narrow, the back low. I tried to curb my impatience and my imagination, which was mounting all sorts of wild theories about why I had been detained, by thinking about the missing key and where it could be. The first place I would have to search would be my father's bedchamber. That was not a prospect that appealed to me. Going straight to the hiding places that I already knew about in search of the money had been an uncomfortable experience, but sifting through his private belongings was too personal. Although of course I would have to do it at some point, I had hoped to be able to leave it until his death was less raw.

I squeezed my eyes shut and allowed a picture of my father's bedchamber to form inside my head, letting my imagination explore any possible hiding places, but there were so many in which to secrete such a small item that I soon gave up and directed my thoughts instead to my cousin. His presence was annoying, and his persistence about the Lady Isabella was as irritating as a fly; no matter how many times you swat it away, it returns for more. His idea about the spices, though, appeared to be a good one and worth exploring, especially since I had conceded I had little alternative but to send the Lady Isabella back out to sea much sooner than I had intended, and would need all the revenue her trip could yield. I must handle the situation with care though, because I did not want to inflate my cousin's good opinion of himself even further, and I was not ready to share the news that our business had heavy debts. Until I knew what my father had done with the money there was still the chance that I could recover some of it, and I was going to cling to that shred of optimism with all of my might.

The shadows cast by the candle began to take on a less dense quality and I looked up to the window. The combination of the thick bars and the dirt that I could now see streaking across the glass and clustering around the frame prevented the ingress of much natural light. The sun must have risen and I longed to see daylight, but I had no sense of how much time had passed since I had been shut in here. My stomach was protesting though; last night's supper seemed a long time ago. I closed my eyes and wondered again why I was here. A key grated in the lock and my head jerked up, eyes now wide open. My breath caught in my throat and a heavy dread descended on me as I watched the door swing slowly on its heavy hinges until a shaft of weak light and a waft of stale air followed a tall and angular man into the room. He was wearing a long gown and knee-high boots and I recognised him at once. Such was my relief, I had to stop myself from leaping to my feet and greeting him as an old friend. I had known Mr Usher for many years. He had been a customer and associate of my father, and a frequent guest at our table. He was also Sir Grey de Wilton's right hand man, the person who sullied his hands dealing with the less desirable elements of the town's society, and those who were so poor or desperate they had no alternative but to steal and sell their bodies, whilst Sir Grey himself polished the veneer.

'Madam Gillhespy,' Mr Usher said. His tone was unpleasant, and quite unlike the jovial person I thought I knew. The relief that washed over me just a moment ago vanished, and I was reminded that he also had a reputation as a hard interrogator. He kicked the door closed behind him and the room descended into semi-darkness again. I did not rise, but watched him light a taper from the dying candle. He brushed past me as if I weren't there, and applied the taper to the sconces mounted in the walls behind me. They flickered into life, casting a half-hearted light that did nothing to lift the oppressive atmosphere that swirled around him.

'Mr Usher,' I replied when at last he sat, brushing the seat of the chair first, and turned to face me. 'Would you care to explain what I'm doing here?' That was something else my father had always taught me. *At times of conflict, don't wait for your adversary to be the aggressor, take the fight to them.*' I'm not sure he envisaged me enacting his advice whilst locked in a prison cell, and I hoped my voice did not betray me.

Mr Usher narrowed his eyes and stared at me, unblinking. The candlelight elongated his shadow, accentuating his sharp angles and projecting his silhouette on to the wall as a sinister black apparition that hung over me, casting judgement. It was almost enough to make me doubt my own innocence. Had I done something of which I had no recollection?

'How is Jennet?' I asked with a smile. Jennet was his daughter. We had been friends once when we were children, but life and marriage had taken us in different directions. I had heard that she had recently given birth to her second child, the thought of which gave me a pang of pain, remembering my own failed attempt at motherhood and the tiny dead body that was wrapped in linen cloth and whisked away from me. My baby, who I had never held. I blinked and rubbed my eyes. It was a mistake to think of him at this moment. I needed to focus.

'How well do you know Arthur Fewell?'

So, this was something to do with Arthur. What had that rascal got involved with now, and why should it concern me? Or it might concern Will – he had been going to meet Arthur for some supper last night. Until I knew why Mr Usher wanted to talk about him, I would not volunteer the information that Will and Arthur had planned to meet. I chose my words with care and aimed for a nonchalant expression in their delivery.

'I know him, but not well.'

'Did you see him yesterday evening?'

'No,' I answered. I was alert now, waiting for him to say more.

'Are you quite sure about that?'

His voice took on an even harder edge, if that were possible. 'I'm going to ask you again. Did you see Arthur Fewell last night?'

'I'm quite sure,' I said, keeping my eyes fixed on his face, even though his countenance filled me with dread. 'I have not seen him since my father's funeral.'

Mr Usher half-raised himself from his chair, and his shadow climbed further up the wall until it was hovering on the low ceiling. Everything about his demeanour was threatening, and for the first time I understood how he could have such a fearful reputation as an interrogator. I recoiled, as a kitten might from a rabid dog, and he lowered himself back into a sitting position.

'It's very important, Madam Gillhespy,' he persisted.

'And I repeat, I have not seen him.' It seemed important not to let him erode my confidence. I knew I was speaking the truth, but he appeared determined not to believe me, and I did not know why. My mind was working quickly, trying to remember Will's precise words when he had said he was going to see Arthur. Whatever this was about, I wondered if Will was involved. If he was, why had I been detained and not him? Or perhaps they were holding Will here as well, in another tiny, airless room.

Mr Usher slipped a hand inside his doublet, pulled out a small card and pushed it across the table towards me. I recognised it, of course, since it was one of the cards I had drawn to give to our customers. His eyes were intense. I pushed my shoulders back and made myself look straight at him, whilst trying to work out where his questions were leading, and what the significance of the card could be.

'We found this in the Black Watch Tower a few hours ago, just after we found Arthur Fewell.'

He was waiting for my reaction, and I hoped that my expression reflected my confusion, but if he was asking me a question I did not know what it was, so I remained silent.

'When we found him dead, this morning,' Mr Usher added, leaning forwards again until I could smell his breath, stale wine and a hint of garlic.

'Dead?' I repeated.

My surprise was absolute. Arthur had always been too full of life to be dead.

'But where? How?'

'We found him at the foot of the tower. His head bears the mark of having been hit with something, perhaps a rock, which caused him to fall to his death.'

'You're saying he was murdered?'

The chill in the room wrapped itself around me like a girdle and squeezed until it hurt to breathe. Arthur, murdered. It could not be true. Arthur was fun, although it was easy to imagine that he might have enemies. I wondered if he'd been caught by a cuckolded husband. My head crowded with thoughts and fear rose within me. Will might know something. He might even have been with Arthur when the attack had happened? He might be lying somewhere, hurt. I knew I should tell Mr Usher that they had planned to meet. I pressed my fingers to my temples and tried to wipe out the visions that my thoughts were conjuring.

Mr Usher's eyes did not waver from my face.

'I don't understand what this has got to do with me,' I said, when it became clear he was not going to answer.

His eyes moved with deliberation towards the card on the table before me.

'We give these cards to our customers. I expect you also have one.'

'Turn it over.'

My hands shook as I removed a glove, reached for the card and did as he instructed. Its texture was no longer that of crisp parchment, but resembled the moss that covered the ground in damp corners of the churchyard. The words printed on the back looked to have been made in a neat hand, but the ink was leaching into the paper, distorting the letters.

8.30 tonight. You know where. A

I dropped the card. 'This has nothing to do with me,' I said, pulling my glove back on.

'I'm thinking it may be an assignation that went wrong. One that you would not want Mr Ord to know about perhaps?'

'Do I look as though I'm capable of pushing a strong, heavy man like Arthur Fewell over a wall?' I had never been on the top of the Black Watch Tower, so I did not know how high the wall was, but even if it was low, the idea seemed ridiculous.

If only Mr Usher could see it that way.

He shrugged. 'Lover's quarrel. You reach for a heavy object – anything that is to hand will suffice, or you could have something on you, for self-defence of course. A lady out alone after dark in a town like this cannot be too careful. You take him by surprise – perhaps you are embracing at the time and his mind is on … other things … and then, whilst he is stunned, you push him. It would not take much strength.'

'No,' I snapped. 'I know nothing of this.' My father's voice in my head urged me to caution, and I held back my fury that he could level such an accusation at me.

'Where were you last night?'

'At home, working,' I replied. Before I could add that I had not been alone, we were interrupted by a rap on the door.

Mr Usher glared at me as though I were somehow responsible and barked, 'Come.'

The door creaked and a clerk entered the small room. He whispered something in Mr Usher's ear and my interrogator pushed his chair back and followed him from the room.

'Wait there,' he said, before locking the door behind him, rendering his parting words ridiculous.

An oppressive silence settled on the room and wrapped its tendrils around my neck and throat until my breath came in ragged gasps. I leapt to my feet to break its grip on me and started pacing up and down – four steps to the wall where the window was, turn, and four steps to the door, turn and repeat, over and over, stamping my heavy boots on the dirty floor – as much to warm my feet as to vent my anger, frustration and fear about the situation I found myself in. Could things get any worse? First, my father's death, then Richard Elliott turning up, the discovery of the debt, and now being suspected of murder.

Moving around eased my breathing and helped me to control my thoughts. It was difficult to think of Arthur as being dead, and I was worrying about Will. Where was he and was he all right? If Mary had done as I had asked and sent George to him with a message, he should know by now of my detention, and he would surely guess where they had taken me, although I could not banish from my head the image of Will lying injured and unable to come to my aid.

Then it occurred to me that I ought to take advantage of Mr Usher being out of the room to have a closer look at the card. I paused in my pacing, slipped my glove off again, picked up the card and examined it on both sides. Its moss-like texture and blurred ink made me certain it had absorbed water, or snow – the town had been wearing its white blanket since the day of my father's funeral. I read the message again, to be certain I had remembered it correctly. The simple signature 'A' had been made with a firm hand pressing the quill into the paper, leaving grooves that had been expanded by the ingress of moisture so the letter would be legible even though the ink was blurred. The logical assumption was that 'A' was Arthur, he had written the note on the card and the recipient – the killer – had then turned up at the designated time, they'd argued, perhaps fought, and the killer had not noticed that he had dropped the card. I wondered if there were signs of a scuffle in the snow.

There were other possibilities though. He might not have delivered it to the intended recipient; it could have fallen from his own pocket whilst he was on duty. Or it could be an old note and have nothing to do with him or his death. The 'A' might not even be Arthur. Even more puzzling, why was he at the Black Watch Tower when he was supposed to be meeting Will at The Sailor's Rest?

Much as I was curious, this had nothing to do with me and I could prove it. The sooner the better as well, because whilst Mr Usher was wasting time interrogating me, the real murderer might be escaping, slipping unnoticed through one of the town gates and disappearing into the wild country beyond the walls.

I leaned over the table, banged my fists on its pitted surface and unleashed a howl of frustration, just as the key grated in the lock again and the door swung open. Framed in the entrance was the clerk who had earlier whispered in Mr Usher's ear. He stared at me with wide eyes and an expression of alarm, as if he thought I were possessed of some demon. I straightened my back, adjusted my cloak and smiled at him. He stepped to one side and waved one arm towards the door. I raised an eyebrow.

'You are free to go,' he said, still watching me warily.

I swept past him, out into the narrow corridor, at the end of which a set of stone steps led up to ground level and another corridor. This one was well-lit, with natural light flooding in from the door that stood open to the street at the far end. My instinct was to run, to get out of there before Mr Usher changed his mind, but the floor was uneven, and my legs were quivering like Mary's blancmange. Instead, I faltered past a number of low, wooden doors, like the one to my recent prison, which punctuated the walls at regular intervals on both sides. A voice I did not recognise boomed from behind one of them. 'I want his chambers sealing and guarding. No-one is to be allowed in – and I mean no-one – until I have had time to conduct a thorough search and am satisfied we have learned all we can. I want to know about everything he was involved with, everyone he met, even where he went for a piss.'

I drew level with a room to which the door was ajar, and as there was a warming fire blazing in the hearth, I judged it to be an office of some sort. Mr Usher was leaning against the door frame.

'Madam Gillhespy,' he said, inclining his head. I stopped and met his eyes. 'I may need to question you further.'

'You know where to find me. I'm sure any further discussions we may need to have can be conducted in the comfort of my closet,' I replied. It was intended as a rebuke, but as soon as the words had left my lips I wondered whether it was a mistake to antagonise him. His expression was as thunderous as the sky over the ocean when it was about to blow in a storm, but I heard a sound like a chuckle. Someone was watching and listening from the room behind him. Perhaps the person whose voice I had just heard.

Mr Usher's parting words echoed inside my head as I hastened past him, desperate to remove myself from this dreadful place. When I reached the open door at the end of the corridor, I stepped out into a clear, crisp day. All trace of the morning's fog had vanished, and the brilliant whiteness of last night's fresh snow dazzled me. My head span and a wave of vertigo nearly sent me toppling down the steps. I closed my eyes and leaned back against the wall, inhaling the fresh, salty air that burned my throat and lungs. Then Will's voice cut through the background noise – the shouts of traders marketing their wares, customers haggling over the price, horses snorting – and never had I been so pleased to hear it.

'God's wounds, Izzy. What are you doing here? I've been so worried since George delivered your message. I didn't know what to think.'

I opened my eyes and there he was, familiar and crumpled in his old brown doublet and creased white shirt beneath a heavy cloak. His dark eyes crinkled and as I rushed towards him he held out his arms. I fell into them and my head landed on his shoulder, relief at being free and seeing Will rendering my legs incapable of holding me upright unaided any longer. It was only then I noticed that standing behind him, wearing a smug smile, was Richard Elliott.

EIGHT

I PULLED BACK FROM WILL'S arms, ignoring my cousin.

'Something terrible has happened,' I said, fearing that I must break the news to him that his good friend was dead, believed murdered. With one glance at his face though, I knew I had been spared that awful task. Will had already heard.

'Shhh,' he said, drawing my arm through his. 'Not here. Let's walk.'

We turned onto Uddyngate, which was busy with traders selling their wares – hot pies, fish and eggs were piled onto small stalls and carts, the legs and wheels of which were embedded in the fresh snow. Men and women were rushing about their business, on foot or on horseback. Dogs pressed their noses to the ground, gulping down any morsels of food dropped by a careless person. The scene was as familiar to me as my own front parlour, but today it shimmered and disintegrated at the extent of my vision. I stumbled and would have fallen were it not for Richard reaching out to steady me and the firm pressure of Will's arm. They both stopped walking and I found myself supported between them like a marionette.

'When did you last eat or drink anything?' Will asked, angling his head towards me and fixing his eyes on mine.

'Last night,' I admitted.

'This way,' he said, steering me across the street and ducking under a low archway into an alley that was so narrow I could touch the walls on either side with outstretched arms. Will squeezed by my side, Richard dropped behind.

'Will, can we not just go home. It's not far. I can walk,' I protested as he stopped at the sign of a ship's anchor hanging above a solid wooden door.

He ignored me and pulled me into the tavern. Its tiny frontage opened into a small room, crowded with tables, benches and chairs, all of them occupied by men, eating, drinking and talking. Wenches weaved between them, low-cut gowns displaying plenty of their own wares. As we passed, one cuffed the back of a man's head and sashayed away from him. He lurched towards her trying to grab her waist, missed, and landed on the floor. She giggled and his companions guffawed. The low ceiling trapped the noise – loud voices engaged in lively debate – and the smell of roasting meat and freshly-baked bread mingled with that of unwashed flesh and spicy ale. It should have been an unpleasant combination, but instead it was uplifting, full of life and energy, a complete contrast to the walls of my recent prison and Mr Usher's sinister silhouette and unsmiling features. Even so, I was grateful that Will led me to a private room behind the bar, calling to the landlord as we passed to bring us food and ale. It was warm and almost cosy, with a fire glowing in the hearth and high-backed chairs arranged around a single table. I sank into one of the chairs close to the fire and loosened my cloak.

'They suspect me of being involved. How could they … I mean, how could they even think that, just because …' I broke off as the door was kicked open and one of the tavern wenches backed into the room. She was carrying a platter of thickly carved slices of roast mutton swimming in juices and chunks of bread with a jug of ale and three mugs. She deposited the platter on the table and I caught the inviting smile she cast in my cousin's direction as she swayed her hips back out of the room. He appeared not to notice.

'Eat, and then we'll talk,' Will said.

He pushed the platter towards me and I fell on it in a most unladylike way. A full belly and the warmth of the room revived my powers of reason. The terrors of the morning retreated, and my head filled with questions all battling for attention. What did Will know about Arthur's death, and what was Richard doing here? How had he known to turn up at the Tolbooth this morning when the message I'd sent with George had been to Will? I mopped up some juices from the platter with my last piece of bread and pushed it away. To my right, Will was pouring more ale into his mug. Richard remained standing opposite me, pulling on his earring, giving a good impression of being lost in his own thoughts.

'You are like a bad penny Mr Elliott,' I said, forgetting that I had decided to match his impudence and call him by his first name. I pushed my chair back and turned to face Will before my cousin had gathered his wits to think of a riposte.

'I bumped into him on my way to the Tolbooth,' Will explained. 'He insisted on coming with me when he heard about you.'

Richard moved to stand behind Will so I could not ignore him. 'I've always been an early riser,' he said. 'I was out walking in the Ness and heard about Fewell. The garrison is in a furore, seeing Scottish spies around every corner.'

'There are a lot of visitors from Scotland in town at the moment, although I doubt many of them are spies,' Will said. He helped himself to another chunk of bread and glared at Richard. 'Cecil and the Scottish Lords are of a mind. They all fear the power of France, and Mary Stuart's new claim to the English throne is something Cecil will not tolerate. A treaty between Scotland and England is therefore desirable. In the meantime, the garrison remains on high alert lest the rumoured French fleet arrives.'

I recognised Will's need to expose my cousin's flippant comment and demonstrate his superior knowledge of Berwick's affairs. However, the machinations and politics of the state did not interest me, even though in this town more than any other in the country, they affected every day of our lives. Since my father's death I had withdrawn into myself and paid little attention to such affairs, but for the sake of my business, I knew I needed to stay informed. That, however, could wait. It was more important to find out what had happened here, under our very noses, to someone we knew and liked.

'Will, you were supposed to be meeting Arthur last night. What happened?' I asked.

'He didn't turn up. You know what Arthur was like. I assumed he'd had a better offer, so I had a few drinks and some supper and went home. I didn't think anything of it. Maybe if I had, and I'd gone to look for him, I could have prevented this happening.'

Will's voice was heavy with anguish. I shook my head and reached for his hands. It was understandable that he would be tormented by the thought that he had failed his friend, but I was grateful that he had not been with Arthur at the time of the attack.

'He might have been set upon. Got caught in a fight, outnumbered. If I'd been there as well there would have been two of us, not so easy to overpower.'

'No. That isn't what happened,' I said.

Will tensed and his foot started a gentle tap, tap on the floor. The atmosphere in the room shifted and Richard's glance slid between us. Will had not appreciated me correcting him in public, whether I spoke the truth or not.

Before I could say anything more, Richard cleared his throat and continued in a loud voice with his account of the morning. 'So, as I was saying. I told Ord the news about Fewell, and he told me about your message, and we surmised that you being seized in the way you were must be connected to Arthur's death. It wasn't until we got to the Tolbooth that we heard they had taken you on suspicion of being involved somehow. I asked the clerk when the murder had taken place and he said something about 8pm last night, so I told him you couldn't possibly have had anything to do with it, since you were with me for much of the afternoon until nine in the evening, when you made it clear you wanted me to leave.' His mouth twitched with the flicker of a smile.

My cousin was clearly enjoying himself, but Will was not. He dropped my hands and his eyes were hard. There was something in his expression that quite changed his features, made him into someone I almost did not recognise. I pressed a hand to my forehead. Richard had sensed Will's tension, I was certain of it, so could he not see what he was implying and how that would make the situation worse? Or was his choice of words deliberate? Was he trying to drive a wedge between Will and me?

'That must have been when the clerk came in and interrupted Mr Usher,' I murmured.

'Yes,' Richard agreed. 'If he's the tall one with the mean eyes.'

Never before had I thought of him as having mean eyes, but Richard was right, and there is no doubt but that I had seen a different aspect of his character this morning than that he had chosen to show to me previously.

'He took me into a side room and I repeated what the clerk had overheard. I must say Isabella, he seemed quite disappointed. He turned without thanking me, said something to the clerk and marched out of the room. I re-joined Ord outside, and a few minutes later you appeared. The rest you know.'

'Thank you. It would seem I owe my freedom to you.' I shuddered, wondering what might have happened if my cousin had not insisted on coming to the house last night and I had been alone. Mary would have told them I had been at home all evening, but would they have believed her? The thought was too uncomfortable, so I pushed it away and turned to Will. He was staring at Richard, and then he turned to me. The expression in his eyes scared me. If I was to say that at that moment I thought Will could murder Richard, I would not be exaggerating. I reached for Will's hands, but he held them in a tight bunch by his side.

Saint Oswald save me from sulking men, the voice inside my head implored as my eyes swept up to the ceiling and back down to the two men in front of me.

I was not going to defend myself or my actions to Will with Richard hanging on to every word. My hands hovered between us and I watched him for a few seconds, hoping he would look at me and see the truth in my eyes, see that I loved him, and not fall for Richard's mischief-making, but his gaze seemed to pass through me and land somewhere over my shoulder. Suppressing a flicker of annoyance I turned away.

'What I don't understand though, is why they thought you had anything to do with it,' Richard mused, twisting the ring in his ear. He paced around the table, dragged a chair towards me and sat down.

'It was the card,' I explained, glancing at Will who was glaring at Richard. 'They found one of the cards I made for the business at the Black Watch Tower, and on the reverse there was a message. It said '8.30 tonight. You know where.' And it was signed simply 'A'. They suggested that Arthur had sent the card to me, that we were having a relationship, in secret, and that I'd gone to meet him, we'd argued and I'd hit him over the head with a heavy object and pushed him over the wall and off the top of the tower. But it doesn't make sense.' I turned towards Will, uncertain how he would react to this suggestion that I had somehow been involved with his good friend. He was staring at me, eyes wide. He could not have appeared more shocked if he'd just seen a sea serpent swimming past Maison Dieu Quay. A shiver of unease rippled around my heart.

'It doesn't make sense,' I repeated. 'I made lots of those cards. It doesn't mean this has anything to do with me.'

'It means they don't have many leads, and it's a tangible connection that they have to investigate,' Richard said.

'I suppose.' There was some sense in his words, but I did not have long to muse over them. Will stood abruptly. 'I'll take you home.'

I rose from my chair. The room started to spin around me, and I leaned against the table, waiting for the moment to pass. I recognised it as a sign of exhaustion, and I wondered what time it was. Mary would be worried. We had not thought to send word to her that I had been released.

'Good day to you, Elliott.' Will nodded to Richard, but there was nothing convivial about his tone of voice. It was a dismissal. Richard bowed. It could have been a polite gesture or one intended to mock, but the hint of a smirk I detected beneath his beard made me think the latter. Will took my arm and steered me out of the inn with none of the gentleness and courtesy with which he had led me in. He marched down Uddyngate at such a pace that I did not attempt to keep up. I could have tripped and been lying in the snow with the day's filth and a twisted ankle, and he would have been none the wiser. So much for taking me home. When I reached my house there was no sign of him. Mary must have let him in because the door was ajar, and then she appeared, casting an anxious glance up the street. She saw me, rushed out and smothered me in an embrace that almost knocked me to the ground.

'Thank the Lord ye're safe. I've been so worried.'

'I told you Mary, I've done nothing wrong,' I said, not mentioning how worried I had been myself just a few hours before. She stepped back and looked me up and down as if to convince herself of the truth of my words. Satisfied, she turned and I followed her inside.

'I need to wash,' I said, removing my cloak and gloves. My thoughts returned to that small room – my prison – the smell and taste of it. The thought alone was enough to make my skin itch. I needed to scrub it away.

'I'll fetch some water,' Mary said, already moving towards the kitchen.

The door to the parlour was open. Will was standing in front of the fire, staring into its flames. I hesitated on the threshold before closing the door and moving towards him. He turned, and one glance at his face told me that this was not going to be a conversation to comfort and soothe me.

'Would you care to fill me in with whatever is going on between you and your cousin?' he demanded, his voice so loaded with fury it could have sunk a ship.

What I would not give to curl up on the settle, in front of my fire, and forget about today. Forget about Richard Elliott and the problems he had brought into my life. Forget about my father's debt. Forget about poor Arthur being murdered. I shunned the chair and met Will's eyes, which were as dark as the night sky. An angry tick was twitching by his right eyebrow.

'There is nothing going on between me and Richard Elliott,' I said, doing my best to remain calm under his unfair accusation.

'You're even calling each other by your first names!'

'Will, you're not listening to me. There is nothing going on between us.'

I moved towards him and we stared at each other. He was so close I could have extended my arm and taken his hand in mine, but the distance between us had never been greater. I knew I could not reach him. A heavy silence descended on the room and wrapped us in it. Will was the first to break away. He poured himself a whisky and knocked it back before topping the tumbler up again.

'Do you think I want to be indebted to that man?'

'But you are. Because you spent the entire afternoon and evening with him. He's your alibi, and soon the entire town will know of that.'

Although he did not raise his voice, I knew that Will was struggling to control his anger. It was threatening to spill over, forcing words to be spoken that could not be withdrawn. My own temper was rising with the unfairness of his accusations, and a dull ache was increasing its pressure behind my eyes.

'Do you think I'm spending time with him by choice? He's been rather foisted on me,' I snapped back at him.

'Don't you see that this is exactly the sort of situation I do not want you to be in. This is why we should marry as soon as we can. Then I can deal with the likes of Elliott.'

He was insinuating that I could not. Did Will think I was incapable because I was a woman, because I was younger than him, intellectually inferior, or because I lacked the skills and experience of life, and business, to be a match for anyone else? I could not argue that I was indeed a woman, and younger than him, but I would contest the rest.

I rubbed my temples, trying to ease the pain that was gathering there. My anger with my father made me less concerned about being disrespectful to his memory, but Will was trying to force me into his way of thinking and my every instinct was to resist.

'I care about you Izzy, and I want to protect you.'

'I don't need protecting,' I flared back at him. 'By you or any other man.'

We were facing each other, both refusing to back down, when Mary's voice interrupted us.

'Your water is ready Isabella,' she said.

'Thank you. I'll be there in a moment.'

I waited for her footsteps to retreat and I could be confident she was out of hearing before pushing my anger to one side and trying again to reason with Will.

'You have to trust me. Richard Elliott means nothing to me. It's you that I love, but I will not be pushed around and treated like a child, or an incompetent who cannot make any decisions for herself.'

Will's expression did not soften and he remained silent.

'Please excuse me,' I said. I left the room, trying to suppress the sensation that there was a chasm opening between us, which, like the ditch surrounding the new town defences, would soon be too wide for us to traverse with any surety that we could safely reach the other side.

NINE

SCRUBBING THE GRIME AND SHAME of the day from my skin and hair revived my body and reinvigorated my brain. Having dressed in a clean gown, perfumed with the heady fragrance of lavender, I scooped up the garments I had worn that morning and carried them downstairs. The stale air of the Tolbooth clung to them still, but Mary would freshen them up. I found her in the kitchen, kneading dough.

'Mr Ord said to tell ye he'll see ye tomorrow.' Mary wiped the flour from her hands on her apron. She took my bundle of clothes, dumped them in a basket, and turned to face me.

'What's happening Isabella?'

If I were small enough for her to pull me into her lap, stroke my hair and whisper soothing words in my ear, until my problems drifted away with the smoke from the fire, I do believe she would have. Part of me wished I could tell her everything that had happened since my father's death, but I knew I could not.

I wondered how much of the argument with Will she had overheard. That relationship was something I could not talk to her about. Besides, Will had said he would see me tomorrow. That, together with my more positive frame of mind gave me new hope that we would resolve our disagreement when we had both had some time to think and calm down. His reaction was not rational. He could not persist in believing that Richard Elliott was his rival for my affections. It must be the shock of Arthur's death, and grief for his friend that was distorting his judgement. I must try to be more patient, more like Mary, who was waiting for me to answer. Her kind eyes did not waver from my face, as though she could see through the skin and bone to the secrets I held inside my head. It was a scrutiny I found unsettling. I picked up the wooden mallet that she used to pummel meat and turned it around in my hand, inspecting it from all angles, surprised by how heavy it was.

The events of this morning would be her biggest concern, and that I did want to share with her.

'You will have heard, I'm sure, that Will's friend, Arthur, has been murdered.'

Mary nodded. 'I went to the market. Everyone is talking about it. But why did they take you? They can't think ye had anything to do with his death.'

'They found one of my cards – the ones we give to customers. It was on top of the Black Watch Tower. There was a note written on it, '*8.30 tonight. You know where. A*'. They thought Arthur had sent it to me. Of course they're wrong, but I'm not sure they would have believed me if Richard Elliott had not told them that he had spent yesterday afternoon and evening with me, so I couldn't possibly have met with Arthur as well, and pushed him off the tower.'

'I haven'y taken to that young man. Trouble maker he is. But at least he's been able to do something useful.'

The glance she cast in my direction was loaded with disapproval.

'Mary, don't. I've had my fill of people cautioning me about my cousin. Well, one person in particular. Do you think I haven't tried to get rid of him, but he sticks like honey.'

'Mr Ord will see him as a threat, especially since ye two are not yet wed.'

'Now you're starting to sound like him. Do you all think I'm so fickle that I would transfer my affections on the turn of a coin? I love Will.'

'I wasn'y referring to your affections.'

'What then?' I asked, puzzled.

'His influence upsets the balance,' Mary pronounced. 'Before, it was just you, but now it's the two of yees. It changes everything.'

She was talking in riddles and I stared at her trying to work out what she meant, but she changed the subject.

'Why would they think Arthur would send one of your cards to you?'

I dragged my thoughts away from Will and Richard.

'I don't know. It doesn't make sense. My cousin thinks it means they have very few leads to pursue. Finding the card established some sort of connection with me and they could not ignore it.'

'But to think that a wee slip of a lass like you could push a man like Arthur to his death,' Mary mused. 'It would take a lot of strength to do that.'

'That was my point too, although it appears he may have been hit on the head with something, and then lost his balance.' I recalled the details with a shudder. In spite of my reassurances to Mary, I knew the memory of that morning would remain with me for a long time. Mr Usher's parting words echoed in my head, *'I may need to question you further.'* It was a warning that I had not heard the last of this matter yet, but I refused to let it consume me. And I remembered something else as well, something that I'd forgotten to mention to Will and Richard; the instruction given by the man I had not seen about searching someone's chambers and wanting to know everything about them. Did this mean Arthur's chambers, and if so what were they looking for?

'Mary, if you listened to the talk in the market you'll know that suspicion is falling on anyone with Scottish connections.'

She frowned, recognising the gentle warning my words contained.

'Douglas has nought to hide,' she said. 'Besides, he only joked this morning that he and others of his countrymen blend in well at the moment. There are so many of them in town.'

Mary paused, and there was that expression again that told me she was considering how much she should say. She brushed some flour from her apron, and I waited. 'He was concerned about ye.'

Douglas Lumsden concerned about me! Why, I hardly knew him.

'That's very … kind of him,' I conceded. 'As you can see though, there's no need. No harm has come to me.'

Mary pursed her lips and resumed kneading the dough, pushing her fists into it to stretch it, and rolling it from one side of the table to the other, grunting with the effort.

I watched her for a few moments, then replaced the mallet and moved to the door. On the threshold I paused. 'Oh, and Mary. If Mr Usher ever visits and you have cause to serve him ale, please lace it with salt.'

'Isabella Gillhespy! That isn'y a very Godly sentiment,' Mary exclaimed, but her reproving words were at odds with the hint of mirth in her voice.

'That's as may be, but he deserves nothing less.'

It would be easier to search in daylight for the missing key, but I could put this off no longer. I had to know what was in that drawer. I paused on the threshold of my father's bed chamber, took a deep breath and pushed the door open. It was only two days ago that I had rushed in here in a desperate hurry to check his hiding places for the money, my thoughts in such turmoil that I had barely noticed the room. So much had happened since then, but I was still no closer to the answers I sought. This time, I had to take greater care. When I had lit the candles that stood on cabinets either side of the bed, I positioned myself in the middle of the room and turned around, taking my time to absorb every detail. Everything was neat and in its place – from his favourite book of poetry on the low table by the settle in front of the fire, to the quill, ink and sheet of paper he kept by the bed, so that he could make a note of anything important that might occur to him in a dream, or in his waking hours during the night. The bed was neat, topped with the thick winter quilt that I had stitched for him using some of our warmest weaves made from the finest lambswool. The fire in the grate was laid. The room was ready to be lived in. All it lacked was its inhabitant.

It was that thought that slew me. My fatigue of earlier was as nothing compared to the emotion that overwhelmed me, like a hammer blow to the stomach. I doubled over and leaned against the solid post closest to me, at the foot of the bed, wrapping my arms around it and hugging it to my body as if it were my father. He had lied to me and let me down, and for that I would never forgive him, but I missed him. No matter what he had done, I still loved him. I clung to the post, shaking, blinded by tears that I could not control. When the torrent of water that flowed from me had dried up, I released the bed post, straightened my back and rubbed at it as if I were an old crone on the wharf. The tears had swept away some of my anger and given me a new resolve. Whatever he had been involved with, and whatever he had done with our money, I was going to work it out.

I looked around me with eyes still stinging from the salty tears, appraising the room, trying to imagine myself as my father. Where would I hide something that I did not want Mary to find by accident whilst she was cleaning? Something as small as a desk key?

The cabinets either side of the bed contained stockings, handkerchiefs and ruffs. Too obvious, and Mary would put those items away with care, but I probed underneath and behind the clothing with my fingers anyway, in case the key was tucked away at the back of one, but there was nothing. I turned around and surveyed the rest of the room. There did not appear to be many hiding places. I stuck my head inside the fireplace and ran my fingers along the cold and unwelcoming stone beneath the mantel. They came away streaked with black but found nothing. I opened the shutters, examined the frames of the windows, and walked every inch of the room listening for the creak of a loose floor board.

Frustrated, I was on the verge of conceding defeat, already wondering what I could use to follow Will's suggestion and force the lock, when I paused by a tapestry hanging on the wall to one side of the fireplace. It depicted a hunting scene, with a large bear ambling through the clearing of a forest, unaware of the archers surrounding it with their bows drawn, ready to release. I knew it well, and usually it did not command my attention – I did not really care for such sport – but there appeared to be a thread extending from the bottom corner. Probably the lining was coming loose, and if it was, where better to hide a key? Sure enough, when I felt behind the tapestry there was a hole, big enough to insert my thumb and forefinger, and resting in there, as cosy as a fledgling in a nest, was a key. I withdrew it, but my fingers were trembling and it slipped through them, bounced on the floor and almost disappeared into a crack between two boards. Just in time, I pounced on it, scooped it up and made a fist around it.

I descended the stairs from my father's chamber to my closet. The room welcomed me with its warm colours, lit up by the flickering light of several candles and a glowing fire. The shutters were open. I pulled the panels together and latched them so the dark of the night could not penetrate and I was safe, and alone, inside the welcoming walls of my private space.

What I was about to do though felt furtive, as if I were spying on someone else's secrets. Except these were my secrets now, and I had to know what they were. I crouched down on the floor behind my desk, took a deep breath and pushed the key into the lock. It turned. I exhaled and my fingers seized the handle.

TEN

MY EYES CLOSED AS THE drawer opened. I suppose somewhere deep inside of myself I did not want to know what it contained. What if I was wrong and it was empty? Or it did not hold the information I sought? No, a voice inside my head insisted. Why hide the key to a drawer if all you have stored in there is unimportant?

What if it held something that was just too terrible to imagine?

I tipped my head back until the bones in my neck creaked in protest. Then I lowered it again, snapped my eyes open and stared into the drawer. It contained a single item. A scroll, tied with a thin red ribbon. I picked it up, lifting it between my thumb and the tip of my forefinger as if the parchment itself might burn me, and placed it on my desk. Without taking my eyes from it, my hands reached behind me for my chair and I lowered myself down until I was perched on the edge. There was no going back – for me, or my father. I reached out with both hands and pulled the two long ends of the ribbon. It unravelled onto the desk, curving and meandering as a river, a blood-red river. Released from its tight roll, the scroll began to uncoil. I steadied it with my left hand, and with my right stretched the thick parchment until it was flat.

It was a certificate, stating that my father owned 100% of the shares of the business known as the Tweedmouth Mining Company. It was a simple enough document, but I had to read it three times before my brain was capable of thinking about what this meant.

'How many more surprises have you left for me father?' I muttered.

Hope flared within me. The situation might not be as bad as I had feared. He had invested the money, so our savings had not just vanished, they had been turned into something more tangible that I might be able to use to negotiate with Mr Young. But like a boat bobbing on the swell of the ocean, no sooner had my hope arisen than it plummeted again. I had never heard of the Tweedmouth Mining Company. Surely I would have if it was a successful enterprise? It was yet another secret.

Since his death, my once solid conviction that my father had kept nothing from me had been broken down and ground into pieces so fine they would be at home in the kitchen, in the jar where Mary stored flour. I supposed I should start expecting them, secrets and surprises. How many more before I uncovered the full truth? I leaned forwards, hunched over the desk, and rested my head in my hands so I could massage my temples. 'Think, Isabella, think.' I urged myself.

If he had invested in another business – no, bought another business – why wouldn't he tell me? I could think of only three reasons, none of which I liked. Either he did not trust me, or the investment was risky and he thought I might try to talk him out of it, or he had not valued my opinion and input into the business as highly as I had thought. Which was it though?

I was not going to find the answer here in my closet. I raised my head from my hands, re-tied the ribbon around the scroll and replaced it in the drawer. As I turned the key I wondered why I was bothering. Who did I have to keep secrets from? Nevertheless, I removed the key and added it to the bunch that I now wore as an ornament around my waist. Until I found out more, I would keep this to myself. The first task I needed to do was ask a few discreet questions in the right places about the Tweedmouth Mining Company.

I found Mary in the kitchen, preparing a tray for my supper. The mouth-watering aroma of freshly-baked bread with a hint of rosemary set my stomach rumbling. She ladled a thick, hearty pottage from a tureen into a bowl and placed it on the tray, brushing away my attempt to pick it up and reproaching me with her eyes as she followed me into the closet. I could have managed it myself, but she liked to keep busy, and without my father to look after her workload was no longer what she had been used to.

'Have you heard of the Tweedmouth Mining Company?' I asked her as she set the tray down on the table at the side of my chair.

She looked at me, her expression a perfect blank canvas, before shaking her head. 'What does it mine?' she asked.

'Coal, I assume.' There was a lot of coal in this area. It washed up on the beach and people would collect it in sacks to barter for goods at the market. Many of the smaller boats that worked from the quay – ours included – would sell it along the coast, although there was a lot of competition, particularly from the Newcastle merchants who controlled the trade. Could that be what my father was thinking? If we owned the mine, all the profit in selling the coal would be ours. Why, then, had that not happened?

Although I was still angry with Will, he was the obvious person to ask about the Tweedmouth Mining Company. He might have heard of it – he might even have done business with it. Nursing my anger with him would not help me find answers, but putting my pride to one side and trying to mend our quarrel might.

The next morning, as soon as it was light, I did not wait to break my fast but slipped out of the back door, past the stores and along the passageway through the walls onto the quay. It was early and I did not pass a single person, but when I emerged onto the wharfside the scene was as busy and familiar as ever, although I noticed at once that the atmosphere was different. Muted, like a mere shadow of itself. I paused to look around, trying to identify what it was. Dockworkers and boys scurried about their business as usual, but the jovial banter was missing. There was a nervousness in the air, and more soldiers were milling around than I had ever seen on the quay before. I wondered if any of them had been on duty two nights ago, and if so whether they had heard or seen anything. Surely Arthur would have called out as he fell to his death? Unless he was already dead, or unconscious, from a blow to the head. Mr

Usher would question them, I was certain, and the entire garrison would be cautioned to be extra vigilant until the killer was caught. No doubt they, perhaps even everyone in town, would have heard about my detention in connection with it, and I bridled at being smeared with unjustified suspicion.

The Custom House where Will would be at work already was to my right, towards the bridge, but I would not disturb him until he took his morning break. I turned left to where I could see the Lady Isabella, anchored alone beyond the end of the quay, where the water at low tide was shallow enough to careen her and enable Captain Thirlwell's men to work on her hull below the water line. They would need to remove the barnacles and other creatures from the ocean that would be clinging to her and repair any holes or rot. Even at this distance her masts towered above the other ships. A lump formed in my throat at the beauty and elegance of her sleek lines. With her sails lowered she was like a tree in winter having shed its leaves, the very essence of her laid bare for all to see.

The tide had just turned and several of the smaller boats were already releasing their anchors and bobbing out on the ebb to join the ocean. I watched for a while, fascinated by its pull, its power to transform the river that flowed with such elegant curves to meet it into a torrent that would carve a deep channel into the centre of the bed. Then, when it had spent all of its energy, the trickle left behind would expose the sand bars that flanked the estuary.

I resumed my progress towards the Lady Isabella. Men were scuttling about her deck like so many black beetles, some spilling over her sides on rope ladders, tools hanging from their belts in canvas sacks. It was slow and laborious work. I noted with approval that Captain Thirlwell had allocated plenty of them to the task. As I drew closer, past the cobbled part of the quay and onto the wet sand which sucked at my boots, I could see one of her sails had been removed from the mast and assumed that too needed repairs. The captain waved to me from the deck and indicated he would climb down and row ashore to join me. He lowered himself over the side and into a small boat that was tied to the lowest rung of the ladder. A few minutes later he was by my side.

'How is she?' I asked.

He stroked his bearded cheek and watched the men swinging on their ropes as they scraped and tapped at the hull. 'So far we've found nothing worse than we expected. I'll be needing wood though, and tar. We've got some rot and some worm holes. I reckon we'll have her seaworthy again in a few weeks, but she's never going to be like new.'

He spoke fondly. His green eyes, directed towards her, wore a soft expression, as if she were a favourite child and I realised he loved the Lady Isabella as much as I did. She, and I, were lucky to have him.

'I know you'll take good care of her,' I murmured. For a few minutes we discussed the detail of the work that needed to be carried out, and then I broached the subject that was consuming me. 'Captain. Have you ever heard of the Tweedmouth Mining Company?'

He thought for a moment before he turned towards me. 'No, can't say as I have. I'm a man of the sea, and I reckon I've been away too long. Why would you be asking?'

'I've just been going through some of my father's paperwork and the name came up on a document. I wondered whether there was something I needed to follow up on, but I don't know how to contact them.'

'If it's important they will know how to find you.'

His words made me think. I had only just heard of the Tweedmouth Mining Company, but if it was a business to which my father used to attend, it must have workers who would be curious by now about why they had not seen him for nigh on two weeks. If they had heard of his death, someone would have contacted me by now, wouldn't they? After all, my cousin had found me easily enough, and he a stranger to the town.

'Yes, well, I must get on,' I said, and took my leave of the captain, promising to check on his progress in a few days.

I made my way back along the quay, joining the throng of men heaving sacks onto carts, clerks delivering messages, and sailors weaving from side to side, their balance impaired as a result of an excess of ale, even at this time of the morning. The Custom House was a small building next to the bridge. This was where the levies due on goods traded were calculated and paid. As I stood outside, leaning against a low wall, watching Berwick's well-dressed merchants entering and leaving, I remembered that I had not yet checked my own statement. It was something else I could no longer put off. Just a few days from now it would be me entering those doors to pay what I owed on the Lady Isabella's latest goods. I had never in my life worried about money, but now I had good cause to, and it was an unsettling thought.

The door opened and Will stepped out. He was about to turn and walk away from the bridge when he noticed me. I smiled and he came towards me instead. 'Izzy,' he nodded. 'What brings you here this morning?' The coldness of his expression left no doubt but that I was an unwelcome visitor. My smile faded, and with it my hopes that our argument might be resolved with ease once we had both had some time to calm down.

'You're still angry about Richard Elliott,' I said.

As soon as I had spoken the words, I wished I could take them back. That was not the approach that would bring about a reconciliation between us, but I lacked the guile to flatter and cajole, especially when it was not I being unreasonable.

'I will not be made to look a fool,' he retorted.

He leaned towards me. His eyes resembled a stormy sky just before it is cleaved apart by a lightning strike. I chose not to heed the warning they conveyed.

'Nobody is making you look a fool. Why won't you believe me?' I protested.

'Why can't you understand?' he snapped back. He raised his arm and I thought he was going to push me, but he lowered it again and turned away so I could no longer see his face. 'It isn't a question of believing you or not.'

'What is it then?'

'It's what others will think. Your behaviour. You're leaving yourself open to insinuation and gossip.'

'Why? Because I had supper with my cousin, who also happens to own half of my business?' I flashed back at him, all thoughts of reconciliation forgotten, buried beneath the unfairness of his accusation. I moved around and stood in front of him so he had to look at me. His arms were folded across his chest, forming a barrier between us, and the stubborn set of his jaw told me my words were not reaching him.

Our raised voices were drawing attention from others. Two merchants interrupted their own conversation, heads turned towards us. Will took my arm and drew me away. I shook his hand off but followed him to the other side of the road that led onto the bridge. It was quieter here, separated from the quay by the people driving carts, or on horseback, flowing into and out of the town.

'Richard Elliott is a stranger in this town and his ways do not make him popular.'

I remembered Captain Thirlwell's dismissal of him as a pasty-faced foreigner. Will was right about that at least.

'He may be your cousin, but that will not stop the speculation that he is also your lover,' he hissed at me.

His words hit me with such force I almost staggered. My head fell and I found myself looking at my boots.

'As a woman, living alone, you are already a target for suspicion and gossip, and your behaviour is making you more so.'

I stumbled away from him so he could not see how much his words hurt. Is that what people thought? Is that what he thought? As the daughter of one successful and respected merchant, and the wife and widow of another, I had never had cause to consider my position in society. With my husband and my father gone, it seemed the rules had changed. I was through Bridge Gate and onto Briggate before I realised Will had not followed me. Had I lost him too? Furthermore, I had not asked him about the Tweedmouth Mining Company.

I reached my house and Mary greeted me at the door.

'Ye've a visitor,' she said, nodding towards the front parlour.

I raised an eyebrow and she pulled me towards her so she could whisper in my ear. 'Says he was sent by Mr Usher.'

Unpleasant memories of yesterday morning hit me and I grappled with a moment of panic. Then I reasoned with myself. If I was to be detained again, it would not be by a lone messenger, and I had not seen any town guards or soldiers outside on the street. Mr Usher had also given me an unequivocal warning that he might have further questions. I was not naive enough to think his suspicions would simply go away. It was still a worry though. What more could he want from me?

I pulled away from Mary, untied my cloak and handed it to her. 'Did he say what he wants?'

She shook her head and I could see beneath her wispy fringe her brow was furrowed with deep creases. Her fingers reached for my hair, tucking the strands that had come loose from my careless plait back beneath my coif.

'I'd better go and find out then,' I said when she nodded that my hair passed her scrutiny.

Inside the parlour the clerk who had eyed me warily, when telling me I was free to leave the Tolbooth yesterday, was warming himself in front of my fire. He removed his hat when I entered the room, which I took as a good sign.

'Can I help you?'

'Mr Usher requires a list of every customer you've had these last twelve months.'

He had found an angle to investigate then. I supposed I should be grateful that it appeared the focus of his attention was no longer on me, but the good name of my business was now to be dragged through the mire. That was sure to be bad for trade, at just the time I needed booming sales.

'Name and address,' the clerk added. His eyes were cast towards the floor and the hat he now held in his hands was doing a jig that any Scotsman would be proud of.

There was nothing to be gained by arguing. I nodded.

'I'll compile a list and have it sent over to him.'

'I've instructions to wait for it.'

He stopped just short of apologising to me for the inconvenience, but nevertheless I clicked my tongue with annoyance. There were so many important issues I needed to resolve, but it seemed that I would have to spend the next few hours going through my ledgers instead.

A sharp retort was on my lips but I bit it back. Throughout my ordeal of yesterday, and then the frustration of opening that drawer and finding that it did not contain the answers to my questions after all, but rather added to the list, I had not given any consideration to who might have killed poor Arthur, and if there was a connection to me or my business. Could the murderer be someone who had dined at my table, or sat in this very room enjoying a nightcap with my father? The thought was quite disturbing, and it planted a seed of something inside me that I was quite unused to feeling. Fear.

'Very well. You could have a long wait. I'll ask Mary to send you some refreshments.'

That was more than he deserved, but he was only the messenger. My generous spirit would not allow me to blame him for carrying out the instructions of his master. I turned my back on him and left the room. Mary was hovering in the shadows by the door into the kitchen.

'It's nothing to worry about,' I reassured her. 'I have to compile a list of our customers. It will take me some time, so please send him some bread and ale, and I'll break my fast whilst I work.'

Mary turned into the kitchen and I went the other way into my closet.

ELEVEN

'WHAT A WASTE OF TIME,' I cursed at the ledgers as if they could hear me, pulling them off the shelf and dumping them in an untidy pile on my desk. I flung myself into my chair and flexed my fingers before reaching for two sheets of paper, a fresh quill and my father's inkpot.

The clerk had been told to wait. So, I'd make him wait. Recent events had prevented me from compiling a tally of goods sold since my last customs bill, but it was a task that needed doing so that I could reconcile the inventory that Richard and I had done a few days ago. What better opportunity than whilst I was being forced to go through the paperwork anyway? Of course, it required precise attention to detail and could not be hurried. I settled down to my work, a smile building from my boots and infusing me with energy as I imagined Mr Usher's frustration waiting for his clerk to return.

Mary brought me a light supper and I continued with my onerous task. My eyes were soon tired and sore from peering at my father's handwriting under the dim candlelight in my closet, the sun having yielded to the moon long before I finished. I delivered the customer list to the clerk, who was fast asleep on my settle, head lolling at what looked to be a most uncomfortable angle and mouth open to reveal yellow teeth. He deserved a reprimand, but I decided to be generous, kicked his shin to wake him up and sent him on his way.

I put off reconciling my customs bill until the next morning, when I could look at it with a clear head and sharp eyes. Had I checked it the night before, I would have thought I had made a mistake, but in the morning I knew I had not. According to the latest inventory, I had too much stock. There could only be one answer.

'Curse him.' I slammed my fist on the desk. Could he not even get a simple stock count right? I meant Richard Elliott of course.

He had been so eager to help, and quite indignant when he thought I was suggesting he was not up to the task. I had allowed myself to be persuaded, and had even been grateful that together we had completed the task in half the time it would have taken me by myself, but it was clear I would have to re-do it.

'I should just have told him to sit and watch. Done it all myself to start with,' I muttered as I pushed my chair back and ducked through the low doorway into the boot room. I kept an old cloak there, which I now draped around my shoulders before stomping out into the cold, morning air. The day was clear but the sun was weak, and if it was casting its warmth anywhere it was not here. The snow lay deep on the ground still, its surface crisp and glittery. I followed the path that George had dug, which was slippery with ice, taking careful steps and placing my trust in my boots, and arrived at the warehouse without mishap. If anything it was even colder in here than it was outside. I did not remove my cloak, but pulled on my fingerless gloves, used the tinderbox to light some candles, seized one of my inventory sheets and set to work.

I knew the side of the warehouse that I had done was correct, so I only had to tackle the other side. Even so it took an age, and I had to keep stopping to blow on my fingers when they got so cold they would no longer grip the quill. I imagined a mug of whisky and a bowl of Mary's broth, swimming with ham and turnips, me wrapped in a shawl in front of the fire in my closet. The image spurred me on. I had almost finished the final aisle when the door latch rattled and a shaft of daylight split the warehouse into two halves for a moment before it was extinguished as the door slammed shut. Heavy boots stamped on the rushes. My first thought was that it was my cousin come to interrupt me again, and I prepared to lambast him for his incompetence, but his fancy London shoes would whisper his presence, not shout about it. Maybe it was a customer, or Will. Yes, it must be Will, come to apologise, and I started to move towards the door, allowing relief that our argument would soon be resolved to wash over me.

But it was not Will.

The head that emerged into the light cast by my candle was topped with delicate white curls. Mr Young. I stopped walking, giving myself a few precious seconds to think. He had said four weeks, and it had not yet been two, so what was he doing here? I had not forgotten the last words he had said to me, *'Repayment in full … or property to the value of.'* Nor had I forgotten his lascivious expression. Was he aiming to intimidate or humiliate me?

I could think of no other person I least wanted to see, except perhaps my cousin, but I told myself to put my distaste for his company to one side and view this as an opportunity. He did not know that I had discovered the share certificate, and that I knew about the Tweedmouth Mining Company. I would not have dreamt of demeaning myself by seeking him out and begging him for information, but since he had chosen to present himself at my door, if I chose my words with care I might be able to learn something. After all, he had lent my father the money to invest, so he must know of it.

'Mr Young! What a pleasant surprise,' I said in my most welcoming voice. My lack of sincerity was bordering on disingenuity. I silently implored Saint Oswald to forgive me whilst I pondered how to broach the subject in a way that might encourage him to answer.

'Madam Gillhespy.' He gave a rather stiff bow. 'I thought I should pay you a visit, see how you are, as I have not heard anything from you since our last meeting.'

'I am quite well, and really very busy.'

I could not bring myself to thank him for asking.

'It's a sad affair about that young officer. I heard of your detention in connection with it. I trust you were well treated?'

His eyes roved over me, examining, probing, as if he might be able to see the signs of any mistreatment lingering on the fabric of my gown. He parted his lips and tapped his teeth with a thick finger. I shuddered with revulsion.

So that was it. He was here to reassure himself that his investment was secure. I did not flatter myself that he was here out of concern for my welfare. He did not own me though, not yet, and if I could help it, he never would.

Satisfied by what he had seen so far, he now looked beyond me, peering into the gloom of my warehouse. He carried a heavy-looking walking stick, although I do not believe he needed one for any practical reason. I noticed it was topped with the head of a snarling dog, made from what appeared to be silver, with amber gemstones set into its head for eyes. He pointed it into the warehouse.

'May I?' he asked, and without waiting for an answer he brushed past me and disappeared into the darkness. All I could hear was the tap, tap of his stick against the floor, which paused every now and then, no doubt to give him time to look up and examine my store in detail.

'You've a lot of stock here.'

Not being able to see his expression as he spoke was quite unsettling, It was very evident that I had a lot of stock, and I could not determine whether his comment was meant in an approving way or not. Maybe he was rubbing his hands, imagining taking ownership of it all himself when I failed to repay the debt. I was reminded that it would do me no good to antagonise this man who held such power over me, and chose to answer him as if he were making a simple observation and nothing more.

'The Lady Isabella returned with a full load, and business has been slow since my father died,' I said, moving into the small office and tidying away my quill and ink. I folded up the inventory sheet I had just completed and placed it in the pouch that held my keys around my waist – in my haste to leave the house, and my frustration with Richard Elliott, I had forgotten to return with the satchel.

The tap, tap of Mr Young's cane grew louder. He stood in the doorway, blocking much of the light.

'Now might be a good time to start selling some of it,' he suggested, with an oily smile.

His earlier comment might have held another message, but he had no right to talk to me as though I were a child and knew nothing of business. I slammed the desk drawer closed.

'I do not need a lesson in how to run my business, but thank you anyway for the advice.' I did not accompany my reply with a smile.

He nodded and half-raised his stick in a farewell gesture.

'Before you leave though, what can you tell me about the Tweedmouth Mining Company?' I flung my question at him and caught him off his guard.

He blinked rapidly, his mouth opening and closing like the fish hauled onto the banks of the Tweed by the fishermen, surprise at the situation they found themselves in reflecting in their glassy eyes. Unlike the fish, Mr Young recovered.

'Ahh, that was a bad business.' He replaced his hat on his white curls and I waited for him to say more. 'I warned your father, but he would insist.'

'And you lent him the money anyway?' The words spilled out of my mouth before I could stop them.

'What could I do Madam Gillhespy? Business is business. Good-day to you.'

He bustled out before I could say another word.

I leaned against the wall, hands pressed flat against it, shaking my head. Why had I snapped back at him when I should have asked him why it had been a bad business?

I pushed myself away from the wall and dashed out of the door after him.

'Wait,' I shouted, but Mr Young was already turning the corner to vanish from my sight. He lifted his walking stick and waved it over his head, a gesture that meant he had heard me, but chosen to ignore me. It was clear that he knew something, and it was also clear he did not want to share that knowledge with me. I had now lost my element of surprise – next time he would be more guarded.

I locked the warehouse and re-traced my steps to the house. Even the boot room felt warm and welcoming after the bitter chill of the raw sea air that permeated the stores, and the gusting wind outside. I shrugged off my cloak and turned towards the kitchen.

'Mary,' I called, pushing the door open.

The room was empty but I could hear voices. I paced across the kitchen and up the steps into the hall, where my smile faded. There was Mary, and hovering behind her, Richard Elliott. His colourful attire had returned today, although it was a little muted – a mustard yellow doublet that complemented his red-gold beard, over dark grey hosen and a small ruff. On his feet, I could not help noticing that his soft city shoes had gone, and in their place was a pair of chunky leather boots, the likes of which even I would be proud.

I closed my eyes and cursed under my breath. It would seem that once again I was being forced into his company. He stepped around Mary, bounced towards me, took one of my hands and raised it to his lips before I gathered my wits and snatched it from his grip.

'Mary, could I have some broth and some whisky please in my closet. Oh, and send George to fix the fire,' I said, being, I thought, quite pointed in my refusal to acknowledge him.

'Certainly,' Mary replied.

'So touched that you are pleased to see me dear cousin. Don't bother George about the fire, Mary. I'll tend to it.'

The man just did not take a hint, and how dare he speak as though this were his house, and countermand my instructions? A rebuke faded on my lips. There seemed little point expending the energy on someone who was so determined to be obtuse. Perhaps when I pointed out his errors with the inventory he would be more contrite.

'Shall I make that broth and whisky for the two of ye?' Mary asked, glaring at Richard, and I nodded.

'Have you thought any more on what I said about spices?' Richard asked as he followed me into my closet.

'No, and now is not a good time to discuss it.'

He opened his mouth to argue, but I waved my arm towards the fire irons and the coal scuttle. 'Be careful,' I warned. 'You don't want to get coal dust all over those fine clothes.'

'Don't mock me Isabella. I'm quite capable of building a fire.'

'You're not capable of doing a simple inventory though,' I retorted, throwing the inventory sheet I had just completed onto my desk and settling myself into my chair.

He had the poker in one hand and a scoop of coal in the other. He paused and cast me an indignant glance. 'Are you saying there is something wrong with my counting?'

I snorted. 'Well I know there's nothing wrong with mine, so the problem has to have been with yours.'

I was already focusing on the inventory sheets. I sensed, rather than saw, him crossing towards me. 'Fix the fire first would you please, and then come and watch me work, if you must.'

It did not take me long to do a new tally from the sheet I had just taken, and I frowned, not believing the results. I repeated it, certain that I must have made a mistake. Then I compared the sheet he had done with mine. By now, he was sitting across the desk from me, watching. Mary had brought in the broth, which was going cold, and the whisky, which I had already drunk.

After I had checked and re-checked, and checked again, all whilst under Richard's silent scrutiny, I had no choice. I raised my eyes to his.

'What's the problem?' he asked. His tone was no longer belligerent but gentle.

I shook my head, still unable to believe what I was seeing. 'We've got too much stock.'

He raised an eyebrow, inviting me to say more.

My neck was stiff from bending over the paperwork for so long. I put my quill down and kneaded the muscles at the top of my spine with my fingers until the tension eased.

'Of the wine specifically,' I added, remembering how he had commented on how much we had. At the time it had struck me as a sign of how little he knew about this business, but maybe he was more observant, and intuitive, than I gave him credit for.

'It seems I owe you an apology.' I had to be fair and admit I had made a mistake, but it was an effort to raise my eyes to his and see his scorn and derision directed at me. But I was mistaken. He was not even looking at me. He was twisting the gold ring in his ear between the fingers and thumb of his left hand, as he pulled the inventory sheets and the customs bill towards him with the other.

I sat in silence and allowed him to study them, whilst I reached for Captain Thirlwell's ledger. I had been so convinced that my cousin must have made an error with the inventory that I had not double-checked against the ledger. I turned to the page that detailed the wine and studied it.

'Could your father have made a mistake with some of the customer orders? Recorded more barrels sold than were delivered?' Richard mused.

'No,' I said. 'Could I have the customs bill back please?'

I held my hand out for him to pass it to me, but instead he moved from his chair so he was standing behind me and placed it on the desk next to the ledger.

'Look.' I pointed to the column where the captain had totalled the barrels brought in on the Lady Isabella. 'It isn't our stock that's wrong. It's the customs bill. I'll go and see Will.'

Normally the anticipation of a trip to the quay to meet Will would be pleasing, but I had not seen him since we had argued outside the Custom House yesterday. I had hoped he would visit me at home and we could resolve our disagreement in private, but he had stayed away. Our next meeting would be one of business. The prospect did not fill me with joy.

'The error is in our favour. We could just leave it,' Richard suggested.

I turned and stared at him, trying to work out if he was being serious but I could not tell. His eyes were wide and innocent. Was he mocking me? I decided to leave him in no doubt of what I thought about that suggestion.

'Do you know what the penalties are for smuggling?' I snapped.

'All right, there's no need to be like that. Of course I do. It was just a thought. I'll come with you.'

'Oh no, no, no. Absolutely not.'

'Isabella, this is my business as well as yours. If there's a problem, I have a right to know about it.'

We glared at each other, each of us unwilling to concede any ground to the other. I had unfairly accused him of incompetence, which had made me appear weak and given him an advantage that he seemed determined to press home, but then he had lost any respect that he might have gained by suggesting that we should ignore the discrepancy. Did he really think I cared so little about this business to risk losing it like that? Allowing him to accompany me to the Custom House though, was out of the question. I could imagine only too well Will's reaction if I turned up there with Richard by my side, and I was surprised that my cousin could not see that for himself. The tension in my neck returned.

'Richard, I realise I'm in your debt for establishing beyond any doubt that it could not have been me who met poor Arthur that night, and I could not have had anything to do with his death, but did you have to be quite so full of insinuation?'

His eyes widened. Taken by surprise with the sudden change in direction of our conversation, or was he mocking me? They narrowed again.

'What do you mean?' His voice had a defensive tone to it.

'I think you know perfectly well what I mean.'

He stared at me but did not reply.

'You must know that you gave Will the impression that you and I have been seeing quite a lot of each other. He has a suspicious nature and he's also very proud.' I stared back at him now, hoping I had made myself clear enough.

'Do you mean I've created a rift between the two of you?'

He raised an eyebrow and I sensed that he was not surprised. That had been his intention. Infuriating man. To rebuke him though would be to admit that he had indeed caused a rift between us, and I did not want to let him think that he had such power.

'I still think I should come with you.'

I pushed my chair back and stood, indicating that this conversation was over. For a moment I towered over him, but then he stood too, and before I could say anything further, he held out his hand towards me and shook his head. 'But out of consideration for you I will wait here.' He took my hand and this time when I tried to snatch it away he tightened his grip and pressed his lips to the back of it before releasing it with a low laugh.

TWELVE

IT HAD NOT OCCURRED TO me before now that there would be times when Will and I might have a different perspective on my business. Nor had I ever envisaged having to challenge him over something when our personal relationship was in such a poor state. Arguments between my first husband and I had been rare – he had instructed and I had acquiesced. He had not shared matters of business with me. My situation now was very different, and I did not know how to approach it.

I'd had no choice but to leave Richard Elliott in my closet whilst I once again set out in the bitter cold air, which had not improved as the day matured. The quickest way to the Custom House was along Briggate and through Bridge Gate, thus retracing my steps from my last, unsatisfactory conversation with Will. I dodged the patches of sheer ice that lingered at the edges of the road and opted instead to join the well-trodden, muddy, and even more slippery route that many pairs of feet, both animal and human, had carved down the centre. I raised my skirts to stop them dragging in the filth, but it was in vain.

Any walk heading towards the quay usually filled me with delight, but not today. Every step I took dragged with the weight of apprehension. And there was something else. A sensation that I had not experienced for a long time. When I was young, perhaps eight or nine years old, if my father was late returning home I would sit in my room, wide awake long after Mary had sent me to bed, listening for his voice in conversation with a companion outside in the street, the sound of the front door opening and his footsteps crossing the hall. To my young mind the time would seem to stretch and stretch until I thought it must snap. My hands would start shaking, and it would hurt to breathe, as if something large was being torn from inside me and then scattered in fragments into the air. This affliction – I could think of no other word to describe it – would not leave me until I knew he was home, and I would curl myself into a tight ball under my blankets until my breathing returned to normal and I would fall into an exhausted sleep.

My breathing was far from normal now. Cold air forced itself into my lungs and I expelled it in a painful rasp. Reliving old and long-buried memories had brought back the frightened child that had experienced them, except this time the fear they carried was associated with Will, not my father.

I concentrated on keeping moving, and emerged onto the quay where the air seemed to mutate into a saltier, denser version of itself. It was like the difference between eating a thin soup and Mary's thick broth. The first does little to restore your strength, whereas on the second, entire armies would flourish. I paused to look around, noting which ships were in and how high the water was, entranced by what I saw. The weak, wintry sun cast a shaft of light on the scene, framing it as in a picture, and I drank it all in; inhaled it through my nostrils, tasted it on the tip of my tongue, and withdrew my hands from my gloves to allow the cold air to brush my fingertips.

The meeting with Will was just a matter of business, and that is how I would approach it. My father's voice whispered in my head, *'Business first Isabella, always business first.'* As usual, it was good advice, and I would follow it, but I did not want to hear it. I shut him out, together with the problems he had left me with, and turned towards the Custom House. I lingered outside for a moment, gathering my thoughts, and then pushed the door and stepped inside. The building had one cramped office on the ground floor and a set of narrow stairs that wound into the darkness above. I had never been up there. Will shared the office with a clerk and the controller, Mr Dixon, a stern, swarthy fellow who rarely smiled. Of him there was no sign, but Will was at his desk. He looked up as I approached, but his eyes were as cold as a bright star in the night sky and my confidence ebbed. I loosened the ties on my cloak to give my hands something to do.

'I've come on business,' I announced. It would be absurd to imagine I would come here, to his office of all places, to discuss our personal differences. No more absurd though than his fancy that Richard Elliott and I were somehow involved, other than him being my cousin, and in his words my business partner. But I did not know what Will was thinking, and unused to his cold demeanour, I found it unsettling.

He nodded at the hard-backed wooden chair in front of his desk and I sat down, withdrew the customs bill from my satchel and placed it between us.

'What can I do to help?'

'You can double-check this bill please.' I met his polite tone with ice of my own. If that's how he wanted to conduct this conversation, so be it. He made no effort to pick up the bill, but watched it with a strange expression on his face, as though it were a small animal that at any moment might leap off the table and start running around the office.

'Is there a problem?'

'Clearly, or I would not be asking you to check it.'

'I'm sure if there is a mistake it will be with your reckoning and not of our making.'

His blunt tone and unsmiling features were bordering on rudeness. I flicked the bill towards him, planted my hands on the desk and pushed myself to my feet.

'There is nothing wrong with my reckoning. It's already been verified. Now please do me the courtesy of double-checking yours.'

He made no move to pick it up, and I stared at him hoping he would raise his eyes, open a window to allow me inside his head. He did not, and nor did he answer me. In fact, he gave every impression of being uncomfortable with the situation.

Whilst we were glaring at each other Mr Dixon bustled into the office, accompanied by a fresh blast of cold air, stamping his feet and rubbing his hands together with vigour. He threw a bundle of papers onto his desk and then appeared to notice that Will was not alone. His eyes shifted between us.

'Is something wrong?' he asked with the flicker of a knowing smile.

His words fell on a stifling silence. There was nothing more I could do here. I'd made my point. As I turned away from both of them, Will picked up my customs bill, folded it and slipped it into his pocket.

'I await your thoughts.' I threw back at him over my shoulder.

I had only been inside the Custom House for a few minutes, but back outside it was as though I was looking at the quay through my father's eye glasses and they'd blurred its crisp edges. I blinked until it returned to normal and my hands had stopped shaking. My body was reacting in a most unusual way, and I did not much like this version of myself. The emotional turmoil and the shocks of the weeks since my father's death must be affecting me in more ways than I could understand. If I was going to work out what was happening in my business and my life – and restore order – I had to keep control of my mind. I could not let it run away with its own fancies.

I felt a tug on my cloak and a voice broke into my thoughts. 'Madam. Are you all right?'

It was George. By his side stood a barrow of coal. I raised my eyebrows.

'Sorry, but you just looked a bit funny.'

'Thank you George. I'm fine. Where are you going with that?'

'Mary needs it at the 'ouse. She's running out.'

'If you are returning there now, will you tell Mary I am going on an errand. Ask her to inform my cousin, Mr Elliott, if he's still waiting for me, that I may be some time and it might be better for him to call back later.'

'Yes Madam.' George scampered away.

I was certain that Richard would be waiting for me, eager to hear about my meeting with Will, but I was not ready to share the detail of that cold exchange with him. Imagining my cousin's frustration when being told I had been delayed lifted my spirits and my lips curved into a smile. I flung my head back and turned my face up to the skies, isolating myself in the midst of all this activity until I began to feel a little dizzy, and a prickling sensation running along my spine told me I was being watched. Pretending I was unaware, I lowered my head and twisted around. My eyes fell on a well-dressed stranger standing just a few yards away wearing a quite extraordinary tall hat, trimmed with a fine yellow ribbon and two feathers in yellow and green set at a jaunty angle. It was the sort of hat my cousin would have been proud to own.

'It's a fine scene,' he said.

I agreed with him, but remained silent.

'And that's a fine ship.' He nodded towards the Lady Isabella.

Again, he was right. She might be shabby and past her best, but she was still beautiful, and today she was the finest on the quay. She was still moored where she had been a few days ago, and her masts and rigging towered over the other ships, reaching for the sky. I allowed myself a swell of pride that she was mine, and was about to say something when the stranger touched the brim of his hat with a faint smile and moved away.

I left the quay with much more energy than I had arrived with. In spite of the unfulfilling exchange with Will, it had worked its restorative effect, and now I was content to just wander, alone with my thoughts. I passed through Segate and walked straight up Uddyngate. At the town well, I could not help glancing to my left, to the Tolbooth, the scene of my incarceration a few days ago. A prisoner in shackles, ragged clothes dangling from his skeletal frame, was being half-led, half-carried towards a cart that stood nearby. The horse stamped its hooves, impatient to transport the wretch to whatever fate awaited him. A small crowd was gathering. I did not want to watch, and hurried by, crossing over the road onto Soutergate and not stopping until I reached the stone wall that marked the boundary of the graveyard at Holy Trinity Church. Nearby, I could hear the industry of men labouring on the new ramparts. Work was continuing at pace, even though the exact location of the wall, particularly to the south of the town, had yet to be decided, and it's possible that even my own street would fall outside it. That would leave many people, as well as the Queen's own stores, vulnerable to attack, and it puzzled me that no-one seemed to think this was a problem.

After watching the men at work for a few minutes, I pushed open the gate and stepped into the graveyard. It had not been with conscious thought that I had directed my steps towards the old church, but as I now sought out the mound of fresh earth, as yet unmarked by a stone, that was my father's resting place, I realised that this is where I had been heading since I'd left the quay.

The churchyard was dark, shaded from the light of day by tall trees. Cold from the ground seeped through my boots. I stood by the side of the grave and closed my eyes.

'Why did you have to die, father?' I murmured.

My father had the answers to all of my questions, but he was never going to share them with me now, so why had I come here? I was doing that little girl thing, running to him for reassurance and guidance, as if he could provide for me, meet those needs even from beyond the grave. It did not occur to me to pray to the Lord for guidance. No, I was on my own now. I was the only person who could resolve my current problems, to which I now added my relationship with Will.

Behind me, a branch snap snapped, crumpled beneath a heavy boot, and seconds later someone cleared their throat close by. Heart pumping, I swivelled around. Although holy ground, this was a lonely spot. Standing not six feet away from me was a burly man, tall and broad-shouldered, with a pale complexion and greying beard.

Douglas Lumsden! Mary's sweetheart.

He removed his hat and bowed to me. His hair was thinning on top and cropped close to his skull. He wore a dark gown, which I knew at a glance was of good quality, and leather boots that reached almost to his knees.

'Madam Gillhespy.' He raised his head and greeted me with smiling eyes.

If it weren't for the fact he was Scottish, I would approve of Mary's choice with all of my heart. But he was. We might have lived in peace with our northern neighbours for nearly two hundred years, but Arthur's murder had rekindled the distrust that bubbled just beneath the surface. I did not need more problems heaping on my shoulders.

I nodded at him and started to walk away.

'Please wait.' His voice stayed me. It was deep and lyrical, quite beautiful in fact. I stopped and turned to face him.

'Can I help you?' I asked. Maybe he had a message for Mary, although it was presumptuous of him to think he could use me to run his errands.

'It's more that I may be able to help you. With information.'

'Really, Mr Lumsden. And what might that be?'

'Tweedmouth Mining Company.'

I raised an eyebrow.

'Mary said ye'd mentioned it.'

'Go on,' I said. Of all the people who might be able to tell me something about the Tweedmouth Mining Company, Douglas Lumsden would not have been top of my list. I tried not to appear too eager to hear what he had to say. It would not do for anyone to suspect how important this was to me.

'It's based down the coast a few miles, towards Holy Island.'

That could explain why I had not heard of it. Why call it Tweedmouth if it was so far away though?

'And it's mining coal?' I asked.

'Aye.' He nodded, stroking his chin. 'But the coal isn't on the surface. They've been digging shafts and tunnelling, bringing it out from underground. The land there is full of it, but there's problems.'

Douglas rubbed his thumb and forefingers together to demonstrate. 'It dinnae come cheap, and then a tunnel collapsed injuring several men. Na body will go down the shafts any more, feart it might happen again. Word has it the project is out of money, and some of the men are owed too.'

Mr Young had said it was a bad business, but nothing had prepared me for this. I stared at Douglas. He was watching, waiting for me to react. My thoughts were racing, like the Lady Isabella with her sails caught in a strong breeze. Surely my financial situation could not get any worse.

'Who are they?' I dreaded hearing my father's name, although reason told me that if Douglas knew of his involvement he would not be talking to me like this.

'The owner was a Mr Young, but I've heard he sold out.'

My jaw fell open and I just stopped myself from gasping. I wanted to turn away from him so he could not see my shock, or understand the enormity of what he had just told me, but my legs were heavy and as rooted in the ground where I stood as the elm tree I reached out to in an effort to stop myself swaying.

'Mr Young, the merchant, here in Berwick?' I asked.

Douglas shook his head. 'Nae, his brother.'

THIRTEEN

THIRTEEN

'THAT LYING, CHEATING, CONNIVING, LOW-LIFE ...'
I ran out of expletives to express how I felt about Mr Young. I
stormed down Soutergate, ignoring anyone who tried to greet me,
and did not stop until I was standing outside the merchant's office.
My father would have cautioned that the course of action I was now
determined on was ill-advised. 'Never act in haste or allow your
emotions to influence business decisions,' he would have said. In
other words, stop to think, but I was beyond caring. I slammed the
door open with such force it almost flew off its hinges, and pushed
past the startled clerk who followed me, protesting that I could not
enter the venerable Mr Young's office without an appointment.

The great man himself had been working at his desk. Alerted
by the commotion the clerk and I were making he was pulling
himself to his feet, his colour heightened by a spattering of pink
spots resembling freckles across his cheeks. He watched me march
towards him, his expression reshaping itself from alarm into faint
amusement, which infuriated me even more. The clerk was gabbling
his apologies as he trailed in my wake. I span around on my heels,
and he just managed to stop himself from running into me.

'Leave us,' I snapped. He opened his mouth to protest and then
backed away, pulling the door behind him.

When I turned around, Mr Young was sitting down. He picked
up his quill and pulled a thick parchment towards him. I rested my
hands on the edge of his desk and leaned forwards.

'You are despicable,' I hissed, projecting the full weight of my
anger into my voice.

'This is a most unprofessional way to conduct yourself, if you
don't mind me saying, Madam Gillhespy. More befitting the nursery
than a place of business.'

He did not raise his eyes from the parchment, as though he was concentrating on something of importance, but I could see it was blank and the quill rested motionless in his hand.

'And I suppose convincing someone to invest money in your brother's business is professional? Especially when that means you get to raise a lucrative loan. Nice little scheme you've got going haven't you? Everyone wins except my father.'

'Business is business. Your father understood that.'

No longer able to control my fury, I swept my right hand across his desk, scattering papers to the floor followed by his ink pot. Black ink leached into the blue and gold rug where it landed. He glanced at it and frowned. The pink freckles had pooled into a tiny red spot on each cheek, but otherwise he appeared quite calm.

The heat of the room was spreading its clammy fingers across my skin, leaving puddles of moisture at the nape of my neck, which were trapped there by the weight of my heavy cloak.

'It's dishonest and immoral and …'

Mr Young interrupted me with what I thought was a grunt but it turned out to be a laugh. There was no smile to his eyes though.

'Madam,' he said, with a staged sigh. 'Whoever led you to believe that business has to be either honest or moral? But you have spirit. I like that. I shall look forward to taming you.'

'Never.' I threw back at him, not stopping to think what he meant. 'I would not demean myself to become like you.'

'I think you should be careful with your choice of words, given the circumstances.'

There was no mistaking the threat that lay just beneath the oily surface, and I was beginning to realise that I was not going to benefit from this encounter, other than the short-term release of my anger.

'And before you start accusing, you should first ascertain the facts. I did not coerce your father. Quite the opposite in fact. He could see the potential in my brother's business and begged us to allow him to invest. He put his own savings in at first. It was only later, when the mine started to experience problems and it was clear a greater investment was necessary, that he borrowed.'

'If it was such a good investment, why didn't you just put the money in yourself?'

'Naturally I did, but your father thought it was such a good opportunity for him to expand your business that he was most insistent, and I deemed it prudent to withdraw. What else could an … honest … merchant do?'

His emphasis of the word 'honest' infuriated me. There was nothing honest about this, but giving in to my desire to yank him by his baby curls and rake my fingernails down his rosy cheeks would get me nowhere. Instead, I tried to match his oily tone with a silky one of my own. 'And then what? Did you and your brother realise that this whole concept was flawed? The shafts and tunnels made it all too expensive, not to mention dangerous?' I was working this out now as I spoke, slotting the pieces together in my mind. 'So you decided to sell all your shares. And my father was there, eager to buy into this great venture. It was too good an opportunity to miss, so … with great reluctance … you sold.'

Mr Young shrugged, self-satisfied and smug. If he had been close enough I swear he would have patted me on the head as if I were a child learning her numbers.

'Time is running out Madam Gillhespy.'

This man sickened me, but I was still in his debt. Not for much longer though.

'You'll get your money, but not a penny more,' I said, and made a vow to myself. I would repay him before his four-week ultimatum expired, and would have nothing more to do with him. In fact, at any opportunity that might arise, I would shame him. From this moment onwards he was my sworn enemy.

Before I turned my back on him to leave the room I thought his patronising, confident air faltered for the briefest of moments, replaced with unease or uncertainty, although I could not be certain, before he lowered his head to his parchment once again.

'Father, how could you have been so stupid?' I directed my question at the portrait of him that hung from the wall of my study, wishing I could take him by the shoulders and shake him until his delusions about coal mining, and that he could deal straight with Mr Young fell from him. Leaves from a tree. Rain from a tar-black sky.

'Be true to what you know.' That was another of his well-worn pieces of advice to me when I'd urged him to expand, to go further, to develop the business. If only he had listened to himself.

I refused to consider, even in my own mind, that the fact I had urged him to expand and be more adventurous might have influenced him. Never had I suggested he should invest in something he did not understand, although I had to consider that this venture might have contributed to his death. Mr Hedley had remarked about the stress of business. My father must have been weighted down with it and there could be little wonder that his heart gave in. It was incomprehensible to me that I had not noticed, but this sentiment was not tinged with guilt, but anger. Directed at myself as well as my father. If I had been more aware before, perhaps I would not be in this mess now.

Richard Elliott had gone by the time I returned home. He had left a message with Mary to say he would see me later. Nor had Will called. The gulf between us was growing ever wider and I did not know how to close it. I badly wanted to talk to him about the Tweedmouth Mining Company, to tell him what I had discovered and ask his views, to have someone by my side who would understand and support me, but I was not going to seek him out. To do so would only strengthen his conviction that I could not cope on my own. It would also have been useful to have the revised customs bill – if he had taken me seriously and looked at it of course. It would mean a larger bill, although those extra levies were as a sprat to a herring compared with the larger debt owed to Mr Young.

I had a plan for that. It wasn't one that I liked, but I could think of no alternative if I was going to be true to my determination that he would have no further influence over my life. It was whilst I had been storming home after our latest encounter that it had occurred to me that this was his true intention. He wanted me to fail to repay the debt, so he could 'tame me,' and I shuddered to think what that might mean. Next time he turned up in my warehouse with his fancy stick tap, tapping around I wanted to be able to forget my manners and tell him to leave.

It was then that the idea had come to me, and when I arrived home I had not even paused to remove my cloak, but hitched my skirts up and bounded up the stairs, taking them two at a time in a most unladylike fashion. Beneath the window in my room there was another false panel, just like the one in my father's chamber. I'd released it, unlocked the second panel behind and pulled out the box that contained my jewellery. I'd carried it downstairs to my closet, ignoring Mary's questioning eyes when she'd delivered the message from Richard.

Now I sat, warm and comfortable in my chair in front of the fire, flickering light from the candles casting a warm glow over the russet of the rug and reflecting from the wood panelling, shutters closed to banish the cold, dark night. My jewellery box was on the low table by my side. I picked it up and put it in my lap. It was locked, so I inserted the key and turned it, pressed a tiny indent in the wood above the escutcheon, and the lid popped open.

My father had always been most generous with my mother, showering her with gifts on every special occasion and other times in between, according to Mary. Most of what was in the box had been hers. I had little need of jewellery, and beyond a gold christening bracelet that was too small for any adult wrist, a diamond-studded choker that had been a marriage gift from my husband and that my father used to insist I wear when we were entertaining clients, and the simple betrothal ring that Will had given me, I possessed little of my own. Although I suppose everything that had belonged to my mother was mine. As was everything that had belonged to my father, debts included.

Sitting on top of my mother's jewellery, as the last items to be placed inside that box, were my father's gold pocket watch, which he cherished, and signet ring. He had seldom been parted from these. Indeed, I had sometimes thought that he even slept in his pocket watch, and as a little girl I would picture him pinning it to his nightshirt before he climbed into bed. I took these out of the box with barely a glance, and placed them on the table. The extravagant ruby tiara, necklace and earrings that my mother was wearing in her portrait followed. There were several large rings and brooches with precious gemstones. I added them all to the pile.

When the box was almost empty, my fingers closed around one final item that was of any worth. A gold locket, quite large, heart-shaped and sparkling with tiny diamonds set all around the edge on both faces. On the back it was engraved. The initials JL and IL were intertwined and the tails of the letters fell away into trailing fronds of ivy that looped around and met above in a crown. I released the delicate filigree, formed in a figure of eight, that kept the locket closed and its contents private. My eyes feasted on the miniature portraits of my parents, younger than I am now. My father, his expression full of love and pride, focused beyond the shoulder of the painter. My mother, impossibly beautiful, glowing with life – her own and the new one that was growing within her. Me. The daughter she would never hold. The mother I would never know.

If I could have cried, would it have made me feel any better? It would not have changed what I had to do. I sat, dry-eyed, the locket open on my lap, lost in my own mind, until the click of the closet door opening roused me. My first thought was that it would be Will, come to make up our argument. But I had not heard his signature rap on the front door, and I could not dismiss the fear, deep inside, that our relationship was over. No, I knew, even before he spoke, that my visitor was my cousin.

'Isabella. I waited for you, then Mary gave me your message that you may be some time, and I must say, I think it was most unkind of you not to return and tell me what they said, about the bill.'

He had made this speech whilst walking across the room and now stood before me. Was it really only a few hours since I had decided to visit my father's grave? The delight I had taken, knowing that delaying my return to the house with news would frustrate Richard, now seemed such a childish emotion when weighed up against my discovery of the scale of the treachery that had been practised against my father. I took no pleasure in the realisation that I had, indeed, frustrated him.

He had stopped speaking, his eyes fixed on the glittering pile of jewels on the table by my side. I waited for the sarcastic comment, but none came. He let out a low whistle. I watched him as his gaze shifted from the jewellery to me, but did not squirm beneath his scrutiny. He turned, and dragged one of the chairs from in front of my desk over to the fire. He did not bother turning it around, but straddled it facing me, leaning forwards on his arms which he folded in front of him and rested on the chair back.

'Why don't you tell me what's going on?' he demanded, although his tone was not unkind.

Why indeed. And then I thought, why not. I'd been guarding these secrets I was discovering, not to protect him but so that I did not appear a fool. But doing so was just heaping more pressure on my own shoulders and I could no longer bear it. I did not care what Richard Elliott thought of me, or how he would no doubt revise his view of our business. Good riddance indeed. So I told him everything.

The effort of remembering and recounting was exhausting, but at the same time, in an unexpected way, it was energising. Richard listened without interrupting, except to utter an occasional curse under his breath that I could not catch. Even when I reached the end of my story, he remained silent, and there was a shrewdness to his eyes that made him less the dandy and more the calculating business man. Maybe I had been under-estimating him.

The locket was still in my lap. Taking great care not to tear the delicate parchment, I removed the portraits of my parents and replaced them in the jewellery box. I closed the locket and added it to the pile on the table.

'What are you going to do?'

'I'm going to raise the money to repay Mr Young.'

His eyebrow arched, but again he did not comment. The silence stretched out between us until I thought it must snap. Then his expression changed. It was as if he had realised, all of a sudden, that he needed to be somewhere else. He rose, nodded to me, and left the room.

So I was right. That was the last I would see of Richard Elliott. He would no doubt be packing his bag and on the first stage back to London. It was not a surprise, and I had thought this would raise my spirits, but instead the prospect of not seeing him again, on top of the loss of Will, left me sad and very alone. It seemed I had got used to his irritating presence after all.

FOURTEEN

'I'LL BE AWAY NOW IF ye're sure ye've everything you need,' Mary said.

We were in the kitchen. Discussing the menus for the week was a routine I was finding difficult to dispense with, although there was no need for it since my father's death, as I was content with very simple meals.

I nodded. "Mary, would you ask Mr Lumsden to meet me after Arthur's funeral this afternoon? Outside the church gates, when everyone has left for the wake.'

Mary had been reaching for her cloak. Her fingers hesitated for a moment before she seized it from the peg where it hung. She had not told me she was planning to spend the day with her Scottish suitor, but I was certain I had guessed correctly from her impatience to leave and the twinkle in her eyes. That had not been placed there by our discussion about how many turnips she needed to buy at the market.

She busied herself fastening her cloak, and I knew she was tempted to ask me what I wanted to talk to him about. I wondered if he had told her that he knew something about the Tweedmouth Mining Company, and that he had spoken to me about it.

Mary could only spend so long fiddling with her cloak, and when she did turn towards me her eyes were shining with curiosity. It was understandable of course, because she knew I disapproved of her relationship with Douglas Lumsden, so why would I want to meet him? But I needed him. What I had decided to do, I could not achieve alone. He was the only person I could think of who might be able to help me. Besides, after he had come to me with the information about the Tweedmouth Mining Company I had started to revise my opinion of him. Allowing my instinct to overrule my head, I was coming to believe I could trust him.

I thought Mary was going to question me, but after staring for a good long while, she simply nodded, picked up her basket and left. No sooner had she gone than there was a rap on the front door. Three raps to be precise. I froze. It was Will. There was no mistaking it. Much as I had been anticipating his visit, I had not expected him to call this morning, on the day of his best friend's funeral. He would find me not looking my best as I had yet to brush and dress my hair. I peered at my reflection in the side of one of Mary's large copper pans and was dismayed by the dishevelled likeness that squinted back at me. A pile of clean kitchen cloths ranging in size were stacked on a chair waiting to be put away. I grabbed one of the largest and fashioned it loosely around my head so it resembled a hood. My steps faltered as I crossed the hall, nerves bubbling up inside me like a broth in Mary's stock pot. What version of Will was waiting for me on the other side of that door? The loving husband-to-be, the man who believes he is being cuckolded, or simply a Custom House official doing his job?

I hesitated on the threshold, not wanting to discover the answer to that question, but of course I had to know, if not now then tomorrow, or the day after. There was nothing to be gained by putting off this moment, so I filled my lungs with air, exhaled very slowly, and then, before I could change my mind, seized and twisted the heavy iron ring to release the latch and flung open the door. One glance at Will's face told me all I needed to know. There was an element of surprise – he had expected to see Mary or George – before his features settled into hard lines. Any remaining scraps of hope about the future of our relationship that I might have been harbouring scattered like so many leaves in the wind.

'Please, come in.' I moved to one side. We were on my territory, and that at least gave me an advantage that I had to use. I led him into the front parlour rather than my closet, in an effort to set a more informal tone for the exchange that was to come, but it did nothing to thaw his frosty mien. Everything about his stance was unyielding. Nor did the natural light filtering through the open shutters do anything to improve the atmosphere. It added no warmth and brightness, just streaks of dull grey.

'Drink?' I asked, gesturing towards the cabinet. He removed his hat, threw it onto a chair, and shook his head.

'I'm here on business.'

That had never stopped him before. My heart had already sunk into my stomach, and his curt reply sent it plummeting to my feet. I had envisaged a cosy chat, me resting on my settle, him in his favourite chair, either side of the fire. A scene we had populated so many times in the past. But I already knew that was not going to happen. I did not sit down, but faced him, both of us standing somewhat awkwardly in the middle of the room.

'Well?' I challenged him to speak first. If we got the business out of the way we might be able to move on to resolve the more personal difficulties that stood between us, a wall as impenetrable as those surrounding Berwick. But like our town defences, every wall has its gates. I just needed to find Will's gate.

In his hands he held a slim leather folder. He withdrew a folded sheet of paper and held it out towards me. It was my customs bill. I took it, opened it out, and needed no more than a swift glance to see that it had not been changed.

'You did not find any error then?'

He must have found something. I had checked my inventory twice, and the physical items sitting in my stores provided the evidence. The bill was wrong, and it was impossible to believe he could not see it.

'I had no need to look.'

I stared at him, trying to make sense of what he was saying. He met my eyes, unflinching. His hair was dishevelled, his boots were clean but worn, and his breeches crumpled. In every way he appeared to be my Will, except he wasn't. There was a stiffness about him that had never been there before.

'Come on, Izzy. You think you're so clever. Work it out.'

One part of my brain wanted to ask him what he was talking

about, but in another part the facts as I knew them started to shift, turning like the gears inside the clock on the table behind me, until they presented a different picture. All of the elements were there still, but viewed from a new angle they did not appear the same. Nothing had changed, but everything had changed.

I started to speak, my voice scrambling to keep up with my head, which was still processing this new view and drawing conclusions.

'You had no need to look because you already knew the bill was wrong.'

Will nodded, a slight smile now broaching those stern features.

'You've been under-declaring the barrels of wine brought in on the Lady Isabella to avoid paying the tunnage.' I frowned, and his smile deepened. 'And then we charge the customer the full amount making an extra profit, which you take a share of. But no, my father would never agree to such a scheme. The penalties for smuggling are too severe and we have no need to take such risks. What did you do, to get him to join you in this? Did you threaten him?'

'Izzy, no. I'm shocked. What do you take me for?'

He sounded quite indignant. I wanted to turn away from him, but my feet would not move. He took a few steps closer, towering over me, blocking my light and my vision. I remembered how he had lost his temper after I had told him about my father's debt, even though I had not admitted to the full amount. It struck me that I was quite vulnerable, alone in the house. He leaned closer until our heads were almost touching, and I could feel his breath on my cheek. 'It was your father's idea,' he whispered.

'No!' My head snapped back, unbalancing me and I flung out an arm to steady myself. It connected with the back of the settle, which I gripped, and I dragged my unwilling feet until I was standing behind it, putting some space between us, much as I had done on that previous occasion. I did not want to believe Will, but something told me he was speaking the truth. In how many other ways had my father betrayed my trust? A coldness settled inside my chest. I had thought I had lost him that day when I'd returned to

149

find him dead at his desk, but since then I had lost him over and over again, because now I no longer had my memories of him to rely on. Everything had been false. Built on lies and deceit.

'Think about it Izzy. It was perfect.' Will's smile now was broad. In his smugness he seemed to have forgotten our row. His hands swept the air in front of him, and I knew he would be unaware of how animated they had become in his eagerness to enlighten me. 'Your father gives me false figures. I do a cursory inspection and generate the paperwork. He pays the bill, always on time, never gives anyone cause to take a closer look, and we share the extra profit. We all share the profit.'

It was the way he emphasised the word 'all' that brought me back to the present moment. He was telling me that I too was complicit in this scheme.

'If you think I will go along with this, you don't know me at all.'

'Don't be foolish.'

I shook my head and his smile faded.

'You're not going to last five minutes in business unless you drop your naivety, and fast.' Will thrust a pointed finger towards me and I shrank back from him. His voice rose a notch, and it was tempered with disbelief. 'Do you truly believe that everyone plays by the rules? To get ahead you have to take the opportunities that life puts in your path. Your father and I, we were in the perfect position to help each other, and there's no reason why that arrangement should not continue.'

No reason? Had I heard him right? There was every reason. His greed was blinding him, and I realised he was prepared to sacrifice everything to satisfy it. But this was not his decision to make, and it angered me that he should behave as though it were.

'You forget that I have recently been detained for questioning and have experienced the unpleasantness of being suspected of some wrongdoing at first hand. I will not put myself in a position where I could lose everything as a result of your greed. Your scheme stops now.'

I tightened my grip on the back of the settle. My anger was mixed with fear, but I was not going to let him suspect that.

'You're already implicated,' he scoffed. 'It's now your business, and it's your favourite boast that you have been running it alongside your father for these last few years. If you want people to believe that, you cannot then claim that you knew nothing of this.'

'You're not listening to me. I repeat, I will have nothing to do with it,' I snapped. 'And nor will my business.'

And then, of a sudden, everything made sense. Will's insistence that we bring forward our marriage, so he could take care of the business transactions and responsibilities that he implied I could not cope with. What he had really been trying to do was take control so that he did not have to tell me about this little scheme that he and my father had been running. Once we were married I would have had no power to oppose him. My vision of our marriage had been very different to his. Will was right about one thing – I had to stop being naive, starting right now.

'I would like you to leave,' I said, fighting to control my voice.

'I'll be delighted to comply,' he retorted. He marched to the door, snatching his hat from the chair where he had thrown it.

'Will,' I called after him. He hesitated, hand on the latch, and I watched him turn slowly to face me whilst I twisted my betrothal ring from my finger. 'Catch,' I said, and threw it at him.

He emitted a sound very much like the snarl of a caged animal. I had taken him by surprise and he was not quick enough to react. The ring slipped through his outstretched fingers and skittered to the floor. He bent down, scooped it up and left the room, without another glance at me. I slumped forward. A sound very much like waves crashed around inside in my head and tears pressed behind my eyes. I blinked them back. Will had been false to me all along, and I would not cry for him. But for the loss of my dreams for my future, and my memories of my past, I could cry waterfalls.

I leaned into the back of the settle, allowing it to support my weight whilst I tried to fathom how my life had taken such a wrong turn, and what I could do to put everything right again. The death of my father had set such a cycle of events in motion. Every time I thought I had found a solution to one problem, a bigger one popped up in its place.

As if to prove me right, I heard a footstep in the hall and sensed the presence of another person. I looked around for something to defend myself with. Neither Mary nor George should have returned yet, so my logic told me there could be no-one there, yet my instinct insisted there was.

I padded over to the hearth and seized the poker. 'Who's there?' I called.

The door swung open. Never had I been so relieved to see my cousin. He started to remove his hat and his eyes widened in alarm at the sight of me brandishing the poker as though it were a sword.

'I'm sorry if I startled you. Will said I would find you in here. He told me to come straight in. I must say, he seemed in quite a hurry.'

A hurry and a rage I would wager. He would not have been at all happy to see Richard arrive at my door. That would have confirmed his suspicions that I had already transferred my affections before breaking off our betrothal. What reason would he give for that, I wondered, when the news got out? He could not admit the truth, but nor would he want to confess that he believed himself to be a cuckold. I shrugged the thought away as the least of my worries, replaced the poker, and focused on my cousin instead.

'This is not a good time,' I said.

'Forgive me for intruding, but I needed to see you, this morning, before you do anything else.'

I had not thought to see Richard Elliott again, certain as I had been that my revelations of the true financial state of our business would make him reconsider his presence here in Berwick. And now I had worse news to share with him. He was in business as a smuggler and stood to lose everything he owned, and his freedom to boot. He cocked his head to one side and cast me a curious look.

'Isabella, if I may ask. Why are you wearing a kitchen cloth around your head?'

My hand strayed to my hair. Was it so obvious that it was not a hood? Will had not seemed to notice.

'If I take it off you will understand why,' I said. 'You'd better come through to the closet.'

He followed me without a word. There was something very odd about his demeanour, a meekness that I had not seen before. Was that because he had realised that Will and I were not on good terms, and that he was in part the cause? If so, he was demonstrating more sensitivity to the nuances of mood and expression of those around him than hitherto.

As soon as we were in my closet he removed his gown and withdrew a pouch from inside his doublet. He tipped its contents onto my desk.

'My contribution,' he said.

I stared at the small pile of coins and jewellery. There was a gold chain, some brooches, a tie pin and a chunky signet ring. Resting on top of them all, incongruous among such masculine items, was a lady's ring. It was set with a large square sapphire, bordered by gold, perched on a band which appeared too fine to support its weight. I could not resist picking it up. It caught the light as I twisted it in my fingers, and the stone shone the deep blue of the ocean under a cloudless sky. It was beautiful.

Richard was watching me. I wanted to ask him about the ring and he must have read the question in my eyes. 'The lady decided she did not want it after all,' he said, in a dismissive tone.

I put it down and pushed the pile away from me towards him. 'Thank you, but I cannot accept,' I said.

'Yes you can,' he pushed it back towards me. We were like players either side of a chess board trading pawns.

'I know you don't have a very high opinion of me Isabella. But I'm serious. I did not come here intent on taking from you anything that is rightfully yours. I came here to start again, to make a success of something. What kind of man would I be if I allowed myself to be defeated by the first obstacle that's set in my way?'

'But it's not your debt. I cannot let you sacrifice …'

'The debt is not yours either,' he interrupted me.

'You might never be able to reclaim these items.'

'I know.'

Silence fell between us. And then he did something that took me so by surprise that I did not realise I was holding my breath until black spots started to blot my vision. He took my left hand and unfurled my fingers, letting his thumb trail over the indentation left by my betrothal ring. I thought he might question its absence, but he said nothing. My skin burned beneath the gentle pressure of his thumb and I could not move. Everything about this was counter to my expectations. I thought of this man as my nemesis, as a self-centred opportunist who was out to make trouble, but he was displaying signs of being honourable.

'We will make a good team, you and I,' he said, in a low voice, which sent a shudder rattling through my chest. 'Together, we can make this business the greatest in this part of the country.'

He released my hand. I exhaled and filled my lungs again with fresh air. He moved away, adjusting his ruff. I unlocked the drawer of my desk into which I had placed my pile of jewellery yesterday evening. It seemed I was going to accept his offer. My pride might want me to rebuff him, but my common sense slammed the door in its face. In Richard Elliott, it appeared I had a most surprising ally, someone who would fight by my side to save my business. Will had accused me of being naive, but I was not so naive that I could not appreciate how important that might be. After all, it did not mean I had to like the man.

'There is just one condition.'

His voice broke into my thoughts. He had moved so he was now standing next to me, behind my desk. He reached over my shoulder, opened the drawer, removed the cloth bag containing my jewellery and placed on the desk top. I watched him pull the drawstring to open it. Did he mean to rob me after all? But no, he would not have offered his own items if he meant to steal mine. He withdrew the chain and locket that had held the miniature portraits of my parents and held it out to me in the palm of his hand.

'This one you keep.'

The last few minutes had taken on a dreamlike quality. A dream within which I was trapped and could not escape. The act of taking the locket from him freed me. I released the filigree and it sprang open. My jewellery box was on the small table by the side of my chair. I slid past my cousin, opened it, removed the portraits of my parents and with great care replaced them in either side of the locket before snapping it closed and fixing the chain around my neck.

'There's something else you should know,' I said, my fingers playing with the fine gold links. I had not given myself time to consider whether I wanted to tell him about the smuggling or not, but he had been so generous that he deserved to know the full truth.

'What I have to tell you might make you change your mind.'

'What is it?'

So I told him, not daring to meet his eyes. A feeling very much like dread crept up on me, that in spite of his promises that he was here to stay, he would decide to leave.

'God's truth Isabella! I used to think life was complicated in London, but since I've met you I realise it was as a mere game for the nursery.'

'None of this is my fault, and you could go back to where you came from.' My former indignation with him returned.

'Do you still doubt me? Have I not made it clear that I'm here to stay?'

He turned away as if offended, drifted to the windows, and sat down in one of the deep seats enclosed by thick stone where he gazed out at the courtyard scene, much as I had done myself on countless occasions – the last just days ago, although it felt so distant it could have been years. Then I'd had Will by my side and a bright, welcoming future ahead of us. Now I was alone, save for this man whom I barely knew, and my faithful Mary.

'I'm still getting used to the idea,' I replied. It might be that I owed him an apology, but I could not bring myself to go that far.

'Do you think anybody else knows about this scheme your father and Will were running?'

'No. Will was hoping I would go along with it.'

'Then I suggest we do nothing more about that at the moment.'

I started to protest, but he waved a hand to silence me.

'Just listen to me please. I want no part of a smuggling operation, any more than you do, but what's done is done and we have so many problems to tackle. Let's leave Will to fry in his own grease and see what he does next. He cannot expose us because that would mean admitting his own part in it, and he cannot force us to go along with it from now on, especially if, unless I'm much mistaken, you've broken off your betrothal.' At this he nodded at my hand and my eyes followed his, to the empty space on my finger where my ring should have been.

'In the circumstances, no one would be surprised if I were to take over dealings with the Custom House and choose to go to Mr Dixon instead of Will. Everyone will assume that is due to your falling out, so that removes the problem.'

He dismissed it with the snap of his fingers. Could it really be that easy? I did not want to move forwards with something like that hanging over my head. A heavy weight that could fall at any moment, without any warning. My preference was to battle to remove it, whereas he just stepped around it. He had said we would make a good team, but if this was an example of what was to come, ours would be a ship sailing stormy waters. On this occasion I had no solution of my own to offer, so I made no comment.

'Where are you planning to take the jewellery?' he asked.

'There's someone my father used to mention who deals in such items. He trades outside the walls to the north east of the town. I'm not sure exactly where, but Douglas Lumsden will know. I've asked him to meet me after Arthur's funeral today. I'll take a few items with me.'

'And who is Douglas?'

'He's a friend of Mary's. He's Scottish, and I don't approve of their relationship, but I think he's honest.'

'Can you trust him?'

Could I? The men I thought I could trust had shown me a different side to their natures since my father died – Will included. Douglas alone had tried to help me. He'd sought me out to provide information that I needed, without knowing any of the detail and without asking for anything in exchange, and he had not tried to deceive or double cross me. At least so far. Did that mean I could trust him? Did I have a choice?

'I'll go with him,' Richard said. He must have taken my hesitation as proof that Douglas was not trustworthy.

'No. Most definitely no.'

Richard cast me a sulky glance. 'There you go again. Doubting me, my loyalties and my abilities.'

'No, I'm not, but you're new to this town, and if you will forgive me for pointing out what to most of us is quite obvious, you look and sound like a foreigner. Douglas is known, he blends in – especially in the less salubrious parts of the town – and he's accepted. It will be much safer for him to go alone.'

'If he agrees.'

It had not occurred to me that Douglas might refuse to help, but I was not going to admit that, so I ignored his protest.

'What if he takes the jewellery and we never see him again? He could pocket the money and run, set himself up somewhere else.'

'He could, but I don't think he will. And I'll offer him a share of whatever we make. If we send the items a few at a time we reduce the risk of Douglas double-crossing us, or of him being robbed.' Not that I could imagine anyone risking their own necks by trying to steal from Douglas. Indeed the thought made me chuckle.

'What's so funny?' Richard asked, a petulant tone creeping in to his voice.

'Nothing,' I spluttered. 'You'll understand when you meet Douglas.'

FIFTEEN

THE SKY THAT HUNG OVER us was slate grey, and a vicious wind whipped between the legs of the mourners in this exposed part of the graveyard where Arthur was being laid to rest. Mr Selby was intoning the burial rites. I retreated from that gaping hole, shivering with cold, not relishing the reminder that just weeks ago it had been my father who was being lowered into the ground, a few feet away from the spot on which I now stood. I could not stop my eyes tracking to the corner where he rested, but it was festooned in shadow and I could not even make out the new marker stone that I'd just had laid. So much had changed in such a short space of time that I found it difficult to recognise myself. I dragged my eyes away and scanned the mourners around the grave again. There were plenty of Arthur's colleagues, wearing their parade cassocks with pride, several young ladies scattered around weeping voraciously, dabbing their eyes with dainty handkerchiefs and scowling at each other. A more elderly couple clung together, the man comforting the woman who was leaning against him as if she was finding it difficult to stand. Were they Arthur's parents, come into town for their son's funeral? I tried to remember where he came from – somewhere south of Holy Island I thought.

The figure that I sought, and dreaded seeing, I could not find. Will was not at his friend's funeral and I could think of no reason why he would not pay his last respects. In spite of our estrangement, I hoped there was a simple explanation for his absence, and that he had not met with an accident.

The wind was making my ears ache. I pulled the hood of my cloak closer to my head and scanned the mourners again. Mr Selby had finished the burial rites and was leading the way out of the churchyard. I started to follow and then stopped, struck by the uncomfortable sensation that someone was watching me. Perhaps Will was here after all. I twisted my head around but could not see him. A man standing apart from the rest of the mourners lowered his head before our eyes connected. I had caught only a glimpse of his face and was certain I did not know him, although there was something familiar about the way he stood and the set of his shoulders. Was it he who had been staring at me, or was my imagination playing tricks? A ragged dog worried at his ankle. He kicked out at it and the dog yelped and scuttled back to the hole, which the gravediggers were already filling in with earth. It sat down on its haunches at the end of the grave, head on one side, peering into the black hole and whimpered. As I passed, one of the gravediggers threw a shovel of soil at it which just missed showering my skirts. He loaded the shovel again and aimed at the dog which had already backed away and was now standing by my side.

'If so much as one ounce of that dirt lands on me you'll regret it,' I snapped at the oaf. He lowered the shovel and tipped the earth into the hole. I swept past him.

Outside the gate to the churchyard the mourners were dispersing, making their separate ways to the wake. Richard Elliott was leaning against a gnarled elm tree. He raised a hand to me with a sheepish smile, which I did not return. If there was a man alive with a thicker skin than my cousin, I had yet to meet him. He pushed himself away from the tree and sauntered towards me, his dark cloak swinging around his knees revealing hosen of a pale brown beneath. At least his clothes blended in with the surroundings, even if they were not in keeping with the occasion.

'What are you doing here?' I hissed at him.

'I know what you said.' He raised his hands in mock defence. 'Don't worry, I got the message. I won't interfere, but I thought, dear cousin, that you might appreciate some support.'

'I've lived without your support for all of my life,' I retorted.

'Yes, but then you had your husband, and your father.'

'Hmmm, and look where he's left me.'

I was about to remind Richard of the many reasons I had to not be grateful for my father's legacy, when we were interrupted by a deep voice calling my name.

Startled, I looked up. I had thought we were alone, but whilst we had been arguing Douglas had emerged from somewhere. For such a large man he had the ability to move around like a mouse.

'Madam Gillhespy,' he greeted me with a nod. 'Ye seem to have strange company.'

'Mr Lumsden, this is my cousin, Richard Elliott.'

Douglas removed his hat and nodded. 'Charmed, I'm sure,' he said, with a dismissive flick of his wrist. 'But I know who he is. I was referring to the other one.'

'What other one?' I asked, puzzled.

He nodded back to the churchyard. 'He was over there, watching, but he's gone now.'

The sense of unease I had experienced earlier returned as I remembered the man I had noticed.

'Did you recognise him?'

'Nae, he isn'y from these parts. I think he's one of Sir William Cecil's men who came to negotiate with the Scottish Lairds. They've mostly left town, with the agreement they wanted, but one or two have lingered.'

I frowned, recalling the details of my previous conversations with Will and Arthur.

'If they've concluded their business here, why haven't they left?'

'Happen they wanted to enjoy a bit more of our crisp air. There's nought like a bit of snow and an icy wind to toughen up their southern skins.'

Douglas cast a meaningful glance at my cousin, and Richard scowled in return.

'If that was a jibe meant for me, I think you'll find my skin is quite tough.'

'He's right about that.' I nodded, and I could not help a smile breaching my lips before the worry returned. 'But why attend the funeral of a man you don't know – or at least, I assume they hadn't met?'

'Hunting out Scottish spies nae doubt.' Douglas chuckled, and his broad shoulders shook at his own joke.

'Don't,' I snapped, memories of a few mornings ago returning. 'I do not find that amusing. Why would Sir William's man be watching me?'

'Aye, probably he wasn't. Happen he was just curious what a soldier of her Majesty's had done to end up murdered, whilst on duty, at the base of one of the watch towers, in this town of all places.'

'I'm sure it's an event of such insignificance that Sir William has not even heard of it,' I retorted. But then was it? My father used to say there was nothing that happened in Berwick that Cecil did not know of, so important was the town to the defence of the country. But even so I found it difficult to believe that Arthur's murder was being investigated by the highest authority in the land.

'Anyway, we don't know that the stranger was one of his men. It's just speculation,' I insisted.

A silence fell between us, and three pairs of eyes turned back to the churchyard, which was full of shadows but appeared to be deserted. No sinister strangers lurking beneath trees, only the unkempt dog hovering by the gate.

'Madam. Ye asked me to meet you.' Douglas reminded me, with the air of a busy man who did not have time to waste.

I shook off the unease that had gripped me and turned back to him.

'Indeed. I was hoping you would help me with some private business that I need to transact.'

At this he glanced at Richard and raised an eyebrow.

'Mr Elliott is aware of this as it relates to my … to our, business. But no-one else is. Not even Mary, and I would like it to remain that way. Do I have your word – even if you choose not to help me?'

'Ye have my word.'

'Let us walk a little.' I had an urge to see the ocean, but I also wanted to be certain that the stranger was not still watching, concealed somewhere out of my sight. I led the way towards the walls, east of the churchyard where there were no buildings and the land opened out, glancing over my shoulder a few times to be certain we were not being followed before I addressed Douglas again.

'I have to raise some money, quickly, quite a lot of money. My father mentioned a man who sometimes trades in small, valuable possessions. I believe he can be found outside the old walls to the east of town.'

Douglas nodded. 'I know who ye mean, and how to find him. But, may I ask, why? Your father was one of the wealthiest merchants in Berwick. You cannot lack resources.'

'It's dangerous to make assumptions, especially in matters of business,' I reprimanded him. He remained silent, watching me with steady, unblinking eyes.

I reached for the pocket inside my cloak into which I had placed the cloth bag containing a few of the items of jewellery, withdrew it, and held it out towards him. He made no move to take it.

'Of course, I'll reward you for your help,' I added, forcing a smile. Maybe I had spoken too harshly.

'Madam, with respect, ye're aware of how precarious my situation could be in this town. Like many of my countrymen, we are distrusted and barely tolerated by those who make the rules. Even though I, and others like me, have fled Scotland and pledged allegiance to your English Queen and the True Religion. Before I can agree to help ye, I need to know what it is ye're asking me to get involved with.'

Clenching my fist around the bag and its contents, I turned away from him, giving myself time to think. I did not want to share the details with him, I just wanted him to help me. Richard took my arm.

'Would you excuse us for one moment Mr Lumsden?'

He drew me away so we were out of earshot.

'What are you doing?' I hissed at him. 'You said you wouldn't interfere.'

'Isabella. He makes a fair point. You said we could trust him not to double deal with us.'

'I think we can.'

'Show him some respect then. You cannot expect him to do your bidding without asking some questions. Especially when you may be putting him in danger.'

I shook his hand from my arm. His words revealed a depth of empathy that I had not expected. What's more, my cousin was making a habit of taking me by surprise. I did not like what he was suggesting though. Sharing such private details went against everything that my father had ever taught me. But then, it was due to my father's poor decision-making that I was in this situation in the first place. It could be that I would do well to listen to the counsel of another and forget everything I had ever learned about business from him.

Enough thinking. I flung my head back and looked at my two companions. We made an awkward triangle. Richard almost by my side, watching me and stroking his close-cropped beard with clean, manicured nails, whilst Douglas had turned his back on us and was standing, legs slightly apart, arms folded across his broad chest, facing the ocean in the distance.

I ignored my cousin and moved so I was standing next to Douglas, sharing his view. As ever, the sea drew me. I watched a gull circling and swooping, a light grey splodge against the darker grey of the sky. What I would not give to have that freedom. The freedom to just be, to exist and not have to worry about anything other than catching a fish for supper.

'I didn't mean to be discourteous,' I said, still watching the gull. 'My father has left me with a considerable amount of debt. It was a big surprise, and indeed a shock, when I discovered the extent of his borrowings. Now I must repay that debt, and I have no time to raise the money in any other way.'

'Would this be something to do with the Tweedmouth Mining Company?'

'It would.' I nodded.

He shifted his position by my side. I turned to face him and he held out his hand.

'Thank you,' I said, passing the bag to him. As its weight transferred from my hand into his, I had the notion that for the first time since my father's death I was taking control. My actions might not produce the results I hoped for, but at least I was doing something. I would show this town, and the likes of Mr Young, that I was not a puppet to be pushed and pulled in whatever direction they chose.

'If the transaction goes well, I have more,' I told Douglas. 'Subject to the gentleman being able and willing to handle them of course. I thought it prudent to break them up into smaller, more manageable parcels.'

'Where will I find ye?'

'Come to the house later, to the back door. I'll be in my closet.'

He nodded and thrust the bag inside his cloak where it was out of sight. I watched him stroll away, his gait surprisingly elegant for a man of his stature, until he turned a corner by the church and I could no longer see him.

'I get the joke.'

What joke?' I asked, frowning at my cousin.

'Earlier, you couldn't stop laughing when you said something about Douglas being robbed. A man would have to be very brave, very foolish, or very drunk.'

He fell into step by my side, and it wasn't until we reached Briggate that I realised the dog from the churchyard had followed us.

'You appear to have a new friend.' Richard smirked.

'It looks hungry, poor thing. I wonder where it lives.'

'Most likely a stray, and full of fleas.'

It was a very ugly brute. Not a big dog, it stood about knee-high with long brownish hair that was dirty and matted, lopsided ears and a head that was too large for its body. There was something about its eyes that struck me. I can only describe them as mournful. The animal was sad. I remembered it whimpering by the side of Arthur's grave.

'I wonder if it was Arthur's.' I pondered.

We had reached my front door now. Without invitation, Richard followed me inside.

'Do you mind?' he asked. 'I thought I should wait with you until Lumsden returns.'

I did not need or desire his company, but what was I going to do for the next few hours by myself?

'We'll go to my closet,' I said, and in a louder voice I called Mary. She met us at the end of the hallway, followed by a mixture of delicious aromas wafting from the kitchen, which made me realise how hungry I was. She must have been full of questions – why I had wanted to meet with Douglas Lumsden, how awful it had been to attend another funeral so soon after my father's, but she did not ask any of them.

'Ye must be frozen to the core,' she said. 'Get yeself in front of that fire – I've kept it stoked and I'll bring you both some hot broth.'

'Thank you Mary. Oh, and could you ask George to go around to the front door and if there is a dog there – tatty, ugly thing – ask him to take it round to the stable and find some food for it please – try and clean it up a bit as well if the hound will let him.'

Richard was already warming himself in front of the closet fire, but his eyes followed me as I crossed the room to join him and they held a flicker of amusement, which was reflected in the set of his mouth.

'Isabella Gillhespy! I do believe you have a heart after all.'

'There's no need for that,' I bridled. What was it with this man that one minute he was full of solid common sense and the next he spoke utter nonsense?

'It wasn't a criticism.'

'Then what do you mean? Of course I have a heart.'

'You just don't like to show it.'

'If it means people mistake it for weakness, then no, I don't.'

I sank into my chair before the fire, grateful for the warmth after the chill of the graveyard, and happy that I could put the ordeals of the day – Arthur's funeral and the interview with Douglas Lumsden – behind me. Without invitation, Richard pulled the matching chair from the corner of the room over so he could sit facing me. Mary brought in bread and soup and we ate in silence, balancing the bowls in our laps. Most unladylike, uncivilised and delicious beyond words.

When we had finished, he took my bowl and placed it with his on the tray that Mary had left on my desk.

'Isabella, I don't want to pry into your private affairs, but did you think it strange that Mr Ord, Will, was not at the funeral of his close friend? Or did you know he would not be there?'

He spoke as though trying to convince me that he had only just thought about this, but even without being able to see his face, the hesitation in his voice made it clear that he had been wondering how to raise the question for some time.

'I thought he would be there,' I admitted.

The concern for his welfare that I had felt whilst standing by Arthur's grave returned. He had lied to me, been complicit with my father in deceiving me, and tried to manipulate me so he could continue with his lucrative scheme without my knowledge. For all of that I could never forgive him, or trust him. Our relationship was over, but the love that I had for him was ingrained deep within me, it was part of my very being, and I could not turn it off with such ease.

'Why do you ask?'

Richard poked at the fire and remained standing, one arm resting against the broad mantel above it. 'I just find it strange, that's all. There is something that doesn't make sense about all of this.'

I sighed. 'None of it makes sense!'

He continued as if I had not spoken. 'I mean, why was one of Sir William Cecil's men at Arthur's funeral? And why did the same man hang around afterwards? I mean, if he knew Arthur, why not go to the wake? And if he didn't know Arthur, I ask again, why was he there?'

I had been asking myself the same questions, and I had no answers.

'Do you think he could have been watching the people who were there. And if so, why?' Richard persisted.

'Please, can we stop speculating. We don't even know that he was one of Sir William's men. Douglas said he thought he was, but he could have been anyone who knew Arthur and was simply there to pay his last respects. Whoever he was, and whatever he was doing in the churchyard, I'm certain it has nothing to do with me. Why would a perfect stranger have been watching me?'

'Hmmm,' he mused, twisting the ring in his ear.

It was clear that he was not convinced. But the stranger could not have been watching me. Douglas must have been mistaken. If I kept telling myself that, maybe the voice of doubt inside my head would be silenced.

'Is there anything else about our business that you haven't shared with me?'

'What more could there possibly be?' I stared at him, taken by surprise. 'Is everything that's happened not enough?'

He shrugged. 'It's more than enough.'

He sat down again and we lapsed into silence for a while, both of us staring into the fire and its mesmerising patterns. The flames danced and flickered – one moment stretching and licking the tip of the blackened stone mantel, the next dipping and twisting through a palette of brilliant red, rusty orange and sunshine yellow. Colours that were shared by my shawl and rug, and to me were the perfect tonic for a cold, problem-filled day. As I stared, my head cleared. No longer full of the man in the churchyard, Will or my financial problems, my thoughts were free to move beyond the present to a more optimistic future. Even so, I had to be realistic and accept that investing in a new ship was going to be beyond my means for quite some time, because borrowing money from Mr Young was no longer an option.

'Whilst we have time to fill, perhaps we should continue that conversation we started a few days ago.'

I blinked, and the hypnotic, soothing effect of the fire was broken. Richard was watching me. He had unfastened his doublet, no doubt prompted by the heat from the fire, and his comfortable appearance – legs stretched out, loose fitting white shirt billowing slightly at his waist – would have convinced anyone who did not know better that he was a man at leisure, relaxing in his own home, in front of his own fire. It should have annoyed me, but instead it was comforting.

'Spices.' He prompted, although he had no need to remind me. I knew what he was referring to. So much had happened since that evening in my closet when he had first suggested this trade that there had been no opportunity to discuss it further. It was a relief to think of something other than the stranger in the churchyard, and I tried to recall my objections, but in truth, there were none, other than our obvious lack of experience.

'Antwerp is awash with spices,' he added.

'What would you get?'

'Saffron, cinnamon, turmeric, nutmeg. There's so much choice.'

'I think we should do it, but I know very little about spices.'

He drew his legs up so they were bent at the knees and leaned forward, supporting himself on his elbows, eagerness shining from his eyes.

'I know a little. My mother has always been a good cook. When times were hard, if my father was away for a prolonged period, she would bake pies and cakes and sell them at the market. And when my father did return he would be full of stories about the Portuguese and the fortunes their boats were making. Of course, they're sailing to the East and bringing the spices all the way back, so our profits would be less, but even so, there's money to be made. I know there is.'

'Okay, but I want you to sail with the Lady Isabella, establish the contacts, make the trades and be clear that if the quality is good and our customers are pleased, then we can take more.'

'I'm not sure how much of a sailor I am,' he hesitated.

'Nonsense, you'll be fine, and Captain Thirlwell will look after you.' I swept his objection aside, although I remembered the captain dismissing my cousin as that 'pasty faced foreigner' and realised I might have to talk to him to ensure he made good on my promise.

'Very well,' he said. 'I would be honoured to go.'

A draft rattled through my closet, rustling my skirts, followed by a scuffling noise in the boot room. It was Douglas.

He had to bend almost double and twist, so he moved in a sideways motion like a crab, to get through the low door. I did not dare ask if he had been successful in his mission. He held the cloth bag out to me, its contents bulky, and I hesitated before taking it, fearing that it contained the jewellery and that Douglas had failed. Then he smiled, and I gripped the bag and realised it was heavy with coins.

'Thank you,' I said. 'And will he take more?'

'Aye.' Douglas nodded. 'Same time tomorrow.'

SIXTEEN

IT TOOK THREE MORE TRIPS for Douglas to take away all of the jewellery. Together with my own meagre savings, the contribution that Richard had made and what my father had not squandered, I now had more than enough to repay Mr Young and fund the Lady Isabella's voyage. I was working at my desk when Douglas returned after the final trip. Earlier, I had counted out some coins that I thought represented a suitable remuneration for the favour he had done me, and placed them in a cloth bag. I held it out towards him, but the look that he threw at me would have soured the milk with no assistance from the kitchen fire.

The bag was heavy in my hand and I lowered it to the desk that stood between us.

'I dinnae want your money,' he said.

'Please forgive me. I didn't mean to offend you, but I wanted to reward you for the risks you've taken, and your discretion, in helping me.'

He mumbled something I did not catch.

'Thank you,' I said.

If he would not accept payment, I would find some other way to express my gratitude, because I could not have done this without him. Douglas had proven himself to be both honest and honourable and I believed I had found a most unlikely friend. Someone I could trust. The value of that was immeasurable.

Douglas left me in my closet, squeezing through the low back door to surprise Mary in the kitchen. I despatched George to fetch my cousin and call on Mr Young, requesting that he wait on me here, today, at his earliest convenience. If he asked why, George was just to say it was a matter of business.

I was determined to relish this moment, and it was only fair that

Richard should be with me after he had helped to raise the money to repay the debt. If I was being truly honest with myself, I was also getting used to having him around, and the more time I spent with him, the more I became aware that beyond the foppish exterior he had very good, sharp, business sense.

Together we staged the room, so Richard would occupy my chair beside the fire and I would sit behind my desk. I hoped that Mr Young's attention would be focused on me, and with the chair set at an angle and draped with my colourful shawl, he would not immediately notice my cousin's presence. I rearranged the quill and ink to my satisfaction, and beat a rhythm with my fingers on the surface of the desk.

'Patience dear cousin,' Richard remarked with a lazy smile.

'What if he doesn't come?'

'He will. He wants his money doesn't he?'

'I'm not sure if he wants his money, or would rather I fail so he keeps his power over me.'

'Either way, he will come.'

And he did.

Mary showed him into the closet. He had already removed his hat and cloak, and sure enough he trotted straight over to me without a glance to either side, my thick rug muffling the tap, tap of his stick, and his baby curls bouncing. I could not help but notice the expression on Richard's face, his eyes widening and his mouth twitching as he tried not to laugh, and I wanted to remind him not to underestimate this man.

'Madam Gillhespy. My dear. To what do I owe the pleasure of this unexpected invitation?'

I did not ask him to sit, but he did anyway, wearing a smug smile. He swept an appraising glance over the shelves behind me and the neatly-labelled boxes of paperwork, business documents and leather-bound books they held, before his eyes came to rest on the wooden casket I had placed on the side of my desk. I lowered my hands so he could not see me clenching my fists.

'I believe there is only one matter of business between you and I.' My voice, I hoped, was icy, but either he did not notice or he was so inured to people demonstrating their dislike for him that it made no impression. I pushed the casket towards him. 'It's all there.'

His fat fingers reached for the box, but I was watching his face. There was surprise, incredulity even, and disappointment. I was right. He had not wanted me to pay off the debt at all. He had wanted to see me ruined, with him taking control of my ships. And where would that have left me? Dependent on him. Even the thought was unbearable, and I thrust it aside. It was not going to happen. I had shown him that I would not submit to his pressure, that I had wits and I would use them to resist. Nothing was going to stop me enjoying that triumph.

He opened the casket and made a pretence of counting the coins, but it was clear that he was not interested.

'If you wouldn't mind signing here to confirm my father's debt has been repaid in full,' I said, handing him an official-looking document that Richard and I had drawn up, along with a quill. He took them and signed.

'It's been a pleasure doing business with you,' he spluttered, pushing the document towards me. 'Next time you find yourself in straitened financial circumstances, you only need to ask.' The oily smile had returned and pink spots once again splattered his cheeks.

'Why, thank you Mr Young, but please be assured that if ever I find myself in a difficult situation in the future, or in need of investment, you will be the last person on this earth that I will come to.' With difficulty, I forced my lips into a smile, refusing to release the anger that was sparking within me, like the flint on steel in a tinderbox.

Behind him, Richard had stood up and I could see that he, too, was angered, but his voice, when he spoke, was calm and so much more sinister as a result.

'I must say Isabella, I'm impressed by your powers of description. Quite uncanny. I feel I would have recognised this man anywhere, and not just from his odious dissembling.'

The merchant leapt to his feet, sending his stick clattering to the floor, and swivelled around to face Richard. He raised one hand to his head as if to fend off a blow whilst the other reached for the belt around his waist where no doubt he had a dagger. I caught my breath. Richard did not move.

'There's no need for that,' he said, not bothering to disguise the contempt that rolled from him like waves hitting the beach. 'I would not waste my energy on someone like you.'

Mr Young's fingers twitched but he made no further effort to reach for his weapon. He lowered his arm.

'Have you met my cousin and business partner?' I asked with a smile so sweet it could have been loaded with the deadly nightshade, sufficient to follow Circe's lead and turn Mr Young into a pig. The thought made me want to laugh, but still I held onto my nerve.

'Ah, the mysterious Mr Elliott,' he said, recovering his composure. 'I do not believe I've had the pleasure, but naturally I have heard about you. Maybe we will have cause to do business, man-to-man, in the future.'

My anger melted into amusement as I watched one of the most influential men in Berwick attempt to reassert his authority over this interview, and fail. He held out his hand to Richard, who made no move to take it, and Mr Young lifted it to his head and scratched his ear with great vigour.

'I would like you to leave now please,' I said. 'And I do not want to see you again, either here, at my warehouse, or any of my ships.'

'I must say, there's no need for that tone. Don't worry, I'll see myself out.' With a loud and self-important huff, he bent to retrieve his stick, hoisted the casket from my desk, tucked it under his arm and strutted from the room. The door had no sooner swung closed behind him than I turned to Richard.

'That went well, I think,' I said, but he was frowning.

'It's all very well Isabella, but you've made him look a fool. That man is our sworn enemy now for sure.'

'We have made him look a fool.' I corrected him. 'It was worth it, and he was our enemy anyway.'

'Even so, it may have been wiser to leave him a little more in the dark about our feelings.'

'It makes no difference. He's only interested in money.'

'And power,' Richard added.

I tidied my desk. 'I think we should go to see Captain Thirlwell. The repairs to the Lady Isabella should be almost complete, and if you are going to sail with her you need to meet the captain properly.'

Richard retrieved his hat and cloak and we left through the back door. The weather was warming and a thaw was turning the top layer of snow and ice into a slush, which only served to conceal the even more treacherous layer that remained beneath the surface. At the stable I paused to stroke Thunder's velvety nose. He whickered with pleasure and from somewhere near his hooves there was a sound like a dog whining. Of course, the hound from the graveyard. I peered over the stable door. George had done a good job of cleaning it up; its hair no longer gathered in matted clumps, but it was still an ugly brute.

'I expect you'd like a walk,' I said and he cocked an ear. I unlatched the door and he watched me for a moment, his liquid eyes guarded beneath his untidy mane before shuffling out and pressing his long body against my legs.

We set off for the quay. I would not have been surprised if the dog had run off as soon as I let him out, but no. He persisted in running circles around us, chasing ahead and then swooping back to make sure we were following. Every so often he leapt into the air, as if a rabbit were being dangled in front of him and he was desperate to catch it.

'That is one energetic beast,' Richard grumbled.

'I like it,' I said.

In truth, I had not given the dog a moment's thought since it had followed me home, but watching its joy in the simple pleasures of life, such as taking a walk, made me realise I did like it, and what's more, I thought I would welcome its company.

'I suppose I had better give it a name,' I mused.

'What? You're not thinking of keeping it?' Richard's tone was one of disbelief.

'I rather think it's … he's … decided to keep me. What do you say to Pepper? It's quite appropriate, given our new venture, and I think it suits him – all ruffled and uneven.'

The Lady Isabella was anchored in the mainstream of the river, the repairs to her hull complete. I had hoped she would be closer to the jetty, which would have enabled me to board via a gangplank to see for myself the progress being made, but the jetty was crowded with other ships loading and unloading. As hoisting myself out of a small boat and up the rope ladder hanging over her bows in a ladylike fashion was beyond my capabilities, I would have to be content with a conversation with the captain instead.

Having made enquiries and established that he was on board, we paid a boatman to row out and request he come ashore to meet with us. We did not have long to wait. Soon the boat was bobbing back to the quay, the captain's stocky frame weighing it down on one side.

'Madam Gillhespy,' he greeted me effusively, with a less expressive nod at Richard. I steeled myself for what could turn into a difficult negotiation. Richard appeared not to notice. Indeed, if anything I would say he was amused.

'Walk with us a little Captain Thirlwell, and tell us how she is doing.'

'She's doing well,' he enthused, and embarked on a detailed list of the repairs carried out, the materials used and the work still to be done. It was an impressive account for such a short period of time. I glanced at Richard, quite expecting his attention to be wavering, but on the contrary, he appeared rapt by the captain's narrative.

'When do you think she'll be ready to sail?' I asked.

'Within the week, I reckon.'

'Good,' I mused. I needed to choose my words with care. 'Captain, you are aware that I have long felt we should be pushing into new territories and expanding this business. The condition of the Lady Isabella, my father's death and present fortunes have made this difficult, but I have decided on a way forward that I'm really quite excited about. My plans will meet as many of those objectives as possible until I can invest in a new ship.'

I watched the captain's face whilst speaking and I had his interest, although it was tinged with suspicion rather than excitement.

'It doesn't involve you travelling any further than recent trips, or making any additional stops, but we will be taking on board a new cargo at Antwerp. Something we haven't tried before.'

'Go on.' He prompted.

'Spices.' I clarified. 'No-one as yet is bringing any volume or variety into this part of the country, and yet I hear spices are in great demand from merchants in London.'

'I don't know nothing about spices,' he said, stroking his hirsute face.

'Don't worry. My cousin, Mr Elliott, to whom I do not believe you have been properly introduced and for which I apologise, knows a good deal about them and will travel with you on the voyage to make contacts, establish the necessary contracts and oversee the first shipment. All you need to worry about is the safe passage of the Lady Isabella and the loading and unloading of the cargo. We will of course be sailing with some of our finest linens and woollen weaves, and I have some other orders to collect as well.'

Richard beamed at the captain, who muttered something into his beard, as he looked my cousin up and down. He could not refuse to do as I asked, but the lack of welcome or enthusiasm in his eyes left me in no doubt that he was not happy to have this particular passenger foisted upon him.

'I know I can rely on you Captain to start making the necessary preparations to sail,' I said, meeting his eyes.

He pulled his hat down low over his forehead. 'Well, since I'm ashore I'd best make use of the time and get started.' He nodded towards us both and strode away.

'Isabella, I must say I think that was most unfair of you.'

My attention was caught by another figure hurrying along the quay, towering over everyone around him, and I did not reply.

'Isabella,' Richard repeated, raising his voice.

'What? Whatever do you mean?'

'Taking credit for my idea to start with, and then setting me up as an expert in spices.'

I smiled. 'My dear cousin.' I took his arm and we strolled towards Segate. 'If I had told him it was your idea, part-owner of this business or not, he would have refused to have anything to do with it. On the Lady Isabella it's his word that counts, not mine or yours. As it is, after he was forced to admit he could not set up the new trade, it was difficult for him to object to you joining the voyage. Although I must admit, I wondered for a moment there if he was going to. You will need to use all of your charm to earn the good will of our captain, I fear.'

'Why does nobody in this town seem to like me?' he protested. 'What have I done to annoy them?'

'Besides turning up unannounced, dressed like a gentleman from her Majesty's court, speaking like a foreigner, and demonstrating some very strange behaviour you mean? You have to work to belong in a place like this. Don't worry. If you tarry for long enough you'll get the hang of it.'

'How many times do I have to tell you …'

But what he had to tell me would have to wait, because the person I had seen a moment ago was now approaching us, and I was right, it was Douglas.

'I have some news for you,' he said, removing his hat. 'It's about the Tweedmouth Mining Company.'

The Jolly Salmon was a small tavern down another of Berwick's tiny alleys, one so narrow that it was not deserving of the term. It was more an enlarged crack where buildings once joined had been forced apart, rather than the walls of two separate structures leaning towards each other. Customers would approach from the south and leave to the north as it was impossible for two people to pass. As the name suggests, the tavern was popular with the fishermen and the merchants that traded the fish south to Newcastle, sometimes beyond, my own small boats included. The painted sign above the door depicted a fish, its mouth turned upwards at the corners into a smile, its body curving into the wind as it leapt out of the river. We settled onto a small table in the far corner of what appeared to be the only room, and the waitress dumped a jug of ale and three mugs onto the sticky surface between us. Pepper sprawled across my feet.

'So, what have you discovered?' I asked, leaning forwards, eager to hear more.

'Good news I think.'

His eyes sparkled as he poured the ale, emptied his own mug in one gulp and topped it up. 'I've been asking around, discreetly, you know, and earlier today this young fellow approached me and asked for a word. He was the foreman there, and it turns out I knew his father, a good man, God rest his soul. It seems that when the tunnels collapsed, which was a great tragedy, the earth continued to shift for many days – weeks even – and no-one dare go near it for feart of being buried alive. A few days ago, he got brave enough to go take a closer look, and he's convinced that there is now coal on the surface. He dinnae know what to do, so he went to see Mr Young (junior), believing he still owned the majority shares in the mine, but that delightful gentleman washed his hands of it. Told the young man with glee that it was nothing to do with him any longer, so he came into town looking for the other investor that he knew of.'

'My father.'

'Aye. They had met on a few occasions, when your father had visited the mine, but the young man – John Bailey is his name – had not heard of his death. He's looking for instruction, what to do. All the workers have been laid off, and some are reluctant to return. They believe the tunnels collapsing was God's way of telling them to stop. That he was angry. But John is a canny lad. He's arguing that if that were the case, why would He have left the coal on the surface like that for anyone passing by to gather. He may be young, but he seems to have a nose for business.'

'Can we meet with him?'

'Aye. That is what he would like.'

'Let's go then.' I started to push my chair away from the table and Pepper flicked his tail. Douglas stayed me with his hand.

'John is no longer in town. He had to return to his village where his young sister and invalid mother are alone. But he will meet with you tomorrow.'

'Why can't we go now?' I demanded, impatience clouding my better judgement.

'Madam. It will soon be dark.'

Douglas was right. Outside the town walls it was a lawless place. Indeed, the thought of riding over the bridge and into the countryside south was only slightly better than going to the north, and into the wild borders between England and Scotland.

'We'll leave at first light,' I said. 'Mr Lumsden, I'll need you to come with me, as my guide.'

'You're not going off on this venture without me,' Richard spoke up. I was not going to oppose him, indeed I had been expecting it.

'We'll need to ride,' Douglas said. 'It's too far to walk, and we'll be safer on horseback.'

'I'll take Thunder. He's getting a little fat and lazy.' My father had been accustomed to ride everywhere, whereas I much preferred to walk, and the town being so small there was really no need to travel on four legs when two would suffice. I suspected Thunder might not have left his stable in the last few weeks.

179

We finished our ale and I returned home alone. I instructed George to prepare Thunder for me to leave at first light, and allowed Pepper to join me in my closet. He sniffed around the room, poking his nose into all the corners and beneath the chairs before stretching out with a satisfied grunt in front of the fire. Wise dog. Mary brought me some supper and I was dozing in my chair when I was disturbed by voices coming from the front of the house. Footsteps crossed the hall and Pepper's ears twitched. The door to my study opened and Mary came in, followed by Mr Usher.

'I'm sorry Isabella. I told him ye were resting, but he said he has orders to speak with ye without delay.'

Pepper sat upright and rumbled a low, soft growl.

'It's all right.' I placed a hand on his head to soothe him and he quietened. If only someone could do the same for me. Memories of the last time that I had seen this man swept through my head, and I remembered challenging him that if he needed anything else from me he could find me at my home. It seems he had taken me up on that. I supposed I should be grateful that he had not had me dragged through the streets again.

'Thank you Mary. You can leave us. Please, Mr Usher, have a seat.' I indicated the other chair, which was still positioned where Richard had left it a few days ago on the opposite side of the fireplace. At that my hospitality ended. I did not offer him refreshments.

'I trust the list of my customers was all in order, and has helped with your enquiries?'

He grunted, and answered me with a question of his own.

'Madam Gillhespy. I need to ask you about the whereabouts of William Ord.'

It was clear that I needed to readjust my expectations of this interview. I had thought he must be following up on the supposed connection between me, my business and Arthur's death. So why was he asking me about Will?

'I don't know where he is,' I admitted. Over the last few days I had been grateful to have so much to occupy myself with that

I'd had little time to brood over Will, and the way he had used me and betrayed me, or allow myself to miss him. Now I thought about it, I had not seen him around the town at all, but then I'd had no further cause to visit the Custom House, so that was not in itself remarkable.

'When did you last see him?' Mr Usher persisted.

'On the morning of Arthur's funeral.'

'Really?' He scoffed at my answer. 'That's a long time for two lovebirds not to see each other.'

'You are not as well informed as you believe,' I advised him, holding out my hand so he could see for himself that my betrothal ring was no longer there.

He stared at my hand and leaned forward. Pepper bared his teeth and the growling started again.

'Shhh,' I whispered to him. It would not be good for me if the brute attacked this man – much as he might deserve it.

'Isn't that Arthur Fewell's dog?' he snapped.

'I don't know. He appeared to be upset at the funeral, followed me home and has not left since. He could have been Arthur's, although I do not recall seeing them together. Why? What is this about?'

Once again he ignored my questions, leaving me trying to fill in the gaps with my own conjectures, which were most likely a long way off the mark.

'Madam, I need some answers please.' His voice took on a new and impatient tone. 'When did you break off your betrothal?'

'The last time I saw Will, on the morning of Arthur's funeral.'

'Why?'

'I don't think that's any of your business,' I snapped.

'I will decide what is my business. Rest assured, I'm acting on a higher authority. If you prefer, we can go to the Tolbooth and you can provide your answers there.'

He stared at me, unblinking, his eyes a cold, hard, flint. His words were not just an idle threat, and I got the impression that he would take great enjoyment from ordering my detention.

'Since my father's death we had been arguing a lot.' I paused, knowing I had to choose my words with care. I had to give him a version of the truth that would satisfy him, without giving him cause to probe any deeper into my business affairs. If he found out about my father's debts, or the scheme he and Will had been running – the smuggling – well, I found it difficult to imagine where they would send me, but I was pretty sure that my previous cell at the Tolbooth would appear as luxury in comparison.

'Go on.'

'He found it difficult to understand why I wanted to postpone our marriage. I felt that to go ahead with our plans would be disrespectful to my father's memory. I insisted on observing an appropriate period of mourning. It angered him. He didn't seem able to understand that my refusal was not an indication that my feelings for him had changed, whereas I didn't think it was unreasonable to insist we wait. Our last argument was quite … fierce … and I thought it best to return his ring. That was the last time I saw him.'

I made sure to stare into Mr Usher's flint-like eyes whilst I made this speech, and was gratified when he looked away first.

'Did you not think it was strange that he failed to attend his friend's funeral?'

'I did, but I was also relieved not to have to see him, in public, so soon after our row. I assumed he must have a good reason for not being there.'

'Thank you, Madam. You have been most helpful.' He stood, bowed, and left the room without another word. The front door slammed and moments later Mary sidled into my closet.

'Is everything all right?' she asked, her face glowing with concern.

'I don't know, Mary,' I admitted. 'He wanted to know about Will. It seems he's disappeared. But I haven't seen him for days, so I cannot help. Mary, I have an early start. I'm going to retire. Can you find some food for Pepper and water. He can sleep in the boot room.'

She raised an eyebrow but did not object.

As I climbed the stairs, listening to Mary's efforts to cajole the hound from his warm spot by the fire and out through the door into the boot room, my thoughts were troubled. Should I be worried about Will? Our relationship might be over, but that did not mean I no longer cared for him. What if he was ill, or had indeed left town, perhaps on business and an accident had befallen him, or he had been attacked? But it was something else that Mr Usher had said that was gripping my insides and squeezing them so tight that I had to stop and catch my breath. What higher authority was he acting on?

SEVENTEEN

THUNDER WAS FRISKY AND I was already regretting that I had neglected to exercise him since my father had died. It took all my strength and concentration to control him as we joined the other early travellers spilling out of the town gates as soon as they opened. Last night's frost was already melting in the bright morning sun, and the surface of the bridge was sure to be slippery. The rush of the water bubbled just beneath the planks as it raced towards us from the land, its undercurrents swirling and churning as the strength of the ebbing tide pulled it out to join the ocean. Many a man and horse had been punished for their lack of caution with a quick dip in that cold river, and I had no intention of following suit. I would far rather we had used the ford that is passable across the mouth of the estuary at low tide, but that would not be for several hours yet, and we could not delay if we wanted to return before sunset.

At the stone tower that was almost at the far end of the bridge we had to wait for a number of carts to pass through the narrow gate, and I turned to look back at the town and the quay. The Lady Isabella was to my side, just a few hundred feet away. It was strange to view her from this perspective. Although the hour was early, her deck was already a hive of activity.

Thunder tossed his head around, impatient to be on the move again. When we got to the other side I would have to lengthen the reins, let him go and hope the others could keep up with us. As it was, I tightened my grip and pulled his head back, leaned forward and stroked the side of his neck, sniffing the air. In the last week the weather had turned and it was fragranced with the arrival of spring.

We passed through the gate and out onto Tweedmouth. Although we had travelled but a short distance, already the atmosphere was different, wilder, more primitive. There were a few poor dwellings spread along the river bank towards Spittal Beach, which we passed without incident. Douglas did not linger, but guided us onto the main road to the south, which hugged the coast before winding inland. I gave Thunder his head, and laughed as the protests from Richard and Douglas fell at our heels.

'You'll have to follow me,' I shouted over my shoulder. After a few minutes we slowed and Douglas caught up with me, Richard close behind.

'Madam Gillhespy, please, you need to stay close to me. It isn't safe out here.'

I looked around. The scene could not appear less threatening. There was not a person, nor a building in sight, although I knew Douglas was right and I had perhaps been reckless.

'Don't worry. Thunder just had some pent-up energy to rid himself of. We'll stick with you now, won't we boy.' I leaned forward to pat his neck and he tossed his head, eager to be on the move again.

The ride was uneventful, although I was aware of Douglas continually looking around us. 'He's making me nervous,' Richard whispered. Several times I wondered if he knew where he was going.

'How far?' I asked after I judged we had been riding for about an hour.

Douglas shrugged. 'We need to turn here.' He pointed to a narrow path between fields to our left, which angled away in the direction of the coast. We had to ride in single file – Douglas in front, me in the middle and Richard at the back. Our progress was slow and tedious, and it was inevitable that my thoughts should turn to Mr Usher and his questions about Will. For the town authorities to come to me for information, they must have already been to his lodgings, and the Custom House, and failed to find him. So where was he? Something must have happened for him to miss his best friend's funeral, and not go to work, and again I feared for his safety, my imagination picturing him sprawled at the base of one of the town's towers having suffered a fate similar to that of Arthur. I could not bear to think of it, so I pushed the images out of my mind and tried to focus instead on the meeting ahead. What would this John Bailey be like, and what information might he have for me?

After a couple of miles the path widened and we emerged onto a headland curving around a horseshoe-shaped bay. A broad, grassy track along the cliff side appeared to lead all the way to a small, rocky beach, and about halfway down a huddle of cottages set a brave face towards the German Ocean. As we approached I could see a young man standing in front of the one closest to us. He was slim and tall, clean-shaven, although as we drew nearer I suspected his youth meant he was not yet able to support a beard. He raised an arm in greeting, and I noticed the cuff of his doublet was frayed and his cloak, if the garment he wore could be described as such, was so short it did not extend to the bottom of his doublet. I let out a sigh of relief that we had arrived at last.

'Mr Bailey.' Douglas nodded to him. 'This is Madam Gillhespy and Mr Elliott.'

The young man removed his cap and nodded at us. 'John Bailey at your service,' he said with a swagger in his voice.

I slid from Thunder's back. 'Pleased to meet you Mr Bailey. Can we leave the horses here and walk?'

For someone as unused as I to spending time in the saddle, it was a relief to be back on my feet, although I was not accustomed to walking in my riding boots and I found myself stumbling on the rough surface. John led us away from the cottages, taking us further along the track before cutting off to our right to follow a gulley that rose gently. Below us, an exuberant stream frothed and bubbled on its way to meet the ocean. Snow lay on the ground in deep patches where the sun could not reach, its surface pitted with the tracks of animals and the lightest tread of birds. The gulley started to curve, and as we entered the bend I could see an opening in the cliff face, like the mouth of a large cave. A rope was stretched across it and tied to posts at either end. A painted wooden sign was nailed to one of them: *'Tweedmouth Mining Company. No entry.'* It was not sufficient to deter anyone who really wanted to enter.

John stopped. 'This is the entrance, but it's too dangerous to go in here.'

I peered into the dark but could see nothing. John led us around the bend and to a track that cut further up the side of the gulley. The undergrowth and overhanging branches had been hacked back, but it was still difficult walking and I cursed my long skirts which kept snagging on brambles. At the top of the track we emerged onto a headland, but the scene here was much different to the one we had ridden over earlier. The land appeared to have collapsed, leaving exposed boulders and rubble scattered everywhere, interspersed with gaping holes through which tufts of gorse protruded. We stood at the edge and looked at a scene of devastation on a grand scale, as if God and the Devil had staged a battle here, using the rocks as weapons.

I started to move closer, but John extended a hand to stop me. 'It aint safe,' he said. 'Come this way.'

He led us around the crater so we could look into it facing in the direction of the ocean. 'Down there.' He pointed. 'Can you see?'

I trained my eyes to follow his finger. The surface of the rock was glistening with moisture, ice maybe, and as it descended further into what must have once been a cavern beneath, it turned black – shiny, coal-black. I clutched Richard's arm and tried to lean further over.

'Isabella, no,' he cautioned me, but he could not disguise the excitement in his voice. It was impossible to tell how deep or for how long the wall of coal extended, but just from what I could see there was enough to solve all of my money problems, but how much would it cost to extract it?

'The men were tunnelling from the back of the cave,' John explained. 'When the ceiling collapsed, this is what it left on the surface. That's an exposed seam of coal and much easier to mine, but the land is unstable.'

'Mr Bailey, do you know what to do, to make the land stable, and safe, so that the mine can be re-opened?' Richard asked.

'I do.' He nodded.

'How long and how much?'

'Depends.' He shrugged. 'If I work alone, and all goes well, just a few weeks, and I need only enough money to feed my family. Of course, when the mine is open and profitable, I would seek a more suitable arrangement.'

It was more than a reasonable suggestion, especially when he did not know me or my cousin, or whether we would honour such an agreement. It would not be difficult to take advantage of his trusting nature. I studied his face. His eyes, dark and intense, met mine, and his mouth widened revealing a row of crooked teeth. He was rolling the dice, and I suspected he had little to lose; scratching a living on this bleak headland must be difficult. Even so, I was reluctant to stretch my financial position to the limit again.

'And the men will come back to work then?' I asked, recalling what Douglas had said about some of the workers being too superstitious to return.

'They will, if they can see that it has been made safe.'

'You're going to have to let us think about this,' I said, shaking my head at Richard to stop his enthusiasm from committing us to something we would be foolish to consider.

John nodded, but his smile faded. We followed him back down the track and through the gulley to the cottages.

'Please forgive my lack of hospitality, but my home is very small and my mother is not well,' John apologised as we prepared to part company. 'But Madam Gillhespy, it has been a great pleasure to meet you and I was very sorry to hear of your father's death. He was well liked and respected here and I do hope you decide to continue what he started.'

I hoped so too, but it was difficult to see how.

We travelled the first part of the return journey in silence. When we rejoined the main road, Richard pulled his horse up alongside Thunder. 'We have to find a way to do this,' he said. 'We cannot just leave it sitting there like that.'

'I know, but how? Everything I have left needs to go into preparing the Lady Isabella to sail.'

'Everything we have left,' Richard corrected me.

'Yes, yes,' I said. Really, did he have to be so fastidious. 'We have to start buying wool and cloth for the voyage now. Perhaps in a few weeks when I've had time to shift some of the wine we have in stock, I … we … can divert some of that resource into the work that needs to be done to make the mine safe. But even then, to get it working we're going to have to pay wages before we've sold any of the coal.'

I shook my head, struggling to work out a solution to this conundrum. I should be elated that the vast amount of money my father had sunk into this company might not be lost to me after all, but realising any return from his investment still seemed far out of reach.

'Perhaps I should not go with the Lady Isabella. Then I could help John and together we could make the land safe and open the mine.'

The thought of Richard labouring and getting his fine, colourful clothes sullied with dirt and coal dust was almost enough to make me burst into most unladylike laughter, but he was so sensitive he would no doubt take offence. With an effort I restrained myself. Anyway, it was out of the question. He was needed elsewhere.

'No, Richard. There will be more profit from the voyage if we are successful with the spices, and you heard Captain Thirlwell. He cannot set up that trade. We are just going to have to be patient.'

Patience and I were not good companions, but in truth I could see no alternative. Richard was brooding now. His countenance resembled that of my father when facing a tricky problem that he was determined not to give up on. I was also reminded of Mr Carr's observation when talking of my aunt, Richard's mother, that being stubborn was a family trait. I knew Richard would have more to say about the mine before he left town. He urged his horse ahead and I let him go. Douglas took his place at my side.

'Forgive me for asking, but did I hear ye say that Richard Elliott will be sailing with the Lady Isabella?'

'Yes.' I nodded, still watching my cousin.

'How well do ye know him?'

'What?' Richard was approaching a bend at a gallop and was almost out of sight. I switched my attention to Douglas. 'What do you mean?'

'It's just, there are some rumours in town.'

'There are always rumours in Berwick, you know that.'

Douglas inclined his head a fraction, acknowledging that my words had more than a ring of truth to them.

'You are well aware that I hardly know him. He's as much a stranger to me as he is to this town. But I think he means well, and he has demonstrated a loyalty to me and to our business that many others, whom I thought I knew well, have not.'

We rounded the bend and the bridge was before us, maybe half a mile away. The town itself lay beyond, shimmering as the setting sun honeyed its defensive walls. Richard had reached the tower and gate on the bridge and appeared to be waiting for us.

'What is it Mr Lumsden? What's concerning you?'

'Sir William Cecil's man, I believe his name is Warde, is still in town.' Douglas did not look at me as he spoke. His eyes too were watching my cousin.

Cecil's man. The one who had been lingering in the churchyard after Arthur's funeral. Mr Usher's words of yesterday evening hit me. '*I am acting on a higher authority,*' he had said. Was that higher authority this Mr Warde, and if so, was he following the direct instructions of the Queen's most important advisor? But what could he possibly want with me, or Will?

'And?' I prompted him. 'What is that to do with me?'

'I dinnae know what he's looking for, but it is said that he's interested in any ships that trade regularly with the Low Countries. He's been asking questions at the quay and the Custom House.'

'Which could be why Mr Usher wanted to know about Will,' I mused. 'Why did you not mention this earlier?'

'I wished to be more discreet,' he said.

The more time I spent with Douglas Lumsden the more I liked him. I supposed he had learned tact and caution from years of being mistrusted in this town just for his Scottish blood, and I almost blushed to remember that I had judged him for that too. Mary had demonstrated much better sense, although she still could not entertain any ambition to marry him unless they left town.

'You wanted to speak to me alone. I understand,' I said. 'But I do believe my cousin is honest. Annoying and irritating, yes, but honest. Besides, if this Mr Warde is investigating something that he suspects is already happening, Richard has only just arrived in town so it cannot be anything concerning him.'

'It could be that the arrival of a stranger, connected to a merchant's business, about to sail to Antwerp, and add to that two suspicious deaths, both with a connection to you, is sufficient to draw such attention.'

'Wait. What are you saying? Two suspicious deaths?'

For the first time during this exchange Douglas hesitated. He tightened his reins and his horse stopped. I did the same, and he leaned towards me.

'Arthur and your father,' he said.

'My father died from natural causes. His heart failed,' I protested.

'Is that so?' Douglas asked.

His voice was so quiet it was almost a whisper. Nevertheless, it blocked out everything else. I could no longer hear the gulls mewing, or see Berwick crouching over the estuary, its walls and the castle protecting the town, and those who lived there, from would-be marauders attacking from the ocean or the river. All I could see was Douglas's face, his eyes, kind but shrewd, fixed on me, gauging the effect of what he had just told me, and all I could hear was a torrent of words rushing through my head. My instinct that something was wrong but I did not act upon it. Mary's impression that he'd had something on his mind. Will's reaction when I had asked him if he knew what that might be and he'd suggested suicide. Mr Hedley had said simply his heart had failed, although he could not tell me why. But Douglas was hinting at some sort of foul play.

His saddle creaked as he twisted in it. I turned as well and my eyes followed his, which were directed towards Richard.

'Are you suggesting that my cousin had something to do with my father's death?'

Douglas did not answer.

'No.' I shook my head. 'There was not a mark on my father's body. No sign of a struggle. Nothing to suggest anyone else was involved. If there had been any reason to suspect that it was anything but natural causes, Mr Hedley would have said so. Besides, what would Richard have hoped to gain? He had his share of the business anyway. He cannot have thought he would inherit from my father.'

It was a ridiculous suggestion that I would not entertain. I had got to know my cousin over the last few weeks and there was no doubt but that he was irritating, but he was no murderer.

Douglas dug his heels into his horse's flank and we set off again, but everything in front of me was a blur. We caught up with Richard and he said something to me, but the wind whipped the words from his mouth and tossed them up into the air before they reached my ears. I nodded anyway, and he threw me a puzzled look. Navigating the bridge required my full concentration to avoid slipping on the surface that was even more treacherous than it had been earlier. The patches of ice that were forming as the temperature dipped were difficult to spot in the fading daylight. My fingers and toes were numb and I longed for my warm fire in my cosy closet.

But it was not to be.

We passed through Bridge Gate in single file, with me in front, but no sooner had I turned onto Briggate than my way was blocked by several town guards on horseback.

'Madam Gillhespy. You need to come with us,' one of them said. Although I could not see his bald patch, I recognised his voice. He was the one who had hammered on my door that time before, and then marched me through the streets like a common criminal. A cold hand of fear gripped my insides. I heard Richard call my name and turned around, but I was surrounded by guards who were preventing him and Douglas from reaching me.

Did I not have enough real problems of my own without someone indulging their imagination about what other schemes I might be involved with? This was wearing thin. The guards started to move as one, nudging Thunder from behind. He flicked his ears and whinnied, but we had no choice but to follow.

My fears were soon confirmed. We were heading back to the Tolbooth. What Douglas had said to me, about this Mr Warde working for Sir William Cecil, was fresh in my mind. I replayed it over and over as we rode, trying not to think of what he had also said about my father, or what awaited me. We stopped and dismounted at the steps to the Tolbooth, and my escort pressed me through the entrance to the building. They led me to the steps at the rear of the ground floor. As we descended them the air grew danker, and the desperation of the poor souls who were incarcerated here, or had been in the past, gripped me. I would have stalled had it not been for the guards surrounding me, propelling me forwards until we reached the same tiny room that I had occupied on the occasion of my previous detention in this building. The one I had thought of as my prison cell.

This time, though, the room was not empty. It was occupied by a single man, seated at the table, hands palm-down on the surface, fingers splayed. He was well-dressed in a dark grey doublet beneath a gown made of a fine woollen weave in an even darker shade of grey. His ruff was modest and his beard was neat and almost entirely white. I could not see his hair because he still wore his hat – tall, yellow ribbon, yellow and green feathers. This was the man I had encountered on the quay after I had argued with Will about the customs bill. He had been looking at the Lady Isabella. Was he also Sir William Cecil's man?

Despite being seated he filled the room, such that had my own good sense not told me it was impossible, I would have sworn that the walls had been moved since I was held here before. The door closed behind me and I loosened the ties on my cloak – not because I was warm, but to ease the choking sensation that had gripped me by my throat.

'Please sit,' the man said. His voice was cultured but not kind. To obey him meant to move closer, when my every instinct was to run. That, however, was not an option. I forced my feet to move. Just a few short steps was all it took to position me in the chair opposite him. His eyes followed me all of the way. I waited for him to speak. His fingers moved as if he were playing a scale on a clavichord. His nails were neat and clean.

'Madam Gillhespy. I've had you brought here because I believe you may have information that would help me in a little matter I am presently investigating. I understand your father recently died and you inherited his business.' He paused to glance at some notes written in a neat hand on a piece of paper in front of him before adding, 'Joseph Lilburne.' It was all for effect … I would wager he did not need to refresh his memory of my father's name.

'I inherited it jointly, with my cousin,' I said. My voice squeaked like a fiddle on the high notes and I cleared my throat.

He inclined his head a fraction.

'Yes, I was aware of Mr Elliott. He sounds as though he's not from these parts.'

'He has only recently arrived in town,' I confirmed, although again I suspected it was unnecessary.

'Let's not waste time with your minor boats. It's the Lady Isabella I'm interested in. I can see from the port book that she sails regularly between Berwick and the Low Countries. Indeed, it appears her turnaround between trips averages a week or two, except this time.'

'She needed work.'

'Of course.' He nodded. 'Bit of an old tub isn't she really? I would have thought you'd be better off investing in a new ship, especially a merchant of your father's standing ... of your standing,' he corrected himself.

I bridled at his description of my beloved ship as an old tub. 'That's not what you said about her last time we met, Mr Warde. Then you called her a fine ship, as I recall.' It would probably have been wiser for me to remain silent, but the words had slipped out before I could stop them.

'Ah, I see you are quite well-informed. My apologies that I did not introduce myself then, or now. You may also know that I remain in Berwick on the instruction of Sir William Cecil.'

I did not fool myself that his apology was sincere. He'd had no intention of introducing himself, but in addressing him by name I had surprised him into divulging more information than perhaps he had intended. I had Douglas to thank for that small advantage.

'Shall we return to the matter of your *fine ship*. I think you and I both know that the Lady Isabella is, shall we say, past her prime. So I repeat, I would have thought a merchant of your standing would invest in a new ship. Unless your financial circumstances are, shall we say, somewhat curtailed?'

He had to be guessing. He must have been listening to the rumours that sweep around the streets of this town as if blown and scattered on the wind, and there had certainly been plenty of those swirling around me of late, fed and sustained by the arrival of my cousin. But the only people who knew about the debt, aside from myself, were Richard and Douglas, and I trusted them both. The trader who had bought my jewellery might have talked, but he did not know who was selling.

Except. Of course, there was one more person. Mr Young. I had not considered that he might talk, since his lucrative business lending some of his wealth to others was thinly disguised usury, which was itself prohibited, but, as Richard had pointed out, it might not have been a good idea to humiliate him. I had made an enemy of him, and this was his first strike in retaliation.

I ran a dry tongue over my lips. It was most important to remain calm. Let Mr Warde show his hand first. He was patient, waiting for me to answer. Watching me with an intense scrutiny.

'My father's nature was always to be cautious.'

'Indeed.' He nodded his encouragement. 'That is always wise in business, although not guaranteed to turn the biggest profit of course.'

I decided to follow his example and remained silent, waiting for him to make his point.

'You see, what interests me is what happens when people who are used to having money find themselves of a sudden without any. Even with debts. Perhaps big debts, that they did not expect. I wonder, what do they do?'

In spite of the chill in the room, a trickle of perspiration began its slow journey from the back of my neck, tickling its way down my spine.

'Do they perchance start to cheat the system? Steal money from the state by not paying their dues?'

He skewered me with his eyes. I was not one to panic, but how could he even suspect this? He appeared to know as much about my business as I did.

'Or …' he lowered his voice, '… do they start to sell things that don't belong to them. Secrets maybe? Information that if it falls into the wrong hands could be extremely dangerous.'

Now he had lost me.

'Sir, I'm afraid I don't know what you're insinuating.'

He raised an eyebrow. 'Really Madam. I find that most difficult to believe.'

We sat in silence, his fingers playing the invisible keyboard on the table, while I tried to work out what he meant. This interview had taken a most peculiar turn. What secrets could he possibly think I knew that would be of interest to anyone else such that they would pay for them?

'Where is William Ord?'

His question changed the direction of the interrogation for which I should be grateful, but I sensed this man wanted answers, which I was not able to give.

'I already told Mr Usher, just yesterday, that I don't know where he is.'

'At the risk of repeating myself, I find that difficult to believe.'

'We are no longer betrothed. I have no reason to know.'

'Except … is he not of importance to your business?'

I wanted to snap at him that no, Will was not important to my business, and it was when I found out what he and my father had been doing that I broke off our relationship, but I stopped myself just in time. To say that would be to admit that I knew of the smuggling. This man would not believe that I had only just discovered it and was entirely innocent of any wrongdoing. My thoughts were doing a jig in my head, whirling and whirling until I began to feel dizzy. I realised Mr Warde was talking again and tried to focus on what he was saying.

'You see, Madam Gillhespy, William Ord is a person of particular interest to me. I believe he may have information about his friend, the late Arthur Fewell. Information that could be important for the security of our country and our Queen, and which my superior, Master Secretary is most keen I should discover before I leave this town.'

'Mr Warde. You have me most confused. I don't know what you're talking about.'

'Would it help if I jog your memory? When we searched Mr Fewell's lodgings we found certain maps and plans, of the town defences, which he should not have been in possession of. What do you think he may have been planning to do with them?'

'I really don't know. I … I … You're talking in riddles. I knew Arthur only as Will's friend, nothing more. Whatever else he may have been involved with, I knew nothing of it …' I almost added that I was certain that Will knew nothing, but something stopped me. I was no longer certain of anything where he was concerned.

Mr Warde's eyes did not leave my face. There must have been something in my countenance, or my voice, that convinced him I was speaking the truth because he pushed himself to his feet abruptly. If I had thought his presence was imposing before, when he was seated, it was more so now.

'That will be all ... for now,' he announced. He took a few short paces to the door, threw it open and stood to one side.

I interpreted that as an invitation to leave and stood, wondering whether I should just go, and half expecting him to reprimand me if I tried.

He clicked his fingers and a guard appeared from the gloomy recess of a doorway across the corridor. I did not hesitate. I gathered my cloak and stepped past him.

'I'm going to be watching you,' he said in a low voice that chilled my blood. I felt his eyes following me until I was swallowed by the shadows as I ascended the steps to ground level and freedom.

EIGHTEEN

THE CHILL OF THE NIGHT air hit me and I started to shake. I hugged my arms to my chest and leaned against the wall, gulping in the crisp air, desperate to banish the stale, fetid taste of the Tolbooth from my mouth. Its smell clung to my clothes and skin, coating me in a shroud of filth that would be less easy to shake off. I waited for one of the guards to fetch Thunder, gazing up into the night sky, which was sprinkled with stars and illuminated by a moon that was almost a full circle. It was truly beautiful. When I dragged my eyes back to the frosty earth, which was glistening in the white light, Richard was crossing the road towards me, his horse's breath rising in misty tendrils as it hit the cold air. The guard arrived with Thunder and held out a hand to help me mount, but I brushed him away.

'Are you all right? I've been so worried. What did they want?' Richard demanded as soon as the guard had left us.

Such a torrent of words was more than I could cope with after the intensity of the interview I had just endured. But give my cousin his due, he did sound concerned. His hat was pulled low over his brow and his gown was wrapped high around his neck to protect against the cold, so I could see very little of his face. I urged Thunder forwards and Richard followed.

'Isabella,' he pleaded.

'I'll tell you everything, but not here in the street. Come, I'll get Mary to prepare some supper for us.'

'I seem to remember she tried to poison me last time you invited me for supper,' Richard grumbled, his tone petulant, and I almost laughed in spite of everything I had just been through.

We returned Thunder to his stable and left Richard's horse there too. I called to George to take care of them. We discarded our cloaks in the boot room. Mary must have heard us because the door to the kitchen opened, accompanied by a scratching of claws on the flagstone floor and I was almost knocked off my feet as Pepper flung himself at me, barking and butting me with his too-large head.

'Thank the Lord ye're safe,' Mary said, and I realised that Douglas must have called and told her I had been detained again. Maybe he was still here.

She read my mind and shook her head.

'I'm all right, truly I am,' I reassured her. 'But it's been a long time since we've eaten. Can you bring us some warm broth please. We'll be in my closet, but I must change first.'

I left Richard tending to the fire. Pepper refused to let me out of his sight. He clattered through the hall with me and squeezed by my side up the narrow stairs. I discarded my riding outfit and left it on the floor of my bedchamber where it fell. It was tainted with the stench of the Tolbooth and I was certain I would not wear those garments again. Besides, I thought that next time I had to visit the mine it would be more practical for me to wear men's clothing. I did not have the energy to dress properly, so contented myself with wriggling into a clean kirtle that would be considered perfectly adequate for most occasions, although perhaps not for a lady of my social standing to wear in public without a gown over the top, draped a shawl over the top, and re-joined my cousin. He stood in front of the fire, warming his hands, his red-gold beard glowing where it caught the light. He heard, or sensed my presence and turned towards me. His clothes were dusty from the day's hard riding and his features had none of that carefree nonchalance that I had come to associate with him. He appeared drawn and older.

He moved towards me, opened his arms and drew me into them. I should have resisted, but I did not. The warmth of another human body was what I needed more than anything. I allowed my head to settle on his shoulder, but my arms fell awkwardly by my side. The embrace was of a brotherly nature, and did not stir me in the way Will's had been wont to. It felt good to know that I had someone who cared, even though that person was Richard; the man who just a few weeks ago had been my arch enemy and I had wanted nothing more than to see him ride out of town, back to where he had come from. We stayed like that for several moments until Pepper inserted himself between us and we broke apart, just in time as Mary entered the room carrying a tray laden with bowls, a tureen of broth, fresh bread and a jug of wine. Richard took it from her, filled two goblets and handed one to me. We ate from our laps in front of the fire, and I told him what had happened at the Tolbooth, recounting the interview with Mr Warde as closely as I could. I did not tell him everything though. The suggestion that Douglas had shared with me that my father's death could be foul play, I kept to myself. Douglas had taken great care to talk to me out of earshot of Richard – was that because he did not like him, or he did not trust him?

'God's truth. What is going on?' Richard put his empty bowl on the floor and Pepper stuck his head into it and licked until it was spinning around like a child's toy. I would have reprimanded man and beast had my energy not been sapped. Richard's fingers moved to the gold ring in his ear and he twisted it in the gesture that was becoming very familiar to me. I believed he was entirely unaware he was doing it.

'I mean, what does Sir William Cecil want with us?'

'With me.' I corrected him, placing my empty bowl on the table by my side. 'Mr Warde knows of you, but he hasn't pulled you in for questioning because you've only been here for a few weeks, and whatever it is has been going on for much longer. He didn't actually say it, but if you had been there, in that tiny cell with him, his implication was clear. He knows that our business is in financial difficulty – I suspect we have Mr Young to thank for that – and he almost certainly knows about the smuggling, but he also believes that the Lady Isabella is being used to trade information for money.'

Richard nodded. 'Information of a sensitive or secretive nature that could be important for the security of the country, and the Queen. Did he accuse your father?'

'No, but who else could it be?'

'Why would he think that though? What evidence does he have?'

I shrugged. 'He cannot have any evidence, because it isn't true. '

'This is serious.' Richard's fingers stopped twisting the earring and he stared at me, his eyes wider than usual as if a realisation had just hit him. He pulled his chair closer to mine so he could speak in a low voice. 'He believes we are complicit in allowing our ship to send information to the French. Information like these plans of the defences they found, that might help the French to collude with the Scottish Regent and her daughter against our own Queen. Was Arthur dealing with your father?'

'Truly, I don't know.'

'You would tell me if you did wouldn't you? Think Isabella. There must be something.'

'My father was a kind man, gentle and loyal. I never knew him to have any association with Arthur. He didn't go out at night and refuse to tell me where he was going, and nor did we have strangers coming to the house for secret meetings. He spent most evenings alone in his closet. He was not involved with anything that could be of any use or interest to anyone who may be plotting against the Queen.'

'But he did manage to invest his fortune in a mining company that you knew nothing about, and smuggle wine that you knew nothing about. What else might he have been doing?'

'How dare you,' I hissed. 'You only met my father once or twice. You did not know him.'

'Nor, it would appear, did you.'

He reached for my hands. I tried to pull away but he was strong, and there was nowhere for me to go. In protest, I balled them into a fist and he enclosed them with his. Trapped, I breathed out my anger. It was habit, to leap to my father's defence, but Richard was right. I could not say with any certainty what he had or had not been involved with.

'I'm sorry if I've offended you,' Richard said.

'No, you're right to speak,' I admitted. 'It's just that it hurts so much, to realise that I didn't know him at all, and that he did not trust me or care for me enough to confide in me.'

'I'm sure he cared for you a lot and that's probably why he didn't share his problems with you. He was trying to protect you.'

Tears were welling up behind my eyes. I would have rubbed them away but Richard still held my hands captive in his own. It would not do to show weakness. I squeezed my eyes, trying to force the tears to disappear, and lowered my head hoping he would not notice. He released my hands and leaned back in his chair. I turned away, grateful for the moment to recompose myself. Pepper stirred at my feet, grunting in his sleep, ears twitching and tail jerking.

'You see, I didn't listen to my instincts. I had thought something was troubling him. He appeared preoccupied. At the time, I assumed it was worry about the Lady Isabella – she was late returning, and I didn't ask him what was wrong. If I had … if I'd taken the time to talk to him then, there's a chance he might have spoken to me, at least about some of this.'

'And he didn't say anything at all that might have been an indication of what he had on his mind?'

'No. Oh, I'd been pushing him for months to invest in a new ship. I was frustrated that he didn't agree, couldn't see that the Lady Isabella needed retiring to shorter trips, and in my arrogance and naivety I thought he might be about to admit that I was right. Little did I know.'

I drained my wine, fetched the jug from my desk where Richard had left it and refilled our goblets.

'After I started to find out about the debts and everything, I asked Mary if she'd noticed anything odd about my father's behaviour. She too had thought he had something on his mind, and had asked him about it, but he'd insisted there was nothing wrong. I asked Will as well. He and my father spent a lot of time together. He was shocked. He thought I was suggesting my father had taken his own life.'

Richard raised an eyebrow. There was something in his expression, an intelligence behind his hazel eyes, compassion too, that convinced me I could trust him.

'Richard, there's something else you should know.'

'Isabella, don't do this to me … the last time you said those words …'

'I know,' I interrupted him. 'It was this afternoon, when you rode ahead. I've not had time to think about this yet, but Douglas told me it was not surprising that Mr Warde should be interested in me, because not only do I regularly trade with Antwerp, but I'm connected to two suspicious deaths.'

A puzzled frown crossed Richard's face, so I elaborated. 'Arthur, and my father. Douglas implied my father was murdered.'

I did not add that he had hinted that Richard himself was suspected, and as I watched my cousin's reaction I was more certain than ever that if there had been foul play he was not involved. He stared at me, shock and disbelief shrouding his face, then he rested his elbows on his knees and dropped his head into his hands.

'What is happening?' he muttered. He raised his head. 'Maybe we should delay the Lady Isabella sailing.'

'What good would that do?'

He shrugged. 'If I leave you on your own, will you be safe? If Arthur and your father were both murdered. You might be next.'

'Don't.' I shuddered. That was a thought that had not occurred to me and I dismissed it at once. 'What would anyone gain from murdering me?'

'What did they gain from murdering Arthur and your father?'

'I don't know,' I admitted.

We were prevented from further speculation by a knock at the door. It was Mary.

'If ye've finished with your supper dishes may I clear them?'

I nodded.

'It's late,' she added, her eyes directed towards Richard.

'Yes Mary.'

I knew she was reminding me to protect my reputation. That people would talk, make assumptions, even though there could surely be nothing more natural than partners in business, cousins, discussing their mutual concerns. Part of me resented that she felt she needed to say something. After all, she was not my mother, and I was not a child. Furthermore, I cared nothing for the views of this town and those I had mistakenly thought were my friends, people who I could trust and turn to if I needed support. I could spit on them all. But it was late.

'Richard, you should leave. I'm tired. We can get no further with this tonight.'

He nodded, and followed Mary from the room.

For the next few days we concentrated on preparations for the Lady Isabella to sail. I left Richard in charge in the stores whilst I visited our regular customers for any specific orders, all the time letting it be known that we had a good stock of quality wine and were open for business. I received many a kind word about my father, and did my best to believe that they were honestly meant and to accept them as such. In equal measure, there were many curious enquiries about my cousin's unexpected arrival, accompanied, from some of our more elderly and long-standing clients, with comments about what a sad affair it had been when his mother, the aunt I had never known, had left in the way she had.

My days settled into a pattern, visiting customers in the morning, and returning to the stores in the afternoon to complete the paperwork, always with Pepper at my heels; he howled like a creature possessed of the Devil if I tried to leave him. I had become quite accustomed to his presence and drew many a strange glance from passers-by who heard me chatting to him as if he were a child.

I had not placed much faith in my cousin's abilities as a salesman, but in this, as in so many other ways, he proved me wrong. When I returned to the stores after my first morning spent visiting customers, weary from making idle talk with people I did not really care for, I noticed a stack of new cards on the table inside the door.

I picked one up and turned it over. It was handwritten in an attractive, cursive style on a thick, cream parchment:

Madam Isabella Gillhespy and Richard Elliott Esq

Fine wines, spices, tapestries, linens, pottery & curiosities

Briggate

It wasn't as prettily drawn as the ones I had done for my father; there was no decoration to the borders, and it was larger, but it was more descriptive, and a solid reminder that although my father might no longer be here, the business he had poured his life into would continue. I slipped a few into the pocket of my gown.

The following day when I returned to the stores I noticed that the racks of wine were beginning to thin out, and Richard was deep in conversation with a gentleman I recognised as being Lord Grey de Wilton's steward.

'What was all that about?' I asked after he had left.

'Spices, my dear cousin. He wants spices for the kitchen.'

I reinvested some of the money from the wine sales in more wool to trade when the Lady Isabella reached Antwerp.

We had several more conversations about Mr Warde's suspicions, but came no closer to any answers. Nor was there any news of Will. I had even asked Douglas, who appeared to be the fount of all knowledge, but he simply shook his head. Will seemed to have melted to nothing, carried away on the air, and I stopped worrying that some accident might have befallen him – it was far more likely that he had left town.

True to his word, Mr Warde was having me watched. Although he had warned me, I had not thought he meant in quite such a literal fashion. There were two of them, and usually when I left the house one of them would fall into step behind me as I turned out of Briggate. They did not try to go unobserved, so I did not pretend to be unaware of their presence. I even started to greet them with a little wave, and once I sent Mary out with some ale whilst they waited patiently for me to make an appearance. Although I tried to seem nonchalant, it was unnerving to be followed. I hoped that Mr Warde thought his efforts worthwhile. Piecing together my movements could not be the most exciting piece of intelligence work he had ever ordered.

Early in the afternoon, on the day the Lady Isabella was due to sail, Douglas paid us a visit, accompanied by John Bailey. The young man was quite excited. I called George to mind the stores and we took them to my closet.

'Sit down gentlemen, please.' I indicated the hard-backed chairs in front of the desk, and seated myself behind it. Richard remained standing by my side. John paused to look around the room, turning slowly. His eyes rested on the portrait of my father. He removed his hat and lowered his head before turning back to me, sitting down and clutching his hat in his lap. I thought I detected a brightness to his eyes that had not been there before, but he blinked and it vanished. It was probably my imagination, but then I remembered what he had said about my father when we had visited the mine, how he was well liked and respected, and it hit me that John had cared for him. For a moment I envied this young man, who was mourning the person he had known, whereas the person I had known had been steadily dismantled in the weeks since his death, so that sometimes it felt that he had never existed at all.

'I've spoken to the men,' John was saying. His voice brought me back to the moment and I forced myself to concentrate on his words. 'Some of them aint keen but I think they can be persuaded. I've had a closer look at the site, and I've put up some fencing to keep people away from the areas that are most unstable. This leaves a partially exposed seam on which we could start work.'

I frowned. He was impatient to return to work. I could appreciate that, but he had acted without my instruction. He was leaning forward in his chair now, explaining in more detail how they could approach the seam and then his plans for making safe the rest of the site. I held up my hand to stop him.

'Mr Bailey. I appreciate your enthusiasm, truly I do. But since we last met I have not had time to consider the mine. Preparations for the Lady Isabella to sail have consumed all of my time.' I did not add my need to be cautious. That keen though I was to recover some of my father's investment if it were at all possible, if what had happened since his death had taught me anything, it was that taking time to plan and gain a thorough understanding of the situation before committing was not just desirable, but prerequisite to success.

'Would you excuse us for a moment gentlemen?' Richard put a hand on my arm and leaned in close to whisper in my ear. 'A word please.'

There was a tone of authority in that whisper that irked me. It was not a request, but a command.

He stepped away, giving me space to move out from behind my desk. I raised my eyes to the ceiling. Saint Oswald save me from interfering men. I did not want to argue with him in front of Douglas and John, so I nodded at them with an apologetic smile, bottling my anger to be unleashed on Richard, and followed him into the hall.

Before he could speak I turned on him. 'What do you think you're doing? Why are you undermining me?'

'You seem to be forgetting that these are not your decisions to make alone.'

'It would be reckless to press ahead with the mine at the moment,' I persisted.

'Why?' he asked, an innocent smile spreading across his face, eyes widening. He was teasing me.

'Stop playing games,' I snapped. 'You know the reasons as well as I do.'

'Were you not listening? I know that John Bailey is an intelligent young man who is eager to get back to work. I know that for very little resource we could start getting coal out of the ground and onto our ships that are sailing anyway up and down the coast. In my view it would be foolish of us not to do it. After all, so much has been invested in this venture already. Now we have an opportunity to start seeing some of that money back. What has happened to your spirit? It's not so very long ago that you were willing to borrow money for a new ship. Now you won't even take the chances that are under your nose. Really, Isabella, I'm disappointed.'

'I can live with that.' I threw back at him. 'Perhaps you would like to explain how I'm supposed to oversee the mine, the stores and the ships by myself. In case you had forgotten, you're sailing with the Lady Isabella tonight.'

He dropped his teasing smile and assumed an expression of mock seriousness; eyes stern, brows drawn together and one finger raised, as though a thought of some significance had just occurred to him.

'How could I forget,' he said. 'I've been looking forward to it for days … and no, you cannot persuade me to stay here and help you when I could be spending weeks on the open seas with Captain Thirlwell – who thinks I'm not up to the task and a foreigner at that – and his band of merry men, most of whom I'm sure are looking forward to nothing more than seeing me hanging over the side of the ship saying goodbye to my supper.'

The absurdity of his words, in contrast to the look on his face, diffused the tension like smoke escaping a room through an open door and I had to laugh. He joined in.

'I'm just being cautious,' I said.

'Don't. It doesn't suit you. What have we got to lose? John Bailey is more than capable of overseeing the mine, and I think we can trust him.'

'Very well. We'll do it your way,' I conceded defeat, and pushed passed him.

Douglas and John had been talking but they fell silent as Richard and I re-entered the room.

'Mr Bailey, you have a deal,' I said.

His face broke into a broad smile. 'Thank you Madam Gillhespy.

209

You will not regret it, I promise.'

It was only later that afternoon, as I was preparing to honour my father's tradition of taking supper on board the Lady Isabella on the evening before she sailed, that I realised I did care that Richard might be disappointed in me. Furthermore, I was going to miss him.

NINETEEN

CAPTAIN THIRLWELL SENT WORD THAT he would be honoured to welcome me on board the Lady Isabella at 6 o'clock. She would sail with the turning tide, just before midnight, but the watch bell would sound at 8 o'clock for the gates to be closed, so I had to be safely back within the walls by then.

The captain had been concerned when I had first told him that I would honour my father's tradition, and questioned how I would manage to climb the rope ladder to board the ship, but I had assured him that I would be more than able. I had a plan, one that I did not share with him, and as I dressed for the occasion – pulling on a pair of dark grey hose that had once belonged to my father, a white shirt, grey doublet and a small ruff, I could not help smiling at the thought of what he, and my cousin, would say when they saw me. Although I wore my own boots, I donned a short black cloak that had also been my father's and which extended to just below my knee. The male clothing would make it easy for me to board the ship, and substituting my cloak for my father's would, I hoped, fool Mr Warde's men. In truth I was becoming tired of being shadowed by them, and thought it would be fun to try to slip past them, mistaken for a messenger or a clerk. To complete the look I coiled my hair, pinned it close to my head and chose a simple felt hat.

The disguise worked. I walked straight past the first of my personal guards, who was leaning against the gable end of the house at the end of Briggate, turned right, nodded to the soldiers at Segate, and reached the quay without a hint of recognition from any of them.

A member of Captain's Thirlwell's crew was waiting on the jetty. A small rowing boat tethered to it was bobbing on the incoming tide. His eyes widened as I approached and he helped me into the boat, although he knew better than to make any comment. Scaling the rope ladder that hung over the side of the Lady Isabella was tricky, even in my male clothing, but the effort was worth it when I reached her deck. This was my ship and I loved her to the soles of my boots. In the gloaming she was beautiful, all shiny brass and polished wood.

The captain greeted me with raised eyebrows. Standing by his side, my cousin smiled. 'Isabella! Glad to see you have dressed for the occasion. And what a picture you make.'

'Don't bother with the witticism dear cousin. You can have no idea how liberating it is to be free of those heavy skirts. I think I may dress like this more often.'

Both men stared at me. Captain Thirlwell seemed shocked, as if he had never seen a woman dressed in men's clothing before – maybe he hadn't – whilst Richard appeared about to dissolve into laughter.

The captain found his voice first. 'This way please.' He led the way to his cabin at the stern of the ship where one of his two rooms was dominated by a large oak table. In my memory of visits to the Lady Isabella as a little girl, this table was always draped in maps and charts that were as fascinating as they were unfathomable. This evening it was laid for supper for three. The mouth-watering aroma of roasting meat mingled with something sweet and filled the small space. I removed my father's cloak and took the chair Richard pulled out for me. He gave a mock bow and his eyes swept over me in a way that I could not help thinking was far from a look suitable for bestowing on a cousin. My skin glowed and I was grateful that Captain Thirlwell chose that moment to hand me a goblet of wine, which gave me an excuse to turn away.

'To the Lady Isabella,' I said, raising my drink and tipping it towards the captain like the doff of a cap. 'You've done well. She feels fresh and invigorated.'

I spoke the truth. The vision I held inside my head of my beloved ship was a faded version of her former self, like a once beautiful young woman now aged and lined with the scars of life, but the beauty is still there if you are bold enough to peer beneath the surface. I was not so naive though that I did not realise that the transformation was superficial. The Lady Isabella was still tired and we still needed to invest in a new ship.

Captain Thirlwell bowed his head in acknowledgement of the compliment and turned the conversation to the detail of the voyage, whilst the ship cook served us with a tasty soup followed by duck and a dessert of steamed, dried fruit and honey. Richard contributed little to the conversation, and nor did he appear to have much appetite; I could not help but notice his plates were removed still laden with food. His father might have been a sailor, but he clearly was not. I had a pang of guilt that I had insisted he should sail with the ship, but I pushed it away. He had suggested the spice trade, and it needed someone to set it up. I could not go, so that meant he had to.

When we had finished supper and one of the crew had cleared the remnants of our meal and left the cabin, the captain poured a whisky for each of us. Richard might have had no appetite for the food, but he knocked the whisky back in one gulp and refilled his tumbler. Captain Thirlwell swirled the amber liquid around in his, before doing the same.

'We had an inspection earlier today,' he said, a serious tone to his voice which drew my immediate attention.

'Is that unusual?' I enquired, knowing that there must have been something out of the ordinary or he would not have mentioned it.

'We always see one of the customs officials, often your Mr Ord.'

I squirmed at the reference. He was no longer my Mr Ord. That piece of news could not have reached the captain.

'But these were strangers.'

'What did they want?' I tried to keep my voice casual, which was not easy when my throat was of a sudden as parched as the sand on Spittal beach at low tide. I downed my whisky and poured another.

'One of them demanded to see the inventory of cargo and a list of crew as well as any other passengers we may be carrying. The others wanted to see it for themselves.'

I raised an eyebrow.

'They wanted a tour of the ship, including the cabins, and I don't think it was because they were considering going into the business themselves. What's happening?'

'I wish I knew.' I forced myself to meet the captain's eyes. It was true that I did not know, although I had my suspicions, and those I was not prepared to share.

He sighed and pushed himself to his feet, lowering his head as it brushed the ceiling of the cabin.

'It's getting late,' he said. 'Someone will row you back to shore and we must start to prepare for departure.'

'You missed a very fine supper there,' I said to Richard when the captain had left the cabin.

'No appetite,' he replied. 'I don't like this.'

'I had realised that you have not your father's sea legs.'

'You misunderstand – I think intentionally. You know what I mean.'

'Richard. We've already had this conversation. I've done nothing wrong, and I can take care of myself.'

'I don't wish to argue with you, but I beg to differ.'

'You're arguing with me then. Don't. It's too late to change our plans now and for what? For some implied suspicion of something I'm not guilty of.'

'If I had a halfpenny for every innocent man that has been falsely accused and found guilty I would be rich.'

'Perhaps we should both be grateful then that I'm a woman.' I looked down at my male attire. 'Although I do find this outfit quite comfortable.'

'Isabella,' Richard was fit to explode with indignation, but I had heard enough. I silenced him with a shake of my head, pulled the cloak around my shoulders and followed the captain out into the cool air. On the deck I paused to allow my eyes to adjust; there were no stars to pierce a hole in the total blackness of the night, and the moon too was hiding. The water slurped as it lapped greedily at the Lady Isabella's hull, its inky depths below me, stretching as far as the quay. The outline of the town walls was just discernible by a different texture to the darkness. I knew Richard had followed me, but I did not turn around, and instead allowed my feet to feel their way across the deck, which was now lurching and swaying in the swell of the current. The captain was giving instructions to one of his deckhands who was lowering himself down the ladder into the small rowing boat that would take me back to shore.

'Wait.'

I turned, ready to reprimand Richard if he started to voice his objections once again, but he did not. Instead, he drew me to him and enfolded me in an embrace that would have made the sirens blush until the captain cleared his throat and I pulled away, shaken.

'I wish you a safe voyage Captain Thirlwell.' I extended my right hand to him. He regarded it warily for a moment and then gripped it. His hand was large and his skin rough. Before he could misunderstand my meaning, I shook it, as a man to a man.

'Will there be no book to take to your relative in Antwerp this time, Madam Gillhespy?'

He released my hand. In the dark it was difficult to read the expression in his eyes, but he was watching me, measuring my reaction. I knew nothing of any relatives in Antwerp, or that my father was in the habit of sending books to anyone. The night closed in around us, reducing my world in that moment to just me, the captain and Richard, and the realisation that this was what Mr Warde had been seeking. Just when I was beginning to think I had discovered all of my father's secrets, this one could be the biggest and most dangerous of them all. Memories, small and insignificant, started to slot into place, like searching in vain for my copy of Le

Morte d'Arthur. So I had been wrong, and my father had been a traitor. I could not believe it, would not believe it.

The air was so close now it was stifling. I filled my lungs but it did nothing to relieve the pressure inside my head. Above me, tiny pin holes had started piercing the clouds with light, the brightness of which I had never seen before.

'Oh. Was this a regular arrangement?' I asked. I was unwilling to appear uninformed, although I had a suspicion that the Captain did not believe this story of a relative. He was not asking me a question, he was trying to tell me something. Something that he thought I ought to know.

'For the last year or so.' He nodded.

'And what were your instructions?'

'Mr Ord was always most particular that your father did not wish me to be inconvenienced in any way, so my instructions were always to give the book to one of the merchants we buy our wine from as the trade was being concluded. Where it went after that, or who may have collected it, I never knew.'

Will! Will was involved in this. It's fortunate that the Lady Isabella's deck had a high wooden railing, because otherwise the step back I took would have tipped me over the side and into the cold waters of the Tweed below. But why was I surprised? I knew he had been involved in the smuggling. What else? And who had coerced who? Will had said the smuggling had been my father's idea, but trading secret documents with our Queen's enemies was something else. It all came back to Arthur. He was the source of the information, and it was Will who had been Arthur's friend, not my father.

Richard had followed this exchange, but remained silent. I could no more see his expression than I could that of the captain, but I did not need to see it to know what he was thinking. Captain Thirlwell's attention was drawn away by one of the crew and Richard leaned towards me. 'God's truth, Isabella. Do you know what this means? I think we should delay our sailing for 24 hours.'

'No.' I swallowed back the bile that was rising in my throat. 'If this plot has all been Will's doing, whatever information is being sent to the Queen's enemies stops now. Will has disappeared and nothing has been slipped aboard. Mr Warde can watch all he likes, but he won't find anything, because there's nothing to find.'

'He won't like it that you sneaked by his guards dressed as a man, deliberately to deceive him.'

'If he finds out.'

'He will find out, and it makes you appear guilty.'

'If we delay the sailing it makes us look guilty and what reason would we give? Besides, I dressed as a man tonight for very practical reasons, which I can explain if I have to.'

'Madam Gillhespy, please, you need to leave us now,' the captain interrupted us and I acted on his words. Turning my back on my cousin I nodded at the captain and swung myself out onto the ladder, making tight fists around the rungs as the ship pitched in the roiling water. Richard leaned over the side and watched me disappear into the night. In the few minutes it took to row me to shore I continued pondering what the captain had revealed. I still found it difficult to believe that my father had been involved at all. He had deceived and betrayed me in so many ways, but a traitor? A secret supporter of the Scottish claim to the English throne? No, that I could not believe. Which had to mean that Will was, and that I found difficult to believe as well. He had always been very vocal about his dislike and distrust of our Scottish neighbours, but that might have been intended to deflect any suspicion.

The question was, what should I do with this new information, and did it have the importance that Richard and I both assumed? All I really knew for certain was that Will had been sending books to someone in Antwerp. I did not know how those books had been used to deliver information – pages cut out so that maps and plans could be concealed within their covers maybe, or secret messages hidden within their words? It could all be very innocent, but it probably wasn't. Mr Warde would know what to make of it, but could I tell him without putting a noose around my own neck?

The light on the shore was less dense. The lanterns hanging at Bridge Gate and Segate cast shadows of boats and towers that shimmered across the black surface of the river. As I hurried across the jetty, aware that the watch bell would sound soon, I saw a familiar figure, keeping close to the wall so he would not be spotted by the guards above, and moving along the quay beyond Segate towards the ocean. I must be mistaken. Thinking of Will, my overwrought imagination had conjured his likeness. I blinked and rubbed my eyes, but no, the figure was still there. It was one I would recognise anywhere.

I should have been relieved that he was alive and well, but after what I had just learned I could have killed him myself, with my bare hands. Maybe it would have been sensible to take time to think before rushing in. My father's words came back to me once again. *'Never act in haste.'* Last time I had chosen to ignore that advice, when I had confronted Mr Young about his involvement with the mining company, I had opened a door not knowing what I would find, but the outcome had at least provided answers. If I had baulked at that, waited to think so I could process what I knew, or thought I knew, I might still be no wiser about the extent to which that odious man had encouraged my father into reckless spending. Besides, I might not get another opportunity. I pushed my father's voice out of my head, ran along the quay, and when the cobbles ran out I plunged through the shallow waters in pursuit of Will.

The wet sand sucked at my boots making my progress slow and noisy, but Will was so intent on his own actions that he did not appear to notice me. By the time I caught up with him, he was dragging a small boat from the shadows at the furthest point of the quay beneath the New Tower, close to where the Lady Isabella had been careened just a few weeks ago. He threw a bundle into the boat and started pushing it into the water. I put my fingers to my lips and whistled in a most unladylike way. I did not dare call out to him though for fear of alerting any guards who might be on lookout in the tower.

Will heard me and stopped. He turned around, his shoulders tense, one hand on the boat and the other behind his back. I was close enough now that I could smell him. The musky, animal scent that I have always associated with Will, but mingled with something else, a staleness that I did not remember. His beard was ungroomed and hung from his chin like ribbons of weed from the sea, and his face was shadowed with several days growth where it had not been barbered. His cloak was as crumpled as ever.

'I know everything,' I said in a low voice.

His shoulders relaxed a little. 'Izzy? Is that you? Whatever are you wearing?'

I ignored him.

'How could you do that. The smuggling was bad enough, but a traitor too. And using my ship.'

He laughed. That low chuckle that used to fill me with delight, but no longer. Now I wanted to ram it back into his throat so hard that he choked.

'You know, that's one of your most irritating features. You think you know everything, when really you know nothing. If we had ever married that is something I would have found very difficult to live with. Although I must say, in that outfit it is clear that you have other attributes that I'm sure I would have enjoyed.'

His eyes travelled over me and I was aware that my male clothing revealed more of my curves than he was accustomed to seeing. I dragged my cloak tight around me and tried to ignore his barbs. His words stung, but I could not let him divert me from what I had to know.

'What was in the books?' I pressed. 'I don't have any relations in Antwerp. So what was in the books? Information that could be used to help the Scottish Regent and her daughter's claim to become Queen of England? But what I don't understand is why. Was it money? How much did they pay you to become a traitor?'

I heard a bell ring in the near distance. The watch bell, signalling curfew and the closure of the gates. Even if I had turned and run, I would not have reached them in time. Will laughed again and took a step closer to me. One of his hands was still on the boat, but as he moved his other arm from behind his back I could see he was holding a knife.

'Like I said. You know nothing. Do you really think I care enough about one Queen or another to risk my life for their cause? No.'

He shook his head. The whites of his eyes were flashing, giving him a beast-like appearance. A man no longer in control of his emotions. My feet were sinking into the sand and the cold water of the Tweed was swirling around my ankles, anchoring me to the spot. This person in front of me was not the man I thought I had known, and for the first time it occurred to me that by approaching him I might have put my life in danger.

'It wasn't me sending information to the French. It was Arthur. He found out about the smuggling and blackmailed me. I had no choice. If I'd refused, he would have told Dixon.'

'You always have a choice. You could have stopped the smuggling. Paid the levies. There would still have been a healthy profit.'

'No, we couldn't. It was too lucrative. But Arthur's scheme was about to come unstuck. He'd been warned to be more careful. That Cecil suspected there was a leak here in Berwick. I told him I wanted no further part in it, and he said he would make good on his threat to expose me.'

Will paused. My instinct urged me to turn and run, but I was held by a horrible fascination. I both needed, and dreaded, to hear what he would say next.

'He angered me, but I had to make it appear as an accident, so I took him by surprise, grabbed him and slammed his head into the wall, then pushed him over the top of the tower.'

I could not help myself from crying out, and I held my hand to my mouth to stifle the noise. A murderer. I had been in love with a murderer.

'And then you, foolish woman that you are, refused to cooperate. I suppose I should have expected that. You're as weak as your father, but I dealt with him. With Arthur out of the way too there was no longer anything to stop us becoming the greatest merchant in Berwick. Your cousin was a setback, but that milksop was not going to stand in my way. The debt too, but that wasn't so great – I knew you had enough to cover it.' He appeared pensive, stroking his beard with the thumb of his hand that held the knife, and then added, 'but no, it was you who spoilt everything.'

The words that were spewing from his mouth hit me with such force that I believe I would have staggered had my feet not been held firmly in place by the wet sand. A cold fist of fear wrapped itself around my heart and squeezed so tight I gasped for breath. 'What do you mean, you dealt with my father?' I spluttered.

He laughed. 'Oh Izzy, if you could only see your face. I didn't kill him. That's what you're thinking isn't it?' He shook his head. 'Although I admit I was prepared to. But no, his heart saved me the bother. You see, we were arguing. He wanted to tell you about the smuggling. Said you were doing so much of the paperwork that you would be sure to spot it. He seemed to think you're smart. He didn't want you to be involved. I told him I could not let that happen. He tried to insist so I pulled out my knife, took a few steps closer to him, and then his face sort of collapsed, one hand clutched his heart and the other tried to hold onto the back of the chair, but he slumped to the floor. I watched until he stopped twitching, waited for a few more minutes until I was certain he was dead, and then I picked him up and placed him in his chair behind the desk, arranged him, well, how you found him.'

Will had become more animated as he spoke, the knife in his hand dancing to the cold and warped logic of his words. Words that could only stem from a mind that was confused, and the wonder was that I had never noticed. I watched and listened in mute horror until the perilous nature of my situation hit me. I was alone, outside the town walls, after curfew, with a murderer, and I was in no doubt he would not think twice about killing me to save his own skin.

I had no time to process what he had just told me. I yanked my right foot out of the sucking sand with a splash, stepped back and was about to repeat the manoeuvre with my left, but Will was too quick. He let go of the boat and lunged towards me. I twisted away from him, but I could not move far enough. He seized my left arm and at that moment the sand released its grip on my foot and I lurched to one side, dragging Will with me. He slashed at me with his right hand, the one still holding the knife. A sharp pain ripped through my forearm and I glanced down to see a dark stain spreading across the white linen of my shirt. Will either did not notice or did not care. He moved so he was behind me, with the knife pressed against my throat and started pushing me towards the boat.

'Get in,' he commanded.

'How far do you think you're going to get in that boat on this ocean?'

'There you go again, being stupid. You need to hurry, you've cost me a lot of time.' He glanced out across the river, where the masts of the Lady Isabella were just visible, and I realised his escape plan was to sail away on my ship.

'Do you really think Captain Thirlwell will just allow you on board?' I shook my head.

'Of course not, stupid,' he snapped back at me. 'He and the crew will be so busy setting sail that they won't notice. But we have to hurry. The tide will soon be turning.'

'We? I'm not going anywhere.'

'I don't think you're in a position to argue.' He pushed me into the little rowing boat, but as he was reaching for the rope he was knocked off his feet by a snarling, long-haired beast with a whiskery face and a head that was too large for its body.

'Pepper.' I gasped.

Will landed on his back in the shallow water and Pepper jumped onto his chest, pinning him down and baring his teeth. The knife fell with a clatter into the boat and I picked it up and clambered out, landing in the water with a splash that soaked me to my waist. Will was wrestling with Pepper and I was certain it would be only a matter of time before he threw my hound off and what then? I had the knife, but I was not strong enough to overpower Will, especially when he was being driven by desperation.

'Help,' I shouted as loudly as I could. I would have to take my chances with the town guard or I would be as dead as my father and Arthur. But it was not the town guard that I saw hurtling towards me. Two burly figures had emerged from the shadows of the town walls and were running across the sands. As they approached I recognised them with some relief as two of the guards that Mr Warde had instructed to follow me.

'Help,' I shouted again. 'Over here.'

TWENTY

I DID NOT KNOW HOW long I had been sitting, huddled on the cold floor, leaning against the stone wall, unable to stop shaking.

I was back at the Tolbooth, only this time I was in one of the ground floor rooms. There was a fire, so I was not shaking from the cold. A pitcher of wine had been left on the table, but I did not have the strength to get to my feet and pour myself a drink.

The door was closed and I was pretty sure there would be a guard on the other side. My surroundings might be slightly more luxurious than on the previous occasions I had been brought here, but I did not fool myself. I was still being detained, not that I was in any fit state to go anywhere. The shock of Will's final betrayal had left me numb, drained of physical and emotional strength. His words replayed on a loop inside my head. That he had admitted to murdering Arthur was bad enough, but that he had stood over my father and watched him die without trying to help him, chilled me to the very core of my being. How could anyone be that evil?

It was the thought of how he had deceived me in the ensuing weeks that started my pulse racing again. He had pretended to sympathise with me, console me when I had blamed myself for not noticing my father might have been ill, and all the time he had known what had really happened, and it was he, not I, who could have done something to change the outcome.

My recollection of the evening's events became hazy after I had seen Mr Warde's men sprinting towards me. I remembered a lot of shouting, and Pepper barking as if he were possessed of a demon. One of the guards had grabbed my injured arm and I'd screamed, which had sent Pepper into an even greater frenzy and the other guard had been forced to restrain him. In the confusion, Will had slipped away. One of the guards had carried me here, Pepper snapping at his heels, and the other had disappeared, I guessed in pursuit of Will.

My arm throbbed and I tried not to look at the blood-soaked sleeve of my shirt, which was sticking to the wound. Someone had fashioned a tourniquet from a torn strip of cloth, which had at least stopped the bleeding.

The pain in my arm was very real, but it was subdued by the pain in my chest. If a heart could break, then mine surely was. I had been planning, and looking forward to, a future with a man who was nothing short of a monster. Even worse, he had deceived me with such ease. Will had never cared for me. His objection to delaying our marriage was not because he could not wait for us to be together, or even because he thought me incapable – much as I had found that sentiment infuriating at the time. He was not interested in me. All he had ever been interested in was the money. If I had told him the full extent of my father's debt, I wonder if he would have left, like I had once thought Richard would, or if he would have continued to press me to marry as soon as possible so he could assume control and strike some agreement with Mr Young. As long as we were not married he was vulnerable. He had no claim to my father's business without me, and he suspected that if I found out about the smuggling I would refuse to allow it to continue. If we had been married by the time I discovered the truth though, I would have had no authority to deny him. My assets would have become his. My voice would have been silenced. He would have had to deal with Richard, though, a further complication. What would my cousin have done? Would he have opposed Will or gone along with him?

The Lady Isabella would have sailed by now and it would be weeks, nay months, before she returned. I lifted my head and closed my eyes. 'Saint Oswald, keep her safe, and all who sail on her,' I whispered.

The door handle rattled. I opened my eyes and was surprised to find my vision blurred by tears. Mr Hedley brushed past the guard, carrying his worn brown leather medical satchel. The guard followed, closed the door behind him and stood in front of it, arms folded across his chest, sword hanging by his side.

The physician's eyes ranged around the room before they alighted on me. He rushed to my side.

'Madam Gillhespy,' he exclaimed. 'Whatever has happened? No, don't answer that. Let me help you to a chair.'

He reached for my injured arm, noticed the bloody sleeve and moved to my other side. I allowed him to extend one arm behind my back and half lift, half pull me to my feet. My legs would not behave though, and he had to support me to a chair. Was I mistaken or did his eyes widen just a fraction when he noticed my clothing? He made no comment, but noticing the pitcher of wine on the table, he poured a mug and held it out to me.

'Drink,' he commanded. 'It will help.'

He wrapped his hands around mine to support the mug and allow me to lift it to my mouth. Teeth chattering, I managed a few sips and felt the syrupy liquid sliding down my throat.

Mr Hedley dragged another chair so it was adjacent to me and reached for my arm. I winced as he released the tourniquet and started to pull at the fabric of my sleeve.

Grim-faced, he reached for some scissors from his case. 'Fetch me some water,' he demanded of the guard, whilst to me he said, 'I'm sorry, but I'm going to have to cut the sleeve off.'

As soon as the guard had left the room, Mr Hedley leaned back and appraised me. 'I'm not going to ask what has happened, or why I'm treating you here and not at your home, but I want you to know that I am a friend, and if there's anything you would like to talk about, I'm willing to listen, and help, if it is in my power.'

His eyes met mine, kind and not judging, before sliding away as the guard returned with a bowl of water. I gritted my teeth whilst he soaked, tugged and snipped at the fabric, and averted my eyes when he cleaned the wound.

'Fortunately the knife was sharp and straight,' he declared. 'A serrated or blunter edge would have made for a nastier wound. This is neat. Long, but not too deep. I'll dress it properly. You'll need to keep it clean, rest the arm, and I'll change the dressing every day until it starts to heal. As long as it doesn't become infected, it should heal well. You'll have a scar though.'

What did I care about a scar? Most of the time it would be covered by the sleeve of my gown anyway. 'Thank you,' I murmured.

He replaced his scissors and dressing materials and clicked his case shut. 'Remember, if there is anything I can do, you have only to ask. Good day to you.'

The guard left with him and I was alone again with my thoughts, but not for long. After a few minutes the door opened and there, framed in the opening, stood the man I had most dreaded seeing. Mr Warde. He closed the door behind him, walked slowly across the room and lowered himself into a chair across the table from me.

'Madam. I think it's time for you to tell me what you know, don't you?'

I remained silent.

'I see you are still reluctant, so let me start. When we last talked you told me you did not know of the whereabouts of William Ord, and yet this evening you were caught with him, and some kind of scuffle was taking place. A falling out between conspirators? A lover's spat?'

'What I told you before is the truth,' I insisted. 'We are no longer betrothed, and I don't know where he has been these last weeks. I had been on the Lady Isabella for a farewell supper with the captain and my cousin before she set sail – it was a custom of my father's and I intend to uphold it. As I'm sure you're aware, she sailed on the turn of the tide. When I returned to shore, I saw Will creeping along the shadows of the town wall and approached him.'

Mr Warde waited, tempting me into saying more. But what could I say? My mouth was dry and I reached for a sip of wine. He watched, and waited.

'Why did you approach him? If you're no longer in a relationship, why not simply go home?'

227

I had fallen into his trap. My mind was not thinking clearly. I had given him a morsel of information and opened myself up to more questions that I did not know how to answer.

'Why did you dress to deceive my men this evening? What were you trying to hide?'

'Have you ever tried to climb a rope ladder to board a ship wearing a woman's gown?'

'Very good Madam Gillhespy,' he nodded. 'But you must admit that it was rather convenient that your attire fooled my men and allowed you to pass unnoticed to meet with whomever you chose. I have only your word that you were on board the Lady Isabella.'

'You're twisting everything,' I protested. Richard had warned me that this would make me appear guilty. What's more, had I not deceived Warde's men – an action I had taken great delight in – they would have been able to verify that I was speaking the truth. 'I admit that I was finding their constant presence annoying, but my choice of dress this evening was for purely practical reasons.'

'Unfortunately, since the ship has sailed we cannot prove that you were on board.'

I opened my mouth and closed it again. What could I say that would not incriminate me further in this man's mind?

'So I ask you again, why did you approach Ord?'

I fumbled for the words, any words, to give him a good reason, one that he would believe. But all I could think of was the truth, and this man might not even believe that, or that I was not aware of any of it until tonight. He leaned back, casual, giving the impression of a man who could wait until he got what he wanted, but his next words conveyed a very different message.

'It will go better for you if you tell me what you know. My men are very skilled at encouraging people to talk, but I think you and I could come to some agreement.'

My skin itched with the feet of thousands of insects. I did not care to think about what pain might be inflicted on flesh and bone by those tasked with securing a confession – whether the victim was guilty or not – or what kind of agreement he might have in his mind. The power that this man held was palpable. He could destroy me with a click of his fingers, and he was giving me little choice.

But it was a choice.

I could tell him what I had discovered and he still might not believe me innocent, but if I did not I had no doubt that he would not hold back until he was satisfied I had told him all I knew, even if that was very little. To expect any clemency would be foolish.

I took a deep breath of the stale air and chose my words with care. 'I learned this evening that Will, Mr Ord, had been deceiving us, and using the Lady Isabella for his own purposes.'

'I know about the smuggling, a little scheme with which I believe your father was wholly complicit.'

I had suspected as much. 'I myself learned of that only recently, after my father's death, and when I refused to continue it marked the end of my relationship with Mr Ord.'

Mr Warde's face gave little away. He had to believe me, but I would not beg him. I might have fallen low, but I still had my pride.

'Go on,' he prompted. 'What did you learn tonight?'

'It was something Captain Thirlwell said. He asked me if I had a book to send to my relatives in Antwerp.'

Mr Warde sat up a little straighter. This was what he wanted. His eyes drilled into me and it took a huge effort to stop mine sliding away to meet the wall over his shoulder. That would make me appear guilty, and my life depended on this man believing I had known nothing prior to this evening.

'I have no relatives in Antwerp. Not that I know of anyway. It seems that on recent voyages, Will had been giving a book to the captain, with instructions to deliver it to one of the merchants we deal with there. I don't know which merchant, or what the books contained, but I was suspicious. There was no time to question him further – and anyway, I don't believe he knew much more, if anything. I had to return to shore, and my head was full of what I had just heard and what it could mean, so when I recognised Will,

I approached him. It may have been foolish of me, but I didn't think he would harm me, and I still had no idea of the extent of his betrayal.'

My voice was croaky and I reached again for my wine with a hand that trembled. Mr Warde watched me in silence. The next part of my story would surely sentence Will to death, but I could find no alternative. This man could see into my soul. He would not rest until he had extracted every morsel of information from me, and I owed no loyalty to Will. Even so, the thought of being the cause of his downfall – and possibly also my own – was not a comfortable one.

'Will admitted to using the books to send information to supporters of the Scottish Queen, but he said he cared nothing for her claim. He said he was being blackmailed by his friend, Arthur Fewell who had learned of the smuggling scheme and threatened to expose him. He …' I paused. A lump was forming in my throat, blocking the words.

'Let me see if I can help.' Mr Warde intervened. 'Ord met with his friend, in the Black Watch Tower. There was a disagreement between them. Perhaps Ord wanted to stop and Fewell said he would make good on his threat, so Ord hit him over the head with a heavy object and pushed him over the edge of the tower to fall to his death.'

I inclined my head. 'Almost,' I whispered. 'He murdered Arthur, and he as good as murdered my father too.'

Mr Warde stood, pushing his chair backwards so it ground against the wall. 'Wait here,' he commanded. Unnecessary, as I could not go anywhere without tackling the guard, which I was definitely not capable of. 'I'll have some food sent.' He cast back over his shoulder.

Alone again, I hugged my arms around myself to try to stop shivering, taking care not to jolt my injured arm. Mr Warde was true to his word, and after a short while a guard arrived with some bread and cheese. I had no appetite so left it untouched, but I did pour some more wine. Mr Hedley had been right, it did help. I mulled over the conversation with Mr Warde. Had he believed me? And where had he gone?

I do not know how long he left me there for. Eventually I slept, with my head resting on my good arm on the table, and awoke to the rattle of the door opening again. The night had lifted, and a weak shaft of sunlight painted stripes across the wall.

'You're free to leave,' the guard informed me. It was one of the men who had been tailing me. 'I'm to escort you back to your home where you are to remain until Mr Warde calls on you later today.'

I rose, groggy, onto shaky legs. The guard held an arm out to help me but I did not take it. He stepped back to let me pass and followed.

Outside, the day was bright. Unlike the previous occasions when I had been released from the suffocating air of the Tolbooth, today there was no-one waiting for me. Or at least, no person, but rather an ugly, unruly brute of a dog launched itself at me.

'Pepper,' I gasped, raising my injured arm so he could not reach it. With my good hand I stroked his shaggy head and his rough tongue licked my wrist.

'He's been out here all night,' the guard said. 'We tried to shoo him away but he wouldn't leave.'

Pepper fell into step by my side. We made an unusual threesome, me still dressed as a man, the dog who stuck to my side like resin oozing from a tree, and the town guard, whose presence meant no-one approached us although we drew plenty of curious glances. I did not care, but longed only for some rose-scented water with which to wash and a change of clothes.

It was clear that Mr Warde did not trust me to obey his instructions. When we reached my house, instead of taking his leave the guard positioned himself outside the front door. I wondered if there would be another at the rear.

Mary was in the kitchen, and to my surprise Douglas was with her. I raised an eyebrow, but said nothing.

'Thank the Lord ye're safe,' Mary said, rushing towards me. She opened her arms to pull me into them and then stopped. 'Ye're injured. And what are ye wearing?'

'It's nothing,' I said, ignoring her disapproving appraisal of my clothes.

Douglas pulled out a chair and helped me lower myself into it. Pepper glanced at him before settling across my feet. 'Ye look all-in, if ye dinnae mind me saying. Mary, why don't ye fetch the lass some clean water and find her some fresh clothes.'

Mary started bustling about the kitchen and it was my turn to stare. This was Mary's kingdom, and she ruled it as though she were its Queen. Never had I seen her acquiesce to another so readily. 'D'ye want to tell us what happened?' Douglas asked.

I should have been affronted by the ease with which he was taking control of the situation, and how comfortable he was in my home, but instead I found I welcomed his quiet authority.

Having recounted these events many times in my head, as well as during Mr Warde's interrogation, there was no longer anything hazy about my memory of last night. It was as sharp as one of my hairpins. Douglas leaned against the table by my side, absorbing every word of my account, silent and intense. Mary muttered the occasional 'Dear Lord' until I got to the part where Will said he had 'dealt' with my father and watched him die. She turned towards me, a bowl of water in her hands. Her face had lost its habitual, healthy glow and was as white as the surf on the ocean in a storm. Her hands started to shake and water sloshed on to the floor. Douglas reacted with the speed of a hare outrunning a fox, took the bowl and eased her onto a low stool.

'You were right,' I addressed him. 'Mr Warde has been watching me. Us. He has a suspicious mind that does not accept coincidence but seeks connection. And he found it.'

'What happens now?' Douglas asked.

'I don't know. I'm no longer to be detained, but I'm not free – there's a guard at the front of the house, and probably one at the back to stop me if I attempt to leave. And where is Will?' I suppressed a shudder, imagining what fate would befall him if Mr Warde's men caught him.

I did not have to wait long for the answers to my questions. Mary helped me to wash, because I could not manage the task myself without getting the dressing on my arm wet, which she assured me was not a good idea. She brushed rose water through my hair until it shone, and I left it loose, flowing beyond my shoulders. When I was dressed in a simple black gown, she fashioned a sling from an old sheet to support my arm and I retired to my closet, grateful for some time alone to think. But I had only been there for a few minutes when she announced I had a visitor. Mr Warde.

His presence here was not as oppressive as it had been at the Tollbooth. Nevertheless, the atmosphere shifted as soon as he took the chair I offered him opposite me in front of the fire. Just by being there, he seemed to suck out any air of contentment from the room, replacing it with apprehension.

He declined my offer of refreshment with a dismissive flick of his wrist and Mary left us alone.

'My men have been searching for Ord, but have been unable to find any trace of him,' he announced, picking some fluff from his black jerkin. 'Do you have any idea where he might have gone to hide? Anyone he was close to, who might have taken him in?'

'No, I ...'

'Come, Madam. You were betrothed to the man. He had been an associate of your father's for many years. Even, I understand, before your own relationship with him developed, when his late wife was still alive. You must know of his other friends, relatives, colleagues.'

He was right. I should know, but I did not. It had never struck me before that I knew so little about the man I had believed myself to be in love with, and whom I had been prepared to pledge myself to for the rest of my life. I would not make that mistake again. Indeed, I do not believe I would ever consider marriage again.

'Truly, I know of no-one. Arthur had been his one good friend that I knew of.'

And look what happened to him, I could have added, but I had no need. Mr Warde could have said it for me. Then another thought occurred to me. Surely he could not have made it to the Lady Isabella after all?

Mr Warde must have also considered that possibility. He shook his head. 'No, I don't think he managed to board the ship. My man saw him running away from the scene, following the river inland towards the castle, and set off in pursuit but lost him. The night was dark and Ord had the advantage. He slipped away in to the shadows, but he could not have re-entered the town until this morning, so must have spent the night outside the walls.'

'So what will happen now?'

'We'll keep searching for him, and make no mistake, we will find him. And when we do, he will be tried, found guilty of treason and executed. Of course, he is also guilty of murder, but I can only hang a man once.'

I closed my eyes, trying not to picture that scene, of Will on the scaffold.

'Madam Gillhespy.' Mr Warde's voice, always soft, dropped a semitone, and broke into my thoughts. 'If you do hear from him, or have any other ideas about his possible whereabouts, you will let me know.'

It was a warning. He did not trust me, but much as the thought of what would happen to Will when they caught him made me tremble, for what he did to my father, he had earned his fate.

'I want him found as much as you do,' I said, meeting his eyes and willing him to believe me. 'He watched my father die.'

Mr Warde nodded and rose to his feet.

'What about me? Am I to be a prisoner in my own home?'

'For the time being I need you to remain here, and there will be a guard at the front and the rear. If Ord does show his face, we will catch him. As for your part in all of this, I'm awaiting instructions.'

'I had no part in any of this,' I protested.

'I believe you, but when it comes to matters that affect the security of the country, the decision is not mine to make. Be patient Madam and do as I ask. After all, if you're not guilty you have no need to run. If you do decide to run, make no mistake but that I will hunt you down. You fooled my men once. They will not be so easy to deceive a second time.'

'Can I at least open my stores to customers?'

He paused and then inclined his head. 'But know that we will be watching. Good day to you.'

I did as I was instructed. If I was not at home I was in my stores, always with Pepper by my side. For a while it was all right. My arm impeded my movements and made even basic daily tasks difficult, but as Mr Hedley had promised it healed, helped by his daily visits to change the dressing and inspect it for any signs of infection. When this was no longer necessary, he still called and we shared wine together in the parlour. After a few weeks though, the restrictive routine and confinement started to become tedious. Douglas was a frequent visitor, sometimes accompanied by John Bailey with news of the mine. Progress was good and we were beginning to trade coal, overseen by the more than capable young man. I missed the quay and the way it brought me to life, but I dare not go there. Nor was there news of the Lady Isabella, and I did not expect there to be any. I missed my cousin more than I had thought possible. I heard that Mr Warde had left town, although his instructions had not departed with him. Our Governor, Lord Grey de Wilton too had left, with a small army of men from the garrison intending to lift the siege of Leith and drive the French out. Douglas kept me informed with the goings-on of the town, but not everything he told me was good. He spoke of increasing unquiet in the prolonged absence of the Governor and the news from Leith, which was not going according to plan. Of Will there was no news. Even Douglas could find no word of him. Once again he had vanished.

Then one day everything changed and my life would never be the same again. It started as a bright spring day like the many that had already passed before it. I was in the hall, preparing to go to my stores when there was a knock at the door.

'I'll get it,' I called to Mary, thinking it might be Mr Hedley. It wasn't. It was the man I feared more than any other.

'Good day to you Madam Gillhespy,' Mr Warde said.

I stood to one side to allow him to enter, but he did not move.

'Come with me please.'

My heart plummeted into my boots. Surely this wasn't all about to start again. I reached for a light cloak and turned to call to Mary that I was going out. She must have heard our voices and was standing at the back of the hall wiping her hands on a cloth. I shrugged and raised my eyebrows to convey that I did not know where I was being taken. Pepper whined a protest when he realised he was not invited on this outing. I ruffled his ears and closed the door behind me.

Mr Warde was not in a communicative mood. I asked him where we were going but he did not answer. We turned up Uddyngate and icy fingers like tentacles stroked my veins and chilled my blood. This was the way to the Tolbooth, but surely if I was being taken there again he would not have come to escort me in person? He would have sent a guard.

The atmosphere in the streets was strange, taut with tension. It might have been because I had become accustomed to being confined to my own home, but I thought not. It added to my apprehension, which was mounting with every step we took. Mr Warde had not lost his ability to make me believe I was guilty of something, even though I knew I was not.

My breathing eased as we passed the town well and carried on beyond the Tolbooth towards Holy Trinity church where my father was buried. One of the consequences of my confinement at home was that I had been unable to visit his grave. My eyes sought out that sheltered, gloomy corner, but I could not see the marker stone from the road. Beneath the trees and in the untended areas of the churchyard, the cowslips had given way to forget-me-nots and poppies. I had also missed the passing of the seasons, and it seemed summer was on its way, but the joy I would usually find in observing the cycle of nature eluded me. I longed for a glimpse of the ocean, but Mr Warde led me beyond the church, turning away from the coast to a stretch of the new town walls. The scene was as busy as that of the quay, with men scurrying around pushing barrows of earth, pulleys swinging larger slabs of stone into the air, foremen shouting instructions. It was already twice my height, and I looked up at it in awe.

'Please Madam. We do not have time to linger. My master does not like to be kept waiting.'

His master! Surely he could not mean … ?

I had no time to prepare my thoughts. We were joined by a man whose imposing presence, in spite of his slight frame, eclipsed everything, and everyone, around him. He was dressed in black, and his broad shoulders extended beneath an elaborate white ruff that stretched up high behind his ears and over which his beard protruded at an unnatural angle. It was quite extraordinary, trimmed in such a way that it framed his chin before spilling out like a gush of water carving its way through a wall of rock. An air of something sinister hung about him and I almost shivered in spite of the warmth of the day.

'Sir William, this is Madam Isabella Gillhespy,' Mr Warde said and backed away. I watched him go, although I could have willed him to stay. He was my tormentor, and I did not desire his company, but to be left alone with the Queen's principal Secretary instilled a whole new level of panic. What could he want from me?

Sir William Cecil cleared his throat. Mr Warde had just told me he was not a patient man. I turned to face him, trying to remember the instructions of various governesses about how to greet someone of his position, but my head was empty, so I followed my instinct and lowered myself into a curtsey. When I stood, he was regarding me in an appraising fashion, as if I were some merchandise he was considering acquiring.

'Walk with me,' he commanded. He set off at a steady pace and I followed, just a fraction behind. He led me to what would be the outside of the walls, and his head moved from side to side as his eyes swept over the ramparts that would one day become an impenetrable fortification of the town. In the distance, now outside the defences, the great bastion built by King Henry stood tall and proud, but to their side, the old walls were crumbling, helped by the stream of labourers who were removing stones, loading them onto carts and driving them to where work was continuing on the new walls.

Sir William was watching them too. 'It's a delicate balance,' he murmured. 'We need so much stone to build these new defences that we cannot afford to ignore the resource that is sitting in these old walls. But at the same time, we cannot dismantle them entirely until the new are fit for purpose.' He stroked his impressive beard and I detected a furrowing of the skin between his brows beneath the velvet cap.

I was saved from venturing a comment by the approach of a gentleman I did not know. He was tall, slim and wiry, with a dark complexion that hinted at familiarity with a warmer climate than we are used to in the north of England. He removed his cap and bowed, throwing a curious glance in my direction.

'Ah Portinari. Excuse me for one moment Madam.' He moved away, beckoning to the other gentleman to follow. Upon hearing his name I knew who he was. Giovanni Portinari was the Italian engineer who had been brought to Berwick to advise on the construction of the new walls. I watched them for a moment but could not hear their conversation, and my attention drifted back to the industry taking place all around me. When Sir William returned, he was alone.

'This is quite some feat of human ingenuity and engineering, although progress is slow and expensive,' he remarked, continuing our conversation as if Portinari's interruption had not taken place. There was an undercurrent of frustration in his tone. 'Necessary though, if we are to protect our country, even though there are those that would seek to help our enemies by selling our secrets.' He leaned his head towards me and his piercing eyes explored my face.

Of course, I knew what he was hinting at. It took all the strength of will I could exert over my feet to stop me from staggering away from him. Something, call it instinct, told me to hold my ground.

'I had nothing …'

He silenced me with a wave of his hand.

'Save your breath. I believe you had no knowledge of the arrangement between Arthur Fewell and William Ord.'

Relief flooded through me, releasing the tension that had been building since I had opened my front door to find Mr Warde standing there. It left me light-headed, and I looked around for something to lean on, to steady myself, but there was nothing.

'Come, let us sit for a moment,' Sir William said. He led me to a wooden plank positioned across two round logs of a felled tree trunk which made a sort of bench. The men occupying it moved as we approached, and I sank down onto the hard surface.

'Thank you,' I muttered, not sure if I was thanking him for noticing I needed to sit down, or for believing in my innocence.

'You will notify me if Ord shows his face.'

So they had not caught Will.

'Sir, he tried to kill me, and he admitted watching my father die. He will know not to show his face to me should he ever return to Berwick.'

'Even so … I cannot take any risks. Keeping our country, and Queen, safe from those who would threaten our sovereignty is my top priority.'

My eyes widened. I sensed he was trying to tell me something. He was placing an extraordinary importance on whatever Will had been involved with, but I just wanted to be allowed to move on, to put these last few months behind me, grieve for my father and re-build my future.

'When do you expect the Lady Isabella, and your cousin, to return?'

I suspected he knew the answer to that better than I. No doubt his spies would have intelligence of the movement of ships out of Antwerp, but I refrained from pointing that out to him.

'I have received no word,' I said. 'But I hope it will be soon.'

He nodded. 'When she returns, Lord Grey or his appointed representative will oversee the customs inspection and ensure it is thorough. Mr Dixon has been informed.'

A lump rose in my throat and I swallowed it. He might believe me innocent, but he was still suspicious that the Lady Isabella was being used to trade secrets. This was not over yet.

'I have decided that you are not to be charged with anything.'

Had I heard him right? I was struggling to keep up with this interview. It was lurching from side to side, mimicking a ship on a stormy sea, raising my hopes one moment and dashing them the next. My heart was thumping inside my chest, like a bird with wings trying to beat its way out of my body, and I tried to contain it.

'Are you saying I'm free to leave my house and go about my own business without Mr Warde's men following me?' I asked.

He inclined his head, but seconds later I was choking back my joy when he added, 'But Madam Gillhespy, it is time for you to do something for me.'

Sir William's words sent spikes marching down my spine. His eyes seemed to strip back my skin, exposing my bones under his scrutiny. It was the most unpleasant sensation that he was turning me inside out. What could he possibly want me to do for him? I remained silent.

'You see, I believe this town has importance beyond its size and stature to the security of our country. I believe Berwick provides a window to what is happening in Scotland, where their allegiances lie, and what plots may be afoot simply by having eyes and ears here. Eyes and ears that are able to move among the people of the town without suspicion. Eyes and ears that will attract confidences, that will see and hear things that my Lord Grey and certain other sources in the town cannot.'

I stared at him. A voice inside my head insisted I must have misunderstood what he was suggesting. His countenance told me otherwise.

'As a successful merchant, you will start to mix in Berwick society. Nothing could be more natural than that. When your cousin returns he may be your escort if one is necessary, but he won't know of our agreement. No-one will know of our agreement. Anything that you hear or see, you will report to me.'

Something flickered at the edge of my vision, but I dare not let my attention waver from the man in front of me.

'You want me to spy for you?' I managed to splutter after a silence that stretched for an inordinate amount of time. This was not my life. I knew about ships and trade. Had I not had enough of lies and secrets this last few months?

'Why me?' I asked.

The movement I had noticed manifested itself into another person, who now positioned himself to the side of Sir William, who acknowledged him with a curt nod. I stared, unable to believe my eyes. It was Douglas.

'I like your spirit,' Sir William was saying, in answer to my last question. His lips turned upwards in the semblance of a smile, but there was no warmth in it, and his next words added to the chill that already had me paralysed in its grip.

'Besides, I know I can trust you, because if I can't, I may have to forget that I believe you know nothing of your ship being used to trade secrets with the Queen's enemies. And that is treason. Good day to you Madam.'

Our interview was over. Sir William turned his attention to Douglas, who cast me a glance over his shoulder – was it of pity or an apology? I followed my feet and they led me to the quay. How I'd missed it. I gulped in the air, which was mellower with the change of season but still tangy with salt, and avoided looking to my left, to where I had confronted Will. Instead, I focused on the castle, and the river racing towards it with the determination of an attacking army.

My mind was bursting with questions that I could not answer. Foremost among them were how long had Douglas been working for Sir William and did Mary know?

I'd been given my freedom back, but on terms that meant I would never be free. I had no interest in spying on my business associates, customers and neighbours, pretending to be their friend when in truth I was anything but.

The quay was busy, but I had scarce paid it any attention, wrapped as I was in my thoughts. A group of dockworkers knocked into me as they hurried past. I shook my head clear and concentrated on the scene around me. The atmosphere had shifted. It was never languid on the quay, but it was now charged with a new surge of energy. I knew what that meant. A ship was on its way in.

The river glittered under the glare of the sun. I screwed up my eyes and looked towards the treacherous entrance to the harbour. Sure enough, making her way through the sandbars that were now covered by the incoming tide, but still lurked beneath the surface, there was a ship, her masthead standing proud and clear. A brown bear with the head of a woman.

I followed the throng of dockworkers towards the jetty. There was much jostling for space and I held back, watching the Lady Isabella's graceful approach, my excitement tempered by trepidation. Would her arrival bring me good fortune this time, or bad? And what about my cousin, how did I feel about him, and how would he react when I told him everything that had happened here since he had left?

LADY OF THE QUAY

As the Lady Isabella drew closer to the quay, I could not stop the tide of optimism rising within me. Sir William Cecil had told me I was going to be his spy and there was nothing I could do to change that. It was not in my nature to brood over something when I had no power to change it. Instead, I turned my face up to the sun, and waited for my beloved ship to drop anchor.

A Note from the Author

Lady of the Quay is a work of fiction inspired by the beautiful, historic and unique town of Berwick-upon-Tweed, which I first visited in 2021. A walk around the ramparts, absorbing the information that was displayed on boards along the way, was sufficient to convince me to set a new series of novels in this town, and the period had to be the latter half of the sixteenth century.

Berwick's defensive walls, in part medieval, were the most expensive construction project of the Elizabethan era, even though they were never finished. The early years of the reign of Elizabeth I were dominated by Roman Catholic plots to claim the English throne for her cousin Mary, Queen of Scots. Mary herself lived in France, whilst her mother, Marie de Guise, ruled Scotland as Regent. Mary's father-in-law, Henry II of France asserted her claim to the English throne. Following his death in 1559, Mary's young husband, Francis, became King with Mary as his Queen Consort. The strategic position of Berwick-upon-Tweed, close to the Scottish border, would have given the town an unprecedented importance for the defence of England at a time when the most senior politician in the land, Sir William Cecil, Elizabeth's Master Secretary, feared the alliance between Scotland and France more than anything.

In December 1559, when Cecil received intelligence that the French navy was preparing to set sail for Scotland with 15,000 mercenaries, he put the garrison at Berwick-upon-Tweed on high alert and increased efforts to neutralise the threat posed by Mary through a treaty with the Scottish Protestant Lords of the Congregation, who also feared the influence of France and supported reformation of the Scottish Catholic church. These were turbulent times, and to me Berwick seemed to be both a perfect, and unusual setting for a new series of historical thrillers with a female protagonist.

Throughout *Lady of the Quay* I have used the old names for the town's streets and gates, as detailed by Jim Herbert in his excellent Berwick Time Lines. My vision for the town is informed by the True Description of circa 1580 and John Speed's map of 1610. I should point out that the Holy Trinity Church is not the church of that name that exists to this day. The present Church of Holy Trinity and St Mary opened in 1652 and was the only Parish Church built during Oliver Cromwell's Commonwealth. My Holy Trinity Church is its medieval predecessor, which would have been located just to the south.

I've tried to recreate the town of Berwick-upon-Tweed as it could have been in the sixteenth century, and I've also tried to maintain historical accuracy. I'm sure I've made mistakes, but I hope that any readers spotting any will immerse themselves in Isabella's 'world' and forgive me.

In researching the history of Berwick-upon-Tweed for this novel I must thank Linda Bankier at the Berwick-upon-Tweed Record Office for her help with accessing relevant materials in the archives and answering my questions. I must also thank Tony Whitelaw for sharing his knowledge, the loan of many of his books on the town and for accompanying me on a day of exploring its history, walking the ramparts and clambering around Lord's Mount. Further thanks go to Ali Edwards at Coostie Illustration & Design for the beautiful, illustrated map and cover, to everyone at West Oxfordshire Writers for their patient feedback during the writing process, and early readers, my sister Tracey, Gill H and Gill B, Stewart and my fellow indie author at Oxford Independent Authors, Jacquii.

I hope you've've enjoyed *Lady of the Quay* and would love to hear what you thought of it. Drop me a line via my website, or find me on social media.

www.amandarobertsauthor.co.uk

Amanda_Roberts_Author/100095191090333/#

amanda-roberts-author

amanda_roberts_author/

For 63 years Annie has looked up to her father as the one man in her life who would never let her down. It isn't until after he dies that she discovers an inconsistency in wedding dates, which leads her to question every memory she has of her parents and who she really is. Shattered by the discovery that the man she spent her whole life looking up to was not her real father, Annie becomes less and less able to cope, and it falls to her daughter, Suzie, to pursue the truth. Delving into the controversial family past, hidden in secret letters, dusty war records and a neglected headstone, Suzie can only hope that what she discovers is enough to bring her own mother back from the brink.

Praise for *The Roots of the Tree*

The Bookbag says:
"An elegant, thought-provoking look at the nature, the very essence of parenting ... A superb read."

Available on Kindle e-book and paperback from Amazon.
Order from a bookshop, or from the author's website:
www.amandarobertsauthor.co.uk

Two women, nearly 400 years apart, and one ring

When Hannah picks up a ring that had lain buried in her garden
for centuries and it gives her a physical shock, she embarks on a quest
to discover who had once owned it, and how they lost it. Her research
leads her to a woman forgotten by history and a heart-breaking
tale of love and loss. As Hannah closes in on the truth it becomes
clear that someone else wants the ring, but to what lengths are they
prepared to go to get it?

Set in the beautiful Oxfordshire village of Islip, *The Woman in the
Painting* is a perfect choice for fans of Lucinda Riley, Barbara Erskine
and Clare Marchant.

**Available on Kindle e-book and paperback from Amazon.
Order from a bookshop, or from the author's website:
www.amandarobertsauthor.co.uk**

Praise for *The Woman in the Painting*

Silver Medal Award Winner
The Coffee Pot Book Club
Historical Fiction Book of the Year Awards 2023
Time Travel / Time-Slip / Dual-Timeline category

Highly recommended
"With its captivating narrative and poetic language,
The Woman in the Painting immersed me in a world of art, war, love,
betrayal, murder, and ultimately, peace and acceptance."
Mary Anne Yarde
The Coffee Pot Book Club

"*The Woman in the Painting* is an intriguing dual-timeline novel. The
characters come alive, especially Catherine, and the setting in
1645 Islip transports the reader to that time and place. The love
story between Thomas and Catherine is beautifully told. Themes
of love, loss, trust and starting anew are adeptly woven into this
heart-touching story."
Historical Novel Society

"A heart-wrenching story and mystery you'll not soon forget."
"It's a perfect mystery with twist after twist."
"I was instantly drawn in and loved it."
"A real page turner right from the start."
"Beautifully crafted, well researched."
Reader comments from NetGalley, Goodreads and Amazon